Oodrechs

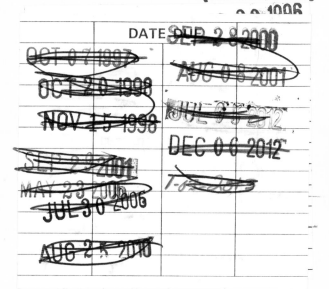

MOST LIKELY
TO DIE

Berkley Prime Crime Books by Jaqueline Girdner

MOST LIKELY TO DIE

JAQUELINE GIRDNER

BERKLEY PRIME CRIME, NEW YORK

MOST LIKELY TO DIE

A Berkley Prime Crime Book
Published by The Berkley Publishing Group
200 Madison Avenue, New York, New York 10016

The Putnam Berkley World Wide Web site address is
http://www.berkley.com

Book design by Maureen A. Troy

First Edition: April 1996

Library of Congress Cataloging-in-Publication Data

Girdner, Jaqueline.
      Most likely to die / Jaqueline Girdner. — 1st ed.
         p.   cm.
      ISBN 0-425-15145-X (hardcover)
      ISBN 0-425-15146-8 (trade paperback)
      I. Title.
    PS3557.I718M67   1996
    813'.54—dc20   95-22449
                                                                              CIP

Printed in the United States of America

10   9   8   7   6   5   4   3   2   1

For Greg

ACKNOWLEDGMENTS

My heartfelt thanks to Neal Ferguson for sharing his expertise as a forensic specialist. And to Barbara Kempster for sharing her expertise as a police dispatcher and former emergency medical technician. And to Eileen Ostrow Feldman, my intrepid first reader. I couldn't have written this without you guys!

Please note, any mistakes in these areas are due to the author's fevered imagination and not to Neal's, Barbara's, or Eileen's generous words of guidance.

MOST LIKELY TO DIE

WHERE ARE WE NOW?

✝

GRAVENDALE HIGH SCHOOL
CLASS OF 1968

HIRSCH, CHARLES (CHARLIE)

Author of six books for children featuring plucky Rodin Rodent, the seafaring rat of many colors. Most recent book published: *Rodin Rodent and the Parrot Pirate*. I also garden.

JASPER, KATE KOFFENBURGER

Run my own small business, JEST GIFTS, a mail-order gag gift company. Spend the rest of my time indulging in vegetarian gluttony, practicing tai chi, and loving sweetie WAYNE CARUSO.

KANICK, JOHN (JACK)

My beautiful and talented wife, LILLIAN, and I own KARMA-KANICK AUTO REPAIR here in Gravendale. Have two children, LARK and JOSH. Still see mom, AURORA, often.

MYERS, MARK

My life's gone to the dogs since I last saw you. And to the cats, the birds, and a bunch of other critters. I'm a veterinarian! Also active in the AIDS Action Committee and Gay Men's Chorus.

NUSSER, NATALIE

B.S. CS/EE, M.I.T. '72. M.B.A., U.C. Berkeley '86.
Have worked in the arenas of aerospace design, electronics, computer programming, and computer chip design. Currently own and manage midsize computer software company.

ORTEGA, PAMELA (PAM)

Local girl makes librarian! I've worked as a city, county, and corporate librarian. Am now managing librarian for WILDSPACE, a nonprofit organization dedicated to the preservation of the planet and its plants and animals.

SEMLING, SIDNEY (SID)

Hey, what can I tell you! Survived Vietnam. Now a handsome, high-paid rocket scientist. Just kidding! Thought I'd get the ladies interested. I AM single though. And a super salesman. Can I sell you something?

TIMMONS, ELAINE SEMLING

I am happily married to husband ED TIMMONS (for over fifteen years), the mother of three gifted children, and head secretary of a growing computer software firm, as well as being an active participant in Sonoma County politics.

VOGEL, REBECCA (BECKY) BURCHELL

Jeez, would you believe I'm an attorney now? (Personal injury.) Still love to party! Single mom of DAVID, "D.V.," 15.

WEISS, ROBERT

Deceased.

ONE

"Louie Louie" was exploding from the loudspeakers, doing its damnedest to compete with the screeches of a few hundred forty-some-year-olds. And I was sweating all over my best-occasion velvet jumpsuit, dancing with Tommy Johnson—no—Jenkins, a kid I hadn't seen in twenty-five years.

"Roar, roar, mmm wawwa mo—"

At least I thought it was "Louie Louie."

I threw my arms out in the spirit of '68 and executed a free-form twirl under the disco lights. A tendril of crepe paper caught me halfway through, flapping onto my moist forehead and sticking there for a moment, then pulling away with an intimate little suck as I completed the turn. The spirit of '68, all right.

"The hotel even did the decorations in Gravendale High colors!" Tommy shouted, pointing at the profusion of purple and red streamers floating under the pulsating lights. Tommy smiled, exposing the gap between his otherwise perfect teeth. "Cool, huh?"

"Yeah, cool!" I screamed back, wondering how a kid that had looked like Alfred E. Neuman twenty-five years ago could have turned into such a good-looking man. Well, not all that good-looking, I told myself guiltily, and glanced over his short shoulders at my sweetie, Wayne. (Twenty-five years might have done a lot for Tommy's looks, but they hadn't added any to his height.)

Wayne was holding his own, gyrating in place across from Gail something-or-other, another classmate I hadn't seen in twenty-five years. And a woman *he'd* never met before in his life. Of course, Wayne hadn't gone to Gravendale High School. This was *my* twenty-fifth high school reunion. But Gail had looked so damned lonely as the other couples had stood up to make their way onto the dance floor that I'd whispered to Wayne, "Ask her to dance," without even thinking. Then I'd watched the ambivalence play out on his homely face. Wayne was used to rejection based on nothing more than his low brows and cauliflower nose. But he was a sucker for anyone needy. So he took a big breath and popped the question. When Gail leapt out of her chair with a big smile of acceptance, I knew it was worth it. A two-for-one cheer-up special.

Actually I was feeling surprisingly cheery myself, out there wiggling my ever-widening hips on the dance floor, sweating all over the most expensive outfit I owned, and feeling some— just a few—of the layered remnants of my teenaged pain, self-consciousness, and insecurity slip-sliding away.

The music felt better too that night than it had twenty-five years before. "Wooly Bully," "Dancing In The Streets," "Shotgun," and "Satisfaction." All I remembered from official high school dances were the Beatles and the Beach Boys.

A few hours ago, Wayne and I had come rushing in late to the ballroom of the Swinton Hotel, nervously snatched a *Where Are We Now?* booklet from a smiling reunion organizer, and plopped down randomly at the nearest big round table to have dinner. I'd only remembered about half of my tablemates. And they'd changed. Tina Reilley, who'd been so shy and plain that I'd worried about her, was currently a gor-

geously glowing physicist. Not glowing from radiation, I
hoped. And former troublemaker Frankie Weems was a corporate attorney. Actually, maybe he hadn't changed.

But no one at the table had been from my old gang of
friends. I suppose I shouldn't have been surprised. For a moment I'd wondered why I'd seen so little of the old gang in
all these years. Not to mention the rest of my former class-
mates. But I didn't come up with an answer.

After dinner, the music started. And hunky Jim Hernandez
asked me to dance. And then Zack what's-his-name. And then
Tommy. And suddenly I was glad I hadn't given in to my
initial impulse to rip my reunion invitation into tiny pieces and
flush them down the toilet. I certainly hadn't been this popular
in high school. So I danced, telling myself I'd hunt later for
the people I'd hung out with twenty-five years ago. I already
knew my old best friend, Patty, wasn't going to be here. And
there had been over five hundred kids in my graduating class.
It wouldn't be easy to separate out the fifteen or so of them
I'd been really close to. If any of them were even here.

"Louie Louie" ended abruptly, and suddenly I could hear
people talking around us.

"This is my fourth husband, he's a keeper . . ."

"And white lipstick. And those awful madras shorts . . ."

"I cheated off you in third grade, do you remember? I copied your paper, but I copied your name too . . ."

"Thanks," I panted to Tommy. Not only was I soaked with
sweat from dancing but my legs were wobbling. And my ears
were ringing.

"You always were a really cool dancer, Koffenburger,"
Tommy said. And then he shouted as another song began,
"Wanna do it again?"

It sounded like "Brown Sugar." And Tommy had said the
magic words, "really cool dancer," even if he had used my
dreaded maiden name. Koffenburger. You would not believe

all the bad jokes that can be made out of a name like Koffen-burger.

I looked over at Wayne. He was still dancing with Gail. What the hell, I decided. My legs were going to hurt tomorrow anyway. I kicked them out in a fancy two-step and started swinging my arms and hips again. And thinking about my old boyfriend, Ken.

Had Ken thought I was a good dancer? Ken who had driven a motorcycle—really a motorbike—but it still had seemed romantic. Ken who had sported shoulder-length brown hair by the time he had disappeared into the cosmos of communes after his first year at Stanford. Ken who—

I looked guiltily over Tommy's shoulder at Wayne again.

Was Ken here in the Swinton Hotel ballroom? I danced faster, avoiding crepe paper. Probably not. I had yet to see even one person from the old gang. I smiled across at Tommy and wondered why he hadn't been part of the group I'd hung out with so long ago. They'd been a mixed crew. A bunch of kids who were smart, maybe smarter than Tommy, but not necessarily super-smart. Kids who were a little on the wild side—that was probably the answer. Tommy had been pretty straight. And most of us had thought of ourselves as hippies, or at least near-hippies, as we banded together to eat lunch on the front lawn and split into smaller groups to talk intimately and earnestly. About sex and society, the Jefferson Airplane, our parents, sex, the Grateful Dead, the war in Vietnam, drugs. And sex again. We even talked about love. And peace, of course. Lots of talk. Very little action.

The Rolling Stones screamed to an end, giving way to the sound of people chattering around us once again.

"I'm really feeling dislocated, you know, I don't mean to be a downer, but my therapist said . . ."

"Remember when we found that shark on the beach and put it in the swimming pool . . ."

8

JAQUELINE GIRDNER

"Your hair has changed, but your aura is just the same as it always was . . ."

"That was really great, Tommy," I said after I caught my breath. "You're a real cool dancer yourself."

He smiled widely this time, revealing the full extent of the gap between his teeth. With a little jolt, I realized *I* might have helped *him* shed a layer of insecurity. It was so easy to forget that other people were vulnerable too. I gave him an impulsive, sweaty hug and then watched as he walked away under the pulsating lights, limping. It looked like I wasn't going to be the only sore ex-dancer tomorrow. Then a woman's voice from behind me caught my ear.

"Whatever happened to Robert Weiss?" she asked someone.

"Don't you remember?" that someone answered. "He blew himself up, right before—"

My whole body clenched. I remembered. I couldn't not remember.

Because Robert Weiss had been one of our group, a talented boy: theatrical, artistic, and elegant. A boy who'd loved magic. He'd promised us all a fireworks show on the weekend before graduation. And he'd given it to us, wearing his top hat and black cape, pulling festoons of light from inside the cape's folds, then making sparklers appear from our ears and our pockets and our noses. Gradually, he'd worked up to the big rockets. Really big rockets, bought out of state. And for the grand finale, he lit the biggest one of all and stepped back. Nothing happened. A frown creased his elegant face as he stepped forward, bending over the malfunctioning rocket to pick it up. It blew up then, blasting away his shoulder and his heart in a huge roar of light and sound and blood.

I don't know how long it was before I realized it wasn't a trick and began to scream.

Twenty-five years later, I shivered under the pulsating lights of the Swinton Hotel ballroom and remembered why my initial impulse had been to rip up my reunion invitation. I felt sick. Sick and cold. I wanted to go home.

I lifted my head to look for Wayne.

But suddenly I couldn't see anything. Even the disco lights blacked out as someone's large, rough hands covered my eyes.

Two

🕭

I turned on my heel the instant I realized those rough hands were blinding me, my adrenaline flowing into tai chi. My paired knee to the groin and fingertips to the throat were almost as automatic. But by the time I got there, the hundred-and-eighty-degree turn had pulled the hands from my eyes and brought me face-to-face with my attacker. Face to laughing face.

I halted my knee's ascent abruptly, just grazing the loose material of his pants crotch, and let my hand drop as if I'd been merely waving. Then I just stared. Because I recognized that laughing face. A broad face with high cheekbones, a wide nose, small close-set eyes, and a big fat grin. My heartbeat began thumping its way back to normal.

"Whoa, Katie, it's me!" the face with the grin shouted. If there was anything I hated worse than being called "Koffen-burger," it was "Katie." Then he threw his big rough hands out as if to embrace the universe and laughed again. Did he have any idea how close my knee had come?

Apparently not. He tilted his head and asked in an affected lisp, "Does the name Sid Semling perhaps refresh your memory?" before crossing his eyes and sticking out his tongue.

God, it was Sid. Sid Semling, master prankster. Sid with

about seventy or eighty more pounds on his big, broad frame, but Sid nevertheless. In a flash, I remembered a few dozen pieces of hilarity sparked by his constant jokes, teasing, and pranks. And a few dozen more chunks of misery. Damn. Sid would be the first person I'd see from the old gang.

I closed my gaping mouth, then opened it again to greet him. "Of course, Sid," I mumbled, but most of my reply was lost in a new blast of music, probably "Proud Mary."

"Lookin' good, Kate!" Sid shouted, undaunted by the cacophony. Then he ran his eyes down my short, A-line body and back up again under the pulsating lights. "At least you've kept the lard off. Me," he patted his ample stomach, "AAA puts out special Sid Semling guidebooks for fat cells. Group tours available."

A smile jerked at my lips. I couldn't help it.

"You know what they say about a fat man though?" he went on with a leer. I had no doubt the question was a setup for a punch line that would be both sexual and offensive. Though possibly funny too. That was the trouble with Sid.

"No, what do they say?" a deep voice asked from behind me. Wayne. I reached back and took his hand. I didn't have to look to know it was him. Or to know that his glare was so deep that his eyes were lost under the cliff of his low brows.

"Jesus, when did they let King Kong out of his cage?" Sid yelped, jumping back in feigned fear.

Or maybe not so feigned. It wasn't just Wayne's brows that were scary. He had over six feet of karate-trained muscles that seemed to throb with menace when he was in protect mode. A helpful habit developed from years of work as a professional bodyguard. Not so helpful in social situations however.

"Wayne Caruso, Sid Semling," I introduced briefly, telling myself if Sid made any more fun of Wayne, I'd finish the knee kick.

The two men grunted and shook hands without further incident. Maybe Sid had grown out of the joy-buzzers he used to carry.

"So you're her . . ." Sid let the sentence dribble out suggestively.

"Her fiancé," Wayne growled as I simultaneously replied, "My sweetie."

I glanced over my shoulder at Wayne. His brows were at half-mast. Much as we cared about each other, trying to reach agreement about our wedding plans had put a gap between us, one that even showed up semantically.

"Well, hey—whatever," Sid said easily. "Point is, I'm having a party for the old gang next Saturday afternoon at my place. A barbecue blowout on my patio. Party hearty—"

"We're coming," interrupted a woman walking up next to Sid.

I stared at her and couldn't remember her for the life of me. She was small and wiry with a pretty Asian face distinguished by a slightly turned up nose. Then she tugged at someone standing behind her. He was tall and skinny with long dark hair, an equally dark beard, and glasses rimmed in black. But it was his stooped shoulders that gave him away more than anything.

"Jack Kanick?" I guessed.

"Uh-huh," he mumbled and flashed me a weak smile before his gaze drifted away to the dancers behind us.

"And I'm Lillian, Jack's wife," said the Asian woman in a slightly accented voice filled with the enthusiasm that Jack's lacked. She put an arm around Jack's waist and squeezed. Jack brought his gaze reluctantly back as I introduced Wayne and myself. Then Lillian went on. "Jack and I are coming to the party. With our kids. And Jack's mom, Aurora—"

"And Becky Burchell," Sid cut in. He pointed to a blond woman dancing a few couples away. At least I thought that was the woman he was pointing to. It was hard to tell beneath the flashing disco lights, but I was pretty sure I saw Becky's delicate features and round blue eyes under a mop of blond permed hair. And it would be just like her to be wearing the sexiest dress in the room, a slinky black number that plunged as dangerously in the front as the back.

"She's Becky Vogel now. Kept the name, lost the husband," Sid added. I crossed my arms uncomfortably. He could have said the same about Kate Jasper. "Becky's a big-shot attorney. But she's still a friggin' wild woman, yeah-uh!"

The woman we were watching let out a *whoop* as if to agree.

"A quarter of a century gone," Jack muttered. At least that's what I thought I heard.

"Now, Jack," said Lillian, tightening her grip around his waist.

"Pam Ortega's coming too," Sid told us. "And Charlie Hirsch." He winked largely.

That's right, I thought, remembering Pam and Charlie's hasty wedding right after high school graduation.

"Are they still married?" I asked.

"No, the baby miscarried and so did the marriage," Sid answered with a grin. I winced. Sid went on without noticing. "And my cousin Elaine's gonna be there. She's not a Semling anymore, she's a Timmons. Married herself a rich one. She's one happy momma now. And Mark Myers, he's . . ." Sid made a swishing motion with his hand. Gay? I wondered. I was having a hard enough time keeping up with the names and the pictures they called up in my mind.

"And Natalie Nusser," Sid added. He turned, put two fingers in his mouth, and whistled. "Hey, Natalie!"

Natalie waved awkwardly from where she was standing beyond the dance floor talking to another woman in a severely tailored suit much like her own. Even at this distance I was sure I recognized Natalie. Her hair was short and blow-dried where it had been long before, but her body was as stiff as ever. She was still a good-looking woman, though, even pursing her lips the way she always had. Natalie had been the smartest of our group. And if rumors were to be believed, the most sexually active. Though I had never been able to believe those rumors. Sex got me thinking about Ken again.

"Is Ken coming?" I asked as quietly as I could and still be heard over the music.

"Uh-uh," Sid said, shaking his head. "I couldn't find the crazy s.o.b." This time he winked so largely, the pantomime could have been sighted in outer Mongolia. "But, hey, you'll come anyway, won't you?"

I looked a question over my shoulder at Wayne, hoping he hadn't caught Sid's innuendo.

"Okay," Wayne mouthed. I could almost hear his brain add, "If you really have to."

"We'll be there," I said to Sid, thinking how good it would be to talk to Pam. And to Becky. Somewhere where we could hear each other speak. Somewhere without disco lights.

"It's potluck," Sid told me. "So bring some munchies. Something for the barbecue too if you want." He winked a tiny wink this time. "Or just cash. Or expensive video equipment—"

"How about tofu burgers and a pinball machine?" I said, getting into the spirit.

"You really have a pinball machine?" he demanded, his little eyes lighting up.

Fifteen minutes later, I wished I'd kept my mouth shut. Because Sid really, *really*, wanted me to bring a pinball machine to his party. I told him it was too much trouble, that pinball machines rarely enjoy a ride. That they're hard enough to keep working without moving them around. But he kept at me, finally talking me into lending him one. He said he'd come with a truck sometime this week—then he turned to Jack and talked *him* into loaning the truck—and that Wayne and I

could help load on our end, and then he'd get someone else
to help unload on his end. I gave in, mentally giving him Hot
Flash, a machine that had been residing in my closet for the
last eight years or so, a machine even my ex-husband hadn't
liked well enough to take with him when we separated. Then
I grabbed Wayne's arm and started circulating.

I still hadn't met up with Pam or Charlie by the end of the
night. Or Elaine or Mark. Though I had talked briefly with
Becky, who'd smelled strongly of alcohol, and Natalie, who'd
smelled more like dry ice. But Sid caught up with us again on
our way out and promised that everyone I'd missed that night,
I'd see at his party on Saturday afternoon.

A week later, Sid kept his promise. He had us all standing
out on the concrete patio of his ground floor condo. The sunlight that filtered through the sheltering stand of oak trees was
a vast improvement over pulsating disco lights. And the only
music that mild June afternoon was the tinny whisper of the
Byrds from a boombox near the unlit barbecue. We could all
hear ourselves speak. Or at least hear Sid speak.

"So my good buddy Jack, here, knows this big-shot investment counselor, Harlan something-or-other, who's traips-
ing off to tour Europe for the summer," Sid was saying. He
slapped Jack on the back fondly. Jack smiled weakly in the
direction of his own feet. "And he talked this goon into sub-
letting the condo to me while he was gone. Right here in
Gravendale, man. At a third of what he pays in mortgage. And
this guy gives investment advice! All I gotta do is keep an eye
on the place. And an ear—"

"And a belly," Sid's cousin Elaine put in, her voice dry.

Sid threw his head back and laughed.

Elaine could talk. She hadn't put on weight. If anything,
she had lost it. Her face still had that Semling look: the high,
broad cheekbones, wide nose, and small eyes. But her body

was anorexically thin and expensively dressed in a white silk pants suit, shot with gold. And matching gold high-heeled sandals. I watched her watch Sid laugh, finding it hard to believe that Elaine, who'd once worn a beaded headband and frequent flowers in her hair, was now a Republican mother of three as she had already mentioned five or six times. Of course, most of us had exchanged business cards and brief occupational histories before Sid had regained the center of attention.

"I don't really know Harlan that well," Jack mumbled belatedly into his beard. "Just fix his car. It's a Volvo."

"Harlan likes you a lot," Lillian put in quickly. "You know that."

Jack shrugged and began humming softly along with the Byrds, his eyes out of focus. I had forgotten that he'd been musical in high school. I wondered if he still was.

"Jack and Lillian are profound centers of the community here in Gravendale," Aurora Kanick piped up. "Their auto mechanic business is a living example of right livelihood."

Aurora was Jack's mom. I remembered her as a Beaver Cleaver kind of mom, shirtwaist dresses and pearls. But no longer. These days, she owned a metaphysical bookstore. And this particular day, she was wearing a short lavender and teal kimono over blue jeans. Her silver hair was pulled back into a chignon. And her eyes radiated spiritual consciousness through oversized glasses. "My son and my daughter-in-law have both touched people's hearts in countless ways—"

"And fixed a lot of cars," Elaine cut back in. "My BMW included—"

"Friends!" Sid enthused, throwing out his arms. "That's the whole point. Came back home with zip and look what my old friends do for me. My buddy, Jack, finds me a place to stay. And good old Natalie gives me a job."

He reached out an arm and pulled Natalie into its enclosure.

She stiffened and jammed her hands in the pockets of her loose linen jacket. But at least she didn't deck him.

"Yeah, I'm Natalie's super salesman now," Sid pressed on. "Got Nusser Networks here a big fat government defense contract lined up. One that'll keep the business in the legal tender for a year at least."

Natalie nodded, then murmured, "I'd better set up the barbecue," and pulled away from his grip.

Sid turned to Lillian, his arm reaching out for a new squeeze. But Natalie had broken his spell.

"I'd better check on the kids," Lillian said, taking a quick side step out of Sid's range.

"They're great kids," I told Aurora. By which I meant quiet and well-behaved kids. Josh, aged five, and Lark, aged eight, had been sitting on the patio drawing on giant pads of paper for more than an hour without a peep. Or maybe it was just that their peeps weren't audible over the adult voices.

"I shouldn't brag, but they are wonderful children," their grandmother agreed. She steepled her fingers together. "So creative. Josh is already an artist like his mother. Lillian is a sculptor as well as an auto mechanic, you know. And Lark draws *and* sings." Aurora paused and something sad seemed to change the shape of her serene eyes. But then she dropped her hands and it was gone. "And they both have such a profound ability to nurture and love." Her cheeks pinkened. "But enough about my grandchildren. I hear you're a vegetarian too."

"Guilty as charged," I admitted. "I brought the tofu burgers for the grill."

"Well bless you," Aurora said. "I brought Tandoori tofu brochettes."

"And I brought a pot of chili *sans* carne, thank you very much," Pam Ortega put in. She kissed her fingertips. "*Mucho* spicy."

I turned to Pam with pleasure. Pam had been a large and beautiful teenager, and was now a large and beautiful woman, with the curves of an Ingres odalisque under her peasant blouse and jeans. Her heart-shaped face and lustrous eyes had a wry look to them that hadn't been there before. It looked good. I smiled at her as Sid turned to Jack and began talking again.

"So I got this deal going on this vintage Chevy for you if you want . . ."

"I believe I'll help Natalie with the grill," Aurora said quietly.

"Be glad to help you help her," Wayne added just as quietly.

Sid was still talking as the odd couple walked away together.

"You could fix up the old clunker, then we could split the cash . . ."

Pam tugged on my hand, pulling me out of blasting range.

"So, Kate," she whispered after we'd moved a yard or so away. "What's the story with you and Wayne?"

Did she want the real story or the easy-listening version? I looked into her eyes and saw real interest there, then took a deep breath. Not just for the air to tell the story, but to ease the tightness in my chest.

"Well, I was married for a long time to this guy named Craig Jasper," I began. "Fourteen years. We got divorced a few years ago and now—"

"Is this thing safe to play?" Mark Myers yelled out, his hands on the sides of the Hot Flash pinball machine where it sat on the opposite side of the patio.

Pam and I both turned to him.

"Mark looks good, doesn't he?" Pam said.

And he did. Mark had filled out since high school. His wiry body had some muscle now. His face was still round though, with alert, intense eyes. Even beneath his receding hairline, those eyes set in that face made him look a lot younger than he was. Younger than any of the rest of us.

"Ask Sid!" I yelled back.

"Ready Freddy," Sid obliged, flashing Mark the go-ahead enthusiastically. "Hot to trot like an old whore—"

"Sid!" Elaine objected, cuffing him on the shoulder.

Sid laughed as Mark hit the reset button on Hot Flash. The machine came to electrical life with an audible hum. It was a vintage Friedman machine with a backglass featuring a lone man being struck by lightning as he stared at three scantily clad women. The look on his face was rapturous. Hot Flash had a wooden top bar on the front, and broad metal bands riveted to the sides. And a playfield that had little more to offer than thumper-bumpers and jellyfish roll-overs. Not a lot of action.

I turned back to Pam.

"Sure is hot in here," came a voice from Mark's direction. Only it didn't sound like Mark. I swiveled my head around to look. Actually, it sounded like the words had come from the pinball machine itself.

"Mark's a vegie too," Pam told me, and I brought my head back around. "Anyway, go on about you and Wayne."

I snuck a glance at the man in question. Wayne and Aurora were standing by Natalie, and Aurora was pouring him some of her home-pressed apple juice. Wayne loved apple juice. And Aurora had brought a couple of gallons.

"Well, Wayne and I met a few years ago," I said, smiling a little at the sight of another glass of juice disappearing down Wayne's gullet. "And we've lived together awhile too. And we're . . . well, we're going to get married."

"But . . ." said Pam.

I reached out and squeezed her hand. She was just as perceptive as she'd always been. Maybe she should have become a therapist instead of a librarian.

"But," I took another deep breath, "I don't want it to be like my marriage to Craig. I want a simple little wedding and then we're out of there. Just married, no big deal. But Wayne wants a 'real' wedding with family and friends and flowers and a best man and—"

"And all the stuff you had at your first wedding."

I nodded violently. Pam got it. If only Wayne would.

"And the worst thing is we're arguing about an event that's supposed to be about love and commitment." I lowered my voice. "Wayne used to be too insecure to argue with me. I'm not sure which way I like him better—"

The sound of bells going off interrupted me. Mark had won a game.

"Hey, Natalie!" he shouted. "Want a shot at Hot Flash?"

Natalie just shook her head. As stiff and dry as ever. That's why I'd never believed her sexual reputation.

Mark yelled at Becky next.

"My turn, my turn!" Becky squealed like a kid and went running over, her pale legs flashing beneath short-shorts. Now with Becky, I'd believed all the rumors.

"It's hard to picture Becky as an attorney," Pam said as if she'd heard my thought.

"And a mother," I whispered back.

We both looked at Becky's fifteen-year-old son, D.V. He had his mother's delicate facial structure, but the inherited blue eyes were pinched and glaring. He wore his blond hair slicked down under a backwards baseball cap, and his jeans were so baggy they looked like they'd slide off at any moment as he stalked after his mother.

"Why do you think Becky brought him—" Pam began.

"So what are you two girls whispering about?" came Sid's voice, closer than it had been a moment before.

"Vegetarian food," answered Pam, managing to plaster a serious look on her face.

I stifled a giggle. Especially when Sid's broad face fell.

"Chard," she added soberly.

But Sid was irrepressible.

"The only thing I like charred is my steak," he told us and slapped his leg.

He was still laughing when Lillian walked up. Sid snaked his arm around her.

"You remind me of a chick I knew in 'Nam—" he began, but Lillian circled out from beneath his arm before he'd even finished speaking. I took a quick glance at Jack, who was now gazing out above us, humming a song I didn't recognize.

"It sure is hot in here," came a voice from the direction of Hot Flash. I swung around in time to see Becky jump back from the machine. "I must be having a hot flash," the voice went on. Becky squealed.

I'd been right the first time. The machine was talking. And it certainly hadn't been talking when it had left home on the truck. I turned back to Sid. He was grinning, one hand in his pocket. Sid Semling, master prankster. He must have done something to the machine.

He turned away from my stare to Charlie Hirsch, standing behind him.

"Hey, Charlie," he prompted. "You were in 'Nam too, right?"

I had almost forgotten Charlie was there. Charlie was a big, shambling man with a long face and wide, dreamy eyes that didn't seem to focus very well on the person talking to him. Especially now.

Charlie nodded without answering Sid, his eyes somewhere else. On Pam, I realized. Of course. How could I have forgotten that Pam and Charlie had been married (for however short a time). And me and my big mouth going on about marrying Wayne. My eyes followed Charlie's to Pam's. She was watching him intently, her lush Ingres body leaning toward him.

"That all you got to say about it, buddy?" Sid demanded.

Charlie nodded again. God, even Wayne was more talkative. Even Jack.

Sid turned back to Jack.

"So how the hell'd *you* beat the draft?" he demanded.

Jack opened his mouth, but before he could answer Lillian interjected, "Bad eyesight."

"Lucky stiff," Sid grumped and then circled in on Pam, his arm around her shoulders in an instant.

"Hey!" Pam said as she pushed his arm away. "What's with the arm bit? Do you get a hundred points every time you put it around someone female?"

Sid just grinned and put his hand back in his pocket.

"It sure is hot in here," the machine across the patio said. "This must be menopause."

Becky shrieked. I didn't blame her. She was my age. Not quite old enough for menopause. Just old enough to start worrying about it. And now I was sure it was Sid's prank. Who else would be tacky enough to make menopause jokes in the first place?

Becky abandoned Hot Flash and came running over to our little group. "Did you hear that?" she wanted to know. "Did you hear that? The machine talked to me!"

Sid didn't surprise us. He put his arm around Becky.

"Did you make it do that, Sid?" she demanded, the lilt in her voice making the demand a flirtation.

"Would it make you happy if I did?" he flirted back.

"Get your arm off my mother," D.V. growled.

I jumped in place. I hadn't seen him follow his mother back. Damn. The kid was scary. And I wasn't the only one who thought so. Sid dropped his arm before D.V. even finished his sentence.

Becky just giggled. "Now, D.V.," she cajoled. "No harm done."

D.V. turned on his heel and stalked back to the pinball machine.

"D.V. is growing up," Becky told us, her blue eyes wide with what looked like affection. "Used to be 'Davie' but now it's 'D.V.' He's a good kid."

We all nodded, even Sid. No one was about to argue the point. Aloud, anyway.

D.V. set up a game on Hot Flash and began whacking the flipper buttons.

"It's hot as a coven's oven in here," the machine said after a few seconds had passed. "Hot as a wizard's pizard. Hot as . . ."

But D.V. went on playing as if Hot Flash were just humming and chiming like any old pinball machine.

This time when I looked at Sid, he pulled something out of his pocket and flashed it at me, something resembling a garage door opener. A remote control?

Then he shoved it back in his pocket and came toward me with his arms extended.

"Oh no you don't," I told him, raising my own arms defensively. "Don't even think about it."

But Aurora got physical before I had to. She walked up to Sid and put her own thin arm around his wide shoulders. Sid jumped and let out a little yip of surprise.

"I've always wanted a boy-toy," Aurora cooed. "Will you be mine?"

Laughter roared over the patio from all directions.

Mark walked up on Sid's other flank.

"Me next," he purred, extending his muscular arm.

"Not without an HIV test," Sid protested. "A squirrelly guy like you."

I laughed again. And was immediately sorry I had.

"I'm HIV negative," Mark said, his intense eyes flashing. "But I've known better men than you who've died of AIDS."

The patio went silent. Aurora lifted her arm from Sid's shoulder. Mark had already told us he was gay. And he'd probably hoped for acceptance of that fact by the very people that might have turned on him if he had come out twenty-five years ago. I tried to think of something to say. But Sid beat me to it.

"Hey, sorry, old buddy," he muttered and gingerly patted Mark's back.

Mark gave him a quick grin of forgiveness, the anger gone from his eyes. "As for being squirrelly," he said lightly. "As a veterinarian, I'll take that as a compliment."

Sid laughed loud and hearty. Too loud and hearty. But it was better than nothing. I could feel the collective sigh of relief as the moment passed.

"Hey, you're an almost doctor. Maybe you can tell me how to lose flab," Sid rambled on. "I'm supposed to take off fifty pounds. I'm forty-three, and I've got a heart condition. Do you believe it?"

Mark tugged at a nonexistent beard on his chin and then answered, "No more canned dog food for you!"

We all laughed at that one.

"At least I've got a job with health insurance," Sid said. "Sales for Natalie's computer firm—"

"I work for a computer firm in Santa Rosa too," Elaine interrupted. "Even if I'm just the head secretary and Natalie owns her own company. But our firm is growing. Natalie's is stagnating—"

"Well, at least she's good to her employees," Sid argued

without apparent rancor. "They like her. She's a good boss, a dynamite programmer—"

But Elaine didn't want to hear anything more about Natalie Nusser.

"So, Charlie, what are you doing these days?" she asked instead.

I'd almost forgotten Charlie Hirsch again. In his khaki shirt and pants, he seemed to blend into the sheltering oak trees.

"Writing children's books," he told her. His deep voice was gruff.

"That's it?" Sid demanded.

Charlie shrugged. "I do some gardening too. And I'm a handyman."

"A handyman, for God's sake," Sid objected. "Wasn't your old man a doctor? What does he think of you gardening for doctors instead of being one?"

"He's dead," Charlie answered.

"Hey, sorry, man," Sid said for the fourteenth time that afternoon.

"Well, Gravendale's seen better times," Elaine opined. At least it was a change of subject.

"Yeah," agreed Sid. "I can't believe all those Mexicans downtown, pissing on the street like pigs—"

"Are you *trying* to ruin your own party?" Pam demanded, her lustrous eyes narrowed in anger. "You know my parents are from Mexico—"

"Those Mexicans aren't like you—" he tried.

"No, they're homeless," she shot back.

Wayne chimed in then with some compassionate words for the homeless. And Aurora followed up, talking about the spiritual connection the community needed to feel with those at every level of prosperity. When Mark started in about the immigrant experience, Sid turned away from us.

"Gotta do a couple of things," he told us. "I'll be back in

a minute.'' Then he disappeared through the sliding glass doors into his living room. I would have bet he was setting up more pranks.

Conversation was pleasant after that, focusing on old memories, mostly the nicer ones.

Becky was the one who brought up Robert Weiss.

"Remember his magic tricks," she murmured. Her fragile face looked even more fragile for a moment. Even tragic. "And the way he could dance like Fred Astaire . . .''

We all nodded. I wondered how many of us were remembering how Robert had looked when fireworks had blown his upper body away. My stomach clenched.

"I always thought he was gay," Mark put in.

"Gay!" Elaine objected. "Whaddaya mean, gay? He couldn't be. He went out with Becky, remember?''

"No," Becky disagreed, with a stronger delivery than I would have expected from her. "I think Mark is right. I didn't understand it then, but later I realized—''

"Remember that goofy cape he used to wear?" asked a voice coming across the patio. Sid, back from whatever mischief he'd put in motion. But I liked him in that instant, recognizing the real affection for Robert in his tone.

"Yeah," Becky answered wistfully.

"Hey, no one's playing pinball!" Sid boomed, waving his arms above his head. "It's party hearty time!''

"Go for it, Sid," Mark challenged him. "See if *you* can win a game.''

"Maybe I just will," Sid replied, straightening his shoulders and sucking in his gut.

He strode up to Hot Flash, pushed the reset button, gripped the machine's metal sides with his large rough hands, slapped the flippers a few times, and then shook the whole machine fiercely as the ball came spiraling down toward the drain.

"You're gonna tilt!" I warned him.

Then suddenly the whole backboard lit up in a flash, as if lightning really had struck the lone man standing there in rapturous worship of the three scantily clad women before him. Sid's body seized, stiffening and vibrating at the same time. I could hear the grating sound of the machine jamming. And the smell of smoke. And a whiff of something else, something like meat cooking.

"He's being electrocuted!" someone yelled from behind me. And still I couldn't put it together.

"Pull him off the machine!" someone else yelled.

I saw Wayne move toward Sid and woke up.

"No!" I shouted.

THREE

"Wayne!" I screamed, burning my lungs and throat with the sound as I began running. "DON'T TOUCH HIM!"

Because Wayne was only a yard away from Sid. And Sid was still gripping Hot Flash. If Wayne touched Sid, the electricity running through Sid's body might . . .

"STOP!" I yelled again.

Wayne seemed to hear me that time. He stopped and turned, his eyes on mine, questioning and then understanding.

"Yes!" was all I could say with the breath I had left.

Because I kept running.

I kept running until I got to the back end of Hot Flash and yanked its cord from the socket.

And finally, Sid was released.

He slumped over the pinball machine for a moment before slowly sliding off onto the concrete patio, his head landing last with an audible *crack*.

"Oh, God. Sid!" someone wailed.

I turned and saw that it was Elaine, her hands flailing in the air as everyone else stood like statues. I was glad to be looking at Elaine. I didn't want to look at Sid. A glimpse had already shown me his gray and blistered hands. And his pale face and blue lips.

"Is he dead?" she asked.

Abruptly, some of the statues began to move. And to speak.

"Who knows CPR?" Pam demanded, swiveling her head around to scan the group.

"I do," Mark shot back, and loped over to kneel by Sid.

He felt for a pulse and put his ear over Sid's mouth as Elaine began wailing again.

"Is he dead?" she kept asking. "Is he dead?"

Mark pinched Sid's nostrils and breathed into his mouth, two slow breaths initially, then five faster ones.

"Call 911," Becky suggested, her thin voice somehow distinct against the backdrop of Elaine's continued wailing.

"I'll call," said Wayne, already heading through the sliding glass doors into Sid's living room.

Was Sid dead? My mind didn't seem clear enough to encompass the question. Had Sid been electrocuted by my pinball machine? I shook my head violently, trying to shake some sense into it, but that just made me dizzier. And sicker to my stomach. Carefully, I sat down on the concrete patio.

"Mommy, what happened?" asked a little voice near me.

I turned my head. Eight-year-old Lark Kanick was looking up at her mother with fear in her eyes. God, I had forgotten there were children here. Five-year-old Josh Kanick grabbed his mother's hand and burst into tears. Lillian murmured something soothing but inaudible and then led both children to the side of the patio furthest from Sid.

When I turned back, Mark was still breathing into Sid's mouth. But it wasn't making Sid look any more alive.

I pulled my eyes away, surveying the rest of the watchers. Elaine was still on her feet sobbing, her fingers splayed as her hands twitched uncontrollably. I knew I should get up and comfort her, but I couldn't seem to make my legs move. I was just too cold, leftover sweat chilled all over my body. Aurora was busy with Jack, her hand on his shoulder, whispering

something in his ear as he swayed his bowed head rhythmi-
cally back and forth. And Becky and D.V. were standing side
by side, hands clasped, more like sister and brother than
mother and son. Natalie, Pam, and Charlie just stared. Stared
at Sid and Mark.

"Damn it, Sid, just try," I heard Mark mutter, and my eyes
strayed back to him. With his elbows locked, Mark placed one
hand on top of the other and pressed on Sid's chest. Hard and
fast. And then he pressed again. And again.

"Police and ambulance are on the way," I heard from
above me.

I looked up gratefully at Wayne. He knelt down in front of
me on the concrete, placing his large gentle hands on mine.
He looked into my eyes.

"Thank you," he said, his voice deep and rough. "You
may have saved my life."

I gazed back at him, astounded. Had I saved his life? With
that question, my mind provided another. Had I killed Sid
Semling with my own pinball machine?

"You okay?" Wayne asked softly.

To my horror, I heard my own bark of laughter at the question. And then I heard the sound of sirens.

The police car and the ambulance screeched up in front of
the condo simultaneously.

Wayne trotted off to greet them.

Seconds later, a uniformed cop came striding out to the
patio from Sid's living room. He was a slender man who
didn't look up to the job before him.

"Okay, everyone stand back!" he ordered in a surprisingly
burly voice.

Natalie, Charlie, and Pam were quick to follow orders,
marching over to the opposite side of the patio where Lillian
and her children were already seated. I was a little slower on
my wobbly legs. Aurora and Jack joined us. And then Becky

and D.V. And finally Wayne, his errand done. I grabbed his hand and held on. Only Mark stayed in place, his mouth on Sid's once more, trying to breathe life into him.

And Elaine, still frozen in place.

"Is he dead?" she asked again, her voice too loud on the quiet patio. "He's my cousin, is he dead?"

"Now, ma'am," the officer said, kindness in his voice. "We'll get to you in a second if you'll just . . ."

I lost the end of his sentence as a tall, red-haired woman and a smaller, brown-skinned man came out onto the patio, weighted down with equipment, duffel bags, and fanny packs.

The red-haired woman tapped Mark's shoulder, and he stood up slowly, shaking his head forlornly.

The redheaded woman took over where Mark had left off, with mouth-to-mouth resuscitation. The brown-skinned man inserted an IV into Sid's vein and a tube down his throat, before lifting Sid's shirt and attaching three round pads connected to a little box with a flip-up screen. All in seconds.

"Maybe they can do something," Mark whispered as he joined our group. His round, youthful face looked haggard, his eyes close to tears. "I sure as hell couldn't. I've saved a German shepherd with mouth-to-mouth, but a human? Why couldn't I—"

"You did all you could do," Aurora assured him. "You acted with loving professionalism and—"

"No, I won't step back!" Elaine's voice burst in. "I want to know what happened! He's my cousin. Almost a brother to me. Don't you understand? He can't be dead—"

The officer looked over at our group hopefully.

"Elaine," I tried softly, not expecting much. I opened up my arms. "Come stand here with us. You're not going to help Sid any—"

But Elaine surprised me as she came rushing, sobbing, into my arms, almost knocking me over with the impact of her small, anorexic body. I wrapped my arms around her, feeling the prominent bones under her thin flesh as she trembled. And then tears came from my eyes too. For Sid, and for this woman I'd never really liked as a girl. I remembered how close Elaine and Sid had been, both only children, more like siblings than cousins. Both obnoxious at times, but always together, always supporting each other.

I heard the sound of something winding up and peeked over Elaine's shoulder. Little paddles shaped like irons were on Sid's chest now, linked to a gray box with coiled cords.

"Stand clear!" the brown-skinned man ordered. Both paramedics stood away and the man pushed a button.

Sid's body jerked, his head, his hands, and his legs.

"Is he alive?" someone murmured behind me.

Elaine's body jerked too, out of my arms to look.

But the electrically induced spasm was all there was to see. Nothing else happened.

The paramedics kept trying as we heard the sound of another police car sirening up. They put more stuff into Sid's IV. They did more CPR. They hooked up the box and made him jerk again. But it was no good.

By the time two more police officers came on the scene, the paramedics were shaking their heads.

"Do we get the body?" I heard the red-haired woman whisper to one of the new police officers, a big man who seemed to be in charge. I winced. If I could hear this, so could Elaine. I wrapped an arm around her thin shoulders. I would have liked to have plugged her ears. Or plugged the red-haired woman's mouth.

"Dead?" the big officer asked in turn.

"Yeah, but we don't get paid unless we give him a ride," she whispered back. "You know that."

"Suspicious death, 187," he replied, throwing out his hands. "*You* know—"

"He's not dead!" Elaine screamed. "You gotta do something!"

The only female officer on the scene turned to Elaine as the two paramedics packed up and left. Quickly.

But Sid was still there, lying on the concrete patio in front of Hot Flash, IV and throat tube in place.

That's when Elaine really began to scream. No words, just long, wailing screams. The female officer grabbed Elaine, taking her arm gently but firmly and leading her into Sid's living room. Then the original officer on the scene began cordoning off an imperfect circle around Hot Flash and Sid's body with yellow tape. The remaining officer turned to the rest of us.

"No one is to leave," he announced. "Your statements will be taken in turn."

A lot of nothing seemed to happen in very active slow motion after that. One by one, we were each taken into the condo to give statements. Becky asked if she could have a beer. Permission denied. Wayne was taken inside for questioning. Pam tried to make conversation. Permission denied. More police came. Aurora wanted to do a "ritual of passing" for Sid. Permission denied. A crime scene technician came and went, sketching, photographing, and measuring.

And then Jack began weeping. Not as dramatically as Elaine, but weeping all the same, softly and hopelessly.

"It should have been me," he whispered. "It should have been—"

"No, Jack," Aurora said and put a hand on his shoulder. "Remember what is written on your heart. Remember . . ."

Lillian jumped up from where she sat with her children and pushed past Becky and D.V. toward her husband.

I bent closer. What did Jack mean, it should have been him? And what the hell was written on Jack's heart? And why was Lillian—

I felt a tap on my shoulder. Damn.

"Ms. Jasper," the officer said. "Please follow me."

Slow motion was over.

The officer waved me into Sid's tastefully decorated living room and onto a comfortable yet elegant sofa, which I suddenly realized was not Sid's at all but some absent investment counselor's, and I was introduced to Detective Sergeant Gonzales.

Detective Sergeant Gonzales was the only officer on the scene who wasn't in uniform, a tall, dark, and handsome man with a Clark Gable mustache. In fact, he looked a bit like Clark Gable, on a morose day. And he was cool. Cool, thorough, and intelligent. He questioned me quietly and efficiently, establishing among other things that Hot Flash was my pinball machine. After about twenty minutes, he finished up with the one question I'd hoped he wouldn't ask.

"Ms. Jasper, in your opinion could Mr. Semling's death have been an accident?"

I clasped my hands together and took a quick breath. I wasn't going to lie. But I wasn't going to give him a straight "yes" or "no" either.

"I don't think so," I told him finally.

And then they let me go.

Wayne reached over and squeezed my leg as I drove home from Sid's. The squeeze seemed to say, I love and adore you and will always stand by you despite our differences. Then again, maybe it was just a squeeze. I reached over and squeezed back just in case.

Communications got even better after we arrived home. Well, at least after we checked for feline marauders. Lately, neighborhood cats had been coming in through the cat door I had so expensively and laboriously installed for my own cat, C.C., coming in to spray the house. Desks, papers, towering bookshelves, a jungle of houseplants, pinball machine legs, swinging chairs. They had marked them all. I wasn't sure if this was a war with C.C. or a war with us. But it was war. So when we came home, we always sniffed.

C.C. came ambling in from the kitchen as Wayne and I were doing our bloodhound act.

"Well, C.C.—" I began and then saw the orange streak of an enemy cat retreating through C.C.'s door.

I sprinted out the front door, shaking my fists and making threatening noises as the orange cat loped across the redwood deck and over the fence. When I came back, panting for breath, C.C. just looked up at me, her smooth black coat unruffled, the little white patches of fur resembling a beret and goatee, respectively, in place. Then she squinted her eyes serenely and opened her little lizard lips to demand food.

"You need assertiveness training," I growled at her.

"Unlike your mother," Wayne muttered.

I turned on him.

"Unlike your mother who is brave and intelligent as well as beautiful and funny," he went on quickly. Then he opened his arms.

Ah, nonverbal communication.

We held each other for what seemed like hours but was probably only minutes, feeling each other's heat and heartbeats and smelling each other's scents. When Wayne ran his gentle hand down my back I began to cry. And then I began to think. Always a mistake, thinking when you're crying.

"Craig," I snuffled.

"What?" Wayne objected, releasing me so suddenly from the warm enclosure of his arms that I would have fallen backwards if not for a quick back step I'd learned in tai chi. I wondered for an instant if the Master had ever used the back step for a similar purpose.

"Craig." I repeated my ex-husband's name stubbornly, watching Wayne's brows lower over his eyes like curtains.

Rock curtains. "He knows more about pinball machines than any other human I know. He'll know if Hot Flash could have malfunctioned."

Wayne straightened his shoulders, closed his eyes completely, and took a long, cleansing breath. As I watched, part of me wanted to scream at him for his attempt to return to reason and another part of me wanted to hug him some more because he *was* trying. And this was the man I was going to marry.

"Fine," he said finally, his voice low and unemotional. "Why don't you call him?"

"All right," I answered and reached out to hold him again. But he had already turned and walked away.

"Hot Flash, huh?" Craig said thoughtfully a few minutes later over the phone. I'd told him everything I could remember of the machine's behavior from the time it left my closet until the time it electrocuted Sid.

"Hot Flash," he repeated. "Boy, that machine sucked. Lousy playfield." He stopped for a moment. "Didn't it have metal side bars and a wooden front rail?"

"Yeah," I answered, my heart giving an eager little hop. That's right. If the front was wood and the sides were metal, then Sid touching the metal sides could have completed an electrical circuit—

"But still," Craig went on, obviously thinking as he spoke. "The guy wasn't standing in water or anything, was he?"

"No." My heart settled back down.

The phone was silent for a moment.

"But wait, now I remember," Craig said finally. "Hot Flash was one of those machines with American and European transformer potential, 120 or 220 volts." His voice took on speed and enthusiasm. "Now if the ground wire of one of those metal side bars was connected to the 220 volt tap of the transformer instead, it could effectively double the power of the house current.''

Then he stopped again.

"But?'' I asked impatiently.

"But it would've had to have been electrically isolated and correctly grounded until the magic moment. Or else the first person to play it would have gotten fried.'' I wished he hadn't used the word "fried.'' My stomach fluttered as a picture of Sid's body seizing accosted my mind's eye. Craig went on obliviously.

"Of course, you could initiate the magic moment through a special relay or two, maybe as a double throw switch with a secure firing mechanism.'' He paused. "But how? Set for a specific sequence? A tilt? Or, hey—how about a remote control?''

"Sid had a remote control,'' I interrupted.

"The guy that got fried?''

"Yeah,'' I answered. "I think Sid was using it to make the machine do the funny voices.''

"But was there a *second* remote control?'' he asked, his voice thick with excitement. "Because if there was—''

"I know,'' I interrupted soberly. "Because if there was, Sid was murdered.''

FOUR

"Jeez, I wish I could have been there to see it," Craig breathed.

"Well I was!" I snapped back. "I saw an old friend die, and let me tell you, it wasn't any fun—"

"I'm sorry, Kate," he said contritely.

I kept my sigh internal. Contrition from Craig was not normal. Just one more sign that Craig still hoped that Wayne and I weren't going to get married. Just one more sign that he still hoped *he* had a chance with me. A romantic chance. For some reason, once Craig had divorced me he'd begun to woo me all over again, and he'd never stopped. I'd tried my best to make it clear that he would never, ever, have another romantic chance with me. Without being too cruel in my rejection. Because Craig was not a bad man. An insensitive man at times. A complete jerk at others. A social idiot—but, anyway, not a bad man.

"Dating any neat new women?" I asked.

"Well," he answered hesitantly. "I met this woman, Tillie, Scottish country dancing. Someone told me it was a great place for computer nerds to meet women."

"And . . ."

"And she's a vegetarian. Plus, she's a technical writer." He paused. "But she has a lot of cats."

"How many is a lot?"

"Twenty-three," he whispered.

I tried to imagine that many cats in one room. And succeeded. Suddenly, I could picture each of them in different colors and stripes and spots, all yowling and racing around. My nose began to tickle allergically.

"And you know what else?" Craig's voice went even lower. "They all sleep with her. In shifts."

I hung up not long after that, glad I was living with Wayne, not Craig. Glad I was living with one cat and occasional visitors.

But I wasn't quite sure Wayne was as happy about our living arrangements as I was. I found him sitting in one of the chairs that hung from the ceiling in the living room, but he wasn't swinging in it like he usually did. He was just sitting, arms crossed, staring out into space.

I put my hands on his shoulders and began to massage. It was like massaging rock. But even rock wears down in time.

"Kate Jasper," he murmured so low I almost missed it. I didn't answer. I was pretty sure I knew what was coming.

"Even if you marry me, you'll still have his name."

Yup, that's what I'd thought was coming.

"Wayne," I said as carefully as I could. "Jasper's not just Craig's name anymore. It's mine. I took it almost twenty years ago. When I called myself Jasper, I didn't have a last name I was anxious to keep. I didn't even have an *identity* I was that anxious to keep. But I do now. I'm the Kate Jasper who owns Jest Gifts. I'm the Kate Jasper who's managed to make my own business from nothing. I'm the Kate Jasper who has a life she loves. And wonderful friends. And a man she adores."

And, I thought, I'm the Kate Jasper who's just seen an old friend electrocuted. By my own pinball machine.

Wayne rose from the swinging chair in one swift motion and had a big hand on my shoulder in another.

"Wasn't your fault," he said.

At first, I thought he meant it wasn't my fault my name was Jasper. But then I realized he knew I was thinking about Sid. Had he felt the guilt tingle through my fingertips into his shoulders?

"Oh, Wayne," I whispered, half in exasperation. How could a man so obstinate in some things be compassionate, verging on telepathic, in others?

"Someone tampered with that machine," he added.

I opened my mouth to tell him what Craig had said about a second remote control, and shut it again just in time. Wayne's hand remained reassuringly steady on my shoulder.

"The thing is," I finally said, feeling my way to the real issue only as I spoke, "I'm not even sure which would be worse. Knowing that Sid was electrocuted by accident, that it was my own machine, maybe my own negligence . . ." I took a breath. "Or knowing he was murdered, that someone hated him that much—"

The phone rang before I could decide. As if I ever could.

Aurora Kanick was on the line.

"Oh, Kate. I'm so glad I caught you in," she said, her tone both crisp and serene at the same time. For an instant, I wondered if I could gain that combination of serenity and crispness in twenty or thirty years time. *Nah*, someone in me decided.

"I've been thinking on Sid's death," Aurora went on. "And the more deeply I consider the circumstances, the more I believe we must act collectively." Then she paused.

Was I supposed to agree?

"Collectively as in, um, what?" I asked instead.

"Well, first off, we all need to sort out our feelings. I'm certain Sid Semling's death had a profound impact on each of us. But times of difficulty can be transformed, don't you think?''

"Yeah," I answered slowly.

"So, I imagined we could all get together for lunch tomorrow around one o'clock. Since it's Sunday, I would think most of us might be available.''

"You mean the people from Sid's party?" I interrupted. My soggy brain didn't seem to be keeping up with Aurora's crisp one.

"Oh, I'm sorry, Kate," Aurora said with a laugh like the tinkle of wind chimes, steel wind chimes. "I'm not being very clear, am I? Yes, I did mean the people who were present at the time of Sid's death. Do you suppose you and Wayne could come?''

I put my hand over the receiver and turned around. Wayne walked toward me, frowning.

"Do you want to meet with the people from Sid's party, at Aurora Kanick's tomorrow?" I whispered.

"Why?" he whispered back, the frown deepening.

"Because . . ."

I saw Sid's face in my mind for an instant, caught as he'd been remembering Robert Weiss with affection. And suddenly I was remembering Sid Semling with affection. And remembering that it was Hot Flash that had killed him.

"You're not thinking of investigating?" Wayne asked softly but urgently.

"No, no," I assured him automatically. But I kept thinking that if I could look into everyone's eyes just once, maybe I'd see . . .

Wayne took another step forward, bent down, and looked into *my* eyes.

"You have to go, don't you?" he said.

I was nodding my head before I even consciously heard his question.

"Okay," he agreed. "Together."

He straightened back up as I took my hand from the receiver to pass on the message.

"I thought it would be best if we all met at Jack and Lillian's house in Gravendale," Aurora told me. "It'll be easier for you to find than mine. I'm living in a cottage out in an experimental community in Lupton now. But Jack and Lillian and the kids are living in the very same house that Jack grew up in. Maybe you remember?" A grainy image of a white house with green shutters floated through my mind as she gave me the address and directions.

"And, Kate, thank you," she added finally. "I know you must be as concerned as I am."

I wanted a translation. But Aurora had said goodbye and hung up the phone before I could ask if "concerned" meant anything like "worried to death that Sid was murdered."

I turned to Wayne to ask him. I even opened my mouth. And then the doorbell rang. Almost as if they were connected.

Wayne and I moved toward the door as a pair, he doing the final honors with the doorknob. But it was my arms that Becky Burchell stumbled into. No, I corrected myself, she was Becky Vogel now. But she was still stumbling.

"Whoa," she breathed into my face. "Hey there, Kate." A connoisseur could have identified the brand of whiskey she'd been drinking from her breath. Even for me, the fumes were enough for a contact high.

Which made me wonder how she'd gotten here. I looked out over her shoulders onto the driveway and saw a Fiat parked at an angle across the gravel. Lucky it was a short car. It would have been in the flowers otherwise.

"Had to come," Becky explained, her voice too high and too loud. She uncurled her spine until she was standing straight on her own two feet. Then she took a deep breath in. And out again.

I backed up a step, holding my own breath, and regretting my earlier impulse to give everyone at Sid's party my business card (with my home address and phone number conveniently stamped on the back).

"Like to come in?" Wayne asked politely from my side. I could hear the forced note in that politeness, but I doubted if Becky could.

"Well, thank you, kind sir," Becky replied with a shaky little bow. Then she tilted her head sideways and stared up at Wayne's face for a moment. And another moment. And another.

I stared at her face as she stared at Wayne's, trying to figure out what she was looking for. What was she thinking? But her face wasn't giving out any clues. She still had the same delicate bone structure and open blue eyes that she used to, though there were a hell of a lot more wrinkles and even a few broken blood vessels in that face. And her smile was just as lopsided as it had been twenty-five years ago. Especially when she drank a bit too much. Or smoked a bit too much. Or—

Something squeezed at my chest. What now? I thought. And then knew. Sadness. It wasn't just Sid dying. It was seeing Becky like this. She'd been wild in high school, but sharp. And witty and fun and kind. And I'd cared for her. How had she become this drunken woman standing in front of me? When in the last twenty-five years had it happened?

Becky gave her head a violent shake, and her face disappeared under a curtain of permed blond hair. Then she took an unsteady step into the entryway. Wayne gave her the elderly aunt treatment, steering her toward the living room with a hand on her elbow.

"Wowie, zowie!" Becky whooped, opening up her arms and knocking away Wayne's guiding hand in the process. "What a cool place. The sixties live!"

I looked at my own living room, outraged. The sixties? True, the room was wall to wall with overflowing handmade bookshelves and a jungle of houseplants. True, our only furniture consisted of a set of swinging chairs suspended from the wood-beamed ceiling by rope, a handmade wood and denim couch, and piles of mismatched pillows. Oh, and a futon. But it was neat. And there wasn't any macramé in sight, by God.

Then she turned her face toward the corner where the two pinball machines, Hayburners and Texan, stood. Her head jerked back as if slapped. Then her eyes filled with tears.

"Oh, Becky," I whispered. "I'm sorry."

I put my arms around her and held her, trying not to breathe too deeply, ashamed of my earlier thoughts. Just because Becky was drunk this night didn't mean she was always drunk. She had seen Sid die just as I had. No wonder she was drinking now. And she had come to me. And I hadn't wanted to see her.

I led her to the wood and denim couch and set her down gently, then sat next to her. I didn't think she could handle one of the swinging chairs.

"My fault," she murmured through her hair, which was hiding her face again. "My fault."

"What exactly is your fault?" Wayne asked softly, still standing.

And for a chilling heartbeat, I wondered if Becky *was* here to confess murder.

"Say again?" she answered, bringing her head up, her blue eyes wet and shining.

"You said something was your fault—" Wayne began patiently.

"Coming here!" she cried, with a wave of her hand. "Coming here, drunk like this. Sorry, sorry. What a dope I am. But I had to. Had to talk to someone."

"About?" I prompted.

"Sid!" she yelped. "Oh, Jeez, Sid. He was always so funny, you know. Making me laugh all the time." She laughed then, a high-pitched laugh that hurt to even hear. "Kate, remember the Jell-O in the swimming pool? Gad, that was hilarious. And when he and the other guys carried Mr. Harper's Volkswagen bug around the corner. And the black lace bra on the flagpole. I know that was Sid's. And the talking toilets."

I nodded unenthusiastically. I'd been one of the idiots who'd sat on the talking toilet. And talked back.

"He made that pinball machine say all that stuff today," she added. "I'm sure of it. And then, and then . . ."

She put her face in her hands.

"It was just like Robert all over again!"

I stiffened next to her on the couch, unable to hear the next few sentences that poured out of her mouth.

Because it *was* like Robert all over again. Robert doing a magic trick, then exploding. Sid doing a prank, then electrocuting. But what did that similarity mean? Nothing, probably. Robert's death had been investigated by the police at the time. Thoroughly. We'd all been questioned. Especially about where the fireworks had come from. They'd finally figured out that Robert had bought the fireworks out of state on a trip with his parents. And there was no way Robert's death could have been rigged. No one could have timed a rocket to fizzle then explode at the same moment the conjuror chose to bend over it.

". . . it's like they were connected," Becky was saying when I tuned back in.

"But how?" I asked seriously.

"I don't know, I don't know," she whimpered, shaking her head. "God playing with the people I love while I watch." She laughed bitterly. "Of course, with me at the center of the universe." Then she sat up straighter, looking as sober as I'd seen her yet that night. "Gad, I've gotta stop this. They were both just horrible, horrible accidents."

I peered into her face, curious if she really believed that. She just stared back, her round blue eyes open and empty.

"Sid's death an accident?" I prodded, going for the jump-start approach.

"Yeah," she said, flinging her hand up suddenly as if to drive the point home. "Sid told us he had a heart condition, remember? So he had a heart attack."

I nodded. That made some sense. I sat a little straighter myself, hoping for a moment.

"And then he shorted out the machine by clutching onto it."

Unfortunately, *that* didn't make sense. Most people clutched pinball machines when they played them. And it didn't short them out.

"Or just two separate events?" Wayne put in quickly. I could hear new eagerness in his low, rough voice. "Sid has a heart attack. Hot Flash shorts out at the same time. And we assume that one event caused the other. What if they were just two separate, coinciding events?"

My heart pumped new hope into my veins. What if they were just two separate events? All right, Sid has a heart attack. Okay, the machine jams. Machines jam all the time. My pulse was racing now.

And then I remembered Sid's hands. They'd been gray and blistered. Burned. As my heart kept pumping, I tried to insert that fact into the theory. Tried to *shove* it in. But I just couldn't. Slowly, my pulse settled back down.

"Hey, you're not worried about negligence or anything, are you?" asked Becky.

"Huh?" I said, peering at her again and seeing concern for *me* in her eyes now.

"I mean it was your machine and all, but who's gonna sue

you," she went on. "Jeez, Sid isn't even married, is he? His parents are both dead, I think." She paused, her eyes half closed. "Anyway, if anyone, the manufacturer would be liable if—"

"I forgot, you're an attorney now," I interrupted. I didn't even want to consider legal liability. Moral liability was enough for one day.

"Personal injury," she said, fumbling through her purse for a card. I didn't remind her that she'd already given me one. "Harvey, Payne, and Putnam. Our motto: 'They screw you, we sue them.' 'Out of court settlements are the best revenge.' 'Follow that ambulance.' Et cetera."

She handed me the card, laughing. I laughed with her. This was more like the Becky I remembered.

But the laughter was short-lived. "Lousy job doing lousy work," she added, her smile a frown now. "And I'll never make partner. But 'hey,' as Sid would say, it's a living."

"Did you see much of Sid when he came back home?" I asked.

I could feel rather than see Wayne's glare. But what would a few questions hurt?

"We went out—oh, I think—a couple of times," she answered, looking at her lap now.

"On dates?" I asked perkily. Just between us girls.

She shrugged.

I riveted my eyes on her, hoping she'd say more.

"Could I have a drink?" she asked after a minute or two went by.

"Apple juice," Wayne answered. "Water, tea—"

Becky stood up, wobbling a little as she did.

"Listen, you guys," she said. "I'm real sorry, busting in on you like this. I just . . ." Her eyes teared up again.

"It's all right," I told her. "I'm shook up too. It was an awful thing to see Sid die."

"Oh, Kate," she murmured. "You were always so good to talk to." She gave me an alcohol-soaked hug, then released me with a moist kiss on the cheek.

"I'll get outa your hair now," she promised and walked unsteadily toward the door.

"Did you drive here yourself?" Wayne asked before her hand had a chance to touch the doorknob.

"Yeah," Becky answered with a quick grin. "D.V. was too busy on the Internet to give me any crap about it."

"Do you really think you should drive home alone now?" he asked, his volume low but his tone stern.

"Haven't had any better offers, mister," she lilted her reply. Then she gave Wayne a big wink.

Wayne's rough cheeks went pink. Flirtation wasn't a game he knew how to play. He swiveled his head around in my direction like a startled giraffe.

"Why don't you let Wayne drive you home in your car," I suggested. I had no desire to drive a Fiat. Driving Wayne's Jaguar's stick shift on occasion was exotic enough for me. And Wayne had to learn to deal with flirtation sometime. "Then I'll follow you and bring Wayne home."

Luckily, Becky's house was only a few highway exits away. And a few winding roads. And a steep concrete driveway. I parked my Toyota behind her Fiat at the top of that driveway, looking out my windshield curiously. Becky's house was small and stucco, surprisingly modest for a trial attorney. I got out of my car to take a better look.

And felt the thud of a hand on my shoulder.

"What the fuck are you doing here?" asked an angry voice inches from my right ear.

FIVE

I turned slowly, raising my arms defensively as I did.
Ready. Lifting my knee ever so slightly too. Just in case.

D.V. Vogel was standing inches from me when I finished
my turn, his scowling face thrust toward mine. Up this close,
I could see the obvious resemblance to his mother in the del-
icacy of his features. He was a good-looking boy, almost
pretty with his large blue eyes and soft mouth. Maybe it was
the fear of that prettiness that kept his otherwise attractive
features contorted so sullenly under his backwards baseball
cap.

I lowered my arms and knee as slowly as I had raised them.

Then I pushed my face even closer to his, our noses almost
touching now.

"Don't you *ever* do that to me again," I told him, keeping
my voice low and serious.

"Didn't mean anything," he muttered, pulling his head
back on his shoulders like a turtle withdrawing. "Anyway—"

"D.V.," I cut in, unwilling to let it go. "I'm serious about
accosting people like that. You may not realize it, but I could
have arrested your hormonal development in mid-puberty just
now."

"Whaddaya mean?" he demanded.

I lifted my knee in explanation. His pants were so baggy it only took a few inches to touch their cloth crotch.

"I could have kicked you in the balls," I added in case he still didn't get it.

He got it. His face went pale as he stepped away, crossing his hands in front of the vital area.

It appeared I had his attention. I looked over my shoulder. Wayne and Becky were still in the Fiat. Time to ask nosy questions.

"So why are you so angry that I'm here?" I demanded.

"Didn't know who you were," he mumbled. "Didn't know Mom was gone till she came back."

"Do you always keep your eye out for your mother?" I prodded. This was weird. Most mothers were keeping their eyes out for their fifteen-year-olds, not the other way around.

He shrugged, then lifted one shoulder and balanced himself on the opposite leg. A teenager trying to turn himself inside out. I remembered the feeling, if not the exact move.

"Is that why you came to Sid's party?" I pressed.

He shrugged then balanced himself on his other leg.

"So, what did you think of Sid?" I tried conversationally.

"He was a total butt-head," D.V. answered.

"Yeah?" I prompted.

"Yeah," he repeated angrily. "Takes her out, gets her totally wasted. And blah, blah, blah, all the time, like he's trying to sell me something—"

"Don't be like that, D.V. Please don't," Becky's wavering voice cut in from beside me. I flushed guiltily, caught mid-interrogation. "Sid's dead." She put her hand on her son's arm. "And Sid was my friend—"

"Some friend," D.V. muttered and marched out from under Becky's hand, toward the house.

"Time to go?" Wayne suggested softly. Softly and firmly.

"Time to go," I agreed.

Becky gave me a quick, fermented goodbye hug and then went tottering off after D.V. Wayne and I looked at each other, shrugged simultaneously, and climbed into the car.

I had to crane my head all the way around behind me to steer the Toyota back down the steep concrete driveway. And I couldn't stop thinking about Becky and D.V. as I did. Not having any children myself, I couldn't really tell just how odd their mother and son relationship was. But it did seem that—

"Hungry?" asked Wayne beside me.

All analysis of Becky and D.V.'s relationship left my mind, blotted out by hallucinations of food. Garlic bread, peach pie, even forbidden visions of roast beef. I could almost taste it. Because I was hungry. Very hungry. Even the thought of Sid's death didn't put a damper on the rebellious growls from my stomach. I couldn't count the number of hours that had passed since we *hadn't* eaten our promised tofu burgers at Sid's party. Lunchtime may have been lost, but dinnertime was at hand.

"New place called Chill-Out in San Rico," Wayne went on. "I called them and they've got six varieties of chili, three of them vegie, plus fresh-baked corn bread—"

"How do I get there?" I interrupted, salivating.

Ten minutes later, we were in opposite self-service lines at the chili bar. One side for vegetarians, one side for carnivores. First you got to ladle out your choice of three chilies: "mild," "hot," and "from hell." Then you got to choose from bowls and more bowls of toppings. Peanuts, jalapeños (in case "from hell" wasn't hot enough, I supposed), two kinds of onions, sprouts, yogurt, sour cream, grated cheese (soy an option), raisins, croutons, and everything else that could possibly top a bowl of chili. And finally there were warmed trays of French bread, whole wheat, and corn bread to go with it. All for six bucks and ninety-five cents. With refills.

I was in near ecstasy, halfway through my loaded bowl of "hot," crunching on a spicy crouton when Wayne spoke up.

"Do you believe Sid Semling was murdered?" he asked.

The crouton went down the wrong way and I grabbed for a glass of water, wheezing. Wayne was up in a shot, slapping my back. I slammed into the table, dislodging the crouton. Wayne's black belt in karate had paid off in a new way.

"Women shouldn't try 'from hell' unless they're ready for it," I heard a male voice comment scornfully a table away.

"I'm fine," I rasped out, tears streaming down my face. If there was anything I hated, it was jalapeño machismo.

Wayne sat back down and busied himself tidying up the mess my frontal assault on the table had left. His face was as red as mine.

"Sorry," he murmured.

"Yes, I do believe Sid Semling was murdered," I whispered back. My throat hurt too much to express myself any louder.

"Thought so," he said miserably. "No separate, coinciding events—"

"His—"

"Hands were burnt," he finished for me considerately.

I nodded, took a drink of water and a small bite of corn bread.

"Any favorite suspects?" he asked.

I swallowed carefully, faces popping into my mind like flashbulbs. Pam's angry one when Sid had talked about the Mexicans downtown. Mark Myers's even angrier one after Sid's HIV crack. Aurora's, teasing. D.V.'s, unable to be teased. Charlie, Natalie, Jack—

"How could Jack go along with Sid's bosom buddy act when Sid was busy trying to get his arm around Lillian?" I asked aloud.

Wayne frowned, as if trying to imagine a reason. And finding himself unable to.

"And how could Natalie hire Sid?" I went on. "I can't believe it was from the goodness of her heart. I'm not sure she even has a heart." I felt petty the minute I said it. I didn't know Natalie very well back then. Or very well now. Maybe she was just shy, not cold.

But Wayne only nodded thoughtfully. I took another small bite of chili.

"Sid might actually have been a good salesman," Wayne pointed out a couple of swallows later. "But . . ."

"But he was a pretty miserable specimen of a human being otherwise," I finished for him. I could hear it in his pause.

He nodded, lowering his head. Wayne generally tried to like everyone. And generally succeeded. Except for my ex-husband, of course. And, it would appear, Sid Semling.

"I know, I know," I agreed. "Half the time he was so obnoxious you wanted to strangle—" I corrected myself mid-sentence. "Not really to strangle, but maybe to scream at him. Or kick him. But there was something occasionally endearing about Sid."

Wayne raised his heavy eyebrows and looked across the chili-strewn table, trying to understand.

"Sid was funny," I tried to explain. "And always determined to have a good time, if nothing else. He played football, but not very well. He didn't take it very seriously. Same with classes. He didn't get very good grades. But he was so damned alive—"

I regretted the word instantly. Because "alive" was the very word to distinguish what had made Sid Semling special. So alive and now so dead.

"His cousin, Elaine, seems to have liked him," Wayne interjected. I could hear the struggle in his voice as he tried to be fair about Sid.

"And Becky went out with him," I added. "Now that, I don't understand. But I guess I don't understand Becky at all anymore."

We both ate in silence for a while after that. The chili still tasted good, actually better after the crouton-ectomy. I even thought about trying a few bites of the "from hell" just to show the guy from the other table.

"What was it that Becky said about someone named Robert dying?" Wayne asked after I had finished what was left in my bowl and taken a last swallow of water. Wayne's a quick learner. This time I didn't have anything to choke on.

I took a big breath and explained slowly. How Robert had put on the fireworks show. How he had lit the big rocket and then bent over it when it hadn't blown up. How it had blown up then.

"Nobody pushed him over? Or nudged him?" Wayne asked.

"No." I played it over in my mind. We had all stood way back from Robert as he did his show. Yards away. "No, he bent over on his own."

"And the rocket wasn't wired to anything?"

I played the scene again from another angle. But I couldn't see any wires. And the police hadn't either. Their only question had been who'd sold Robert the fireworks.

"I don't see how it could have been anything but an accident," Wayne finally concluded, just as I had. "Even if you could get the rocket to blow up when you wanted, how could you get him to bend over it?"

"What if someone blamed Sid anyway?" I asked, sitting up a little straighter with the thought.

"And then waited twenty-five years to kill him?"

"Oh, right."

We left the Chill-Out on that note.

All the way back in the car, I asked myself why come to a

reunion after twenty-five years in the first place. Murderer or not. Each of us must have had our own agenda. I was pretty sure Mark's had been to talk about his gayness, to be accepted as he was.

I understood that agenda implicitly. I had gone to the reunion and to the party partly out of curiosity. But mostly to be accepted. To face the very people who made me feel "not good enough" when I was in high school. Not pretty enough, not popular enough, not cool enough. (Smart was barely an issue then; "girls" weren't supposed to be smart.) And to face those same people, bringing twenty-five years of hard-won adult self-esteem to those memories. For a moment, I felt a tingle of pleasure in my chest. I was glad I'd overcome the pain of the old self-consciousness. I'd faced the old devils, and they weren't devils at all, just a bunch of adults, a lot of whom had probably felt just as worthless as I had as a teenager.

And then I remembered that one of them was probably a murderer. The tingle of energy turned to mass, a mass of lead in my chest.

I had barely closed the front door behind us, when I pulled Wayne to me for a kiss. My self-esteem needed a recharge. And anyway, I loved him. Loved the way he listened to me. The way he held me. The way he tried to be fair. The way his body felt beneath my fingertips. The way his mouth—

The doorbell rang, rudely interrupting love's inventory.

Wayne and I looked into each other's eyes, still holding on to each other. Maybe if we were very quiet . . .

"Guess we'd better answer," he whispered a few heartbeats later. All right, I didn't always love the way he tried to be fair.

At least Charlie Hirsch stood at the front door instead of stumbling in like Becky had.

"Okay time to visit?" he asked, without looking either of

us in the face. He leaned his weight on one foot and then the other.

"Sure," Wayne answered, stepping back from the door.

Charlie remained standing where he was, squirming in place.

"Felt like I needed to talk," he added softly.

"Fine," I said, my voice taking on the volume his lacked. I motioned him forward with my hand. "Come on in."

"If it's okay," he murmured.

It was close to ten minutes before we actually convinced Charlie that it was okay to shamble on in and take a seat on the wood and denim couch, Wayne and I on either side of him. Then he sat and stared out across the room without speaking, looking down at his hands at times, turning them over as if to inspect them for dirt. They actually were a little dirty. And calloused. Gardening, I remembered. He did gardening. He certainly didn't speak for a living.

I looked at him, trying to see him through Pam Ortega's more positive eyes. Charlie Hirsch was good-looking in his own way. Tall and lean-faced, with large, dreamy eyes and dark, wavy hair. But where were his social skills? Then I remembered how shy Wayne had been when I'd first met him. Maybe there were hidden depths of wisdom and kindness and wit within Charlie too. Or maybe not.

"Here to talk about Sid?" Wayne finally hazarded.

"Sid?" Charlie shot back, his head jerking up, focus in his dreamy eyes abruptly. "What about Sid?"

"Well, what are you here to talk about?" I demanded, my voice sharper than I intended.

"Pam," he whispered and looked down at his hands again.

"Pam?" I asked.

Charlie took a quick little breath, fastened his eyes on his lap, and then started talking as fast as his mouth would carry him.

"See, Pam and I were both accepted at U.C. Berkeley," he said, wringing his calloused hands together. "She had a scholarship. And we were really in love. We knew we were too young to marry. But then she got pregnant a few months before graduation." He looked out across the room for a moment, shaking his head. "My fault, all my fault."

"And then?" I prompted after a few moments passed in silence.

He looked at me for a moment, then at Wayne and then at the ceiling. I resisted the urge to poke him in the ribs to get him going again.

"We had to get married," he whispered finally. "And nobody was happy. My parents were pissed. Her parents were pissed. I got a job as a bank teller. Neither of us went to U.C. And then, after all that, she miscarried."

I waited for him to blame himself again, but he just kept looking up at the ceiling. And talking.

"We split up after that. My parents sent me to school in the East. I got a useless degree in English. But Pam never got her scholarship back. And she was the smart one. And then . . ."

He brought his eyes down from the ceiling and stared across the room, his eyes as out of focus as a puppy's on Quaaludes.

This time Wayne did the honors. "And then?" he prompted.

"And then I saw her at the reunion," Charlie said, his voice going even faster. "Pamela Ortega. I've gone out with other women, but never married. Never even gotten serious. There was never anyone like Pam. And . . . and, damn it, there still isn't. See, I think I'm in love with her. Really, really in love with her."

He turned to me and actually looked me in the eye. "Kate, am I completely *meshuga*?"

"No," I said slowly, remembering the way Pam had leaned

toward him, watching him intently. Had there been romantic interest in her eyes too? "There's always a chance—"

"I wanted to say something to her today," he interrupted. "But Sid messed everything up."

Meshuga suddenly took on new meaning. Was the man really a little crazy? Sid had messed things up far more for himself today than for Charlie. I peered a little closer. Was there a Jeffrey Dahmer look in those dreamy eyes?

"Sid even asked about my sex life in front of Pam," Charlie went on. "It was almost like he knew how I felt and wanted to screw it up."

I had missed that interaction. But it sounded like Sid all right.

"See, Sid is a lot like this evil captain in the Rodin Rodent books I write. He looks all good-natured and boisterous and harmless on the outside. But inside, ho-ho-ho and a bottle of rum—hang 'em from the yardarms!"

Charlie leaned his head back, flung out his arms, and laughed deeply and violently. I edged away from him on the couch. Was he really nuts? Or was he just illustrating his fictional captain? He went on roaring out his laughter without appearing to notice my strategic withdrawal, and then abruptly resumed his normal voice. If supersonically breathless can be considered normal.

"But, in truth, the captain is really capable of doing monstrous, monstrous harm without realizing that he himself is the monster. That's the truly diabolical part. And he just keeps on and on with his black-hearted deeds until someone—"

And then he stopped. Just like that.

"Until someone what?" I asked.

Six

"Oh, nothing," Charlie said, his shoulders slumping.

"Nothing!" I protested. "What about the evil captain and—"

"Oh, Rodin always figures out a way to make sure the captain doesn't harm people too seriously."

"Rodin?" I parroted, trying to remember who the hell Rodin was. Finally, it came back to me. "Is Rodin a character in your books?"

"Yes, of course." Charlie peered at me for a moment as if *he* was now doubting *my* sanity.

"Rodin Rodent is my series protagonist, a seafaring rat of many colors. See, he's this plucky little rat, with a coat that's brown and gray and white. And he hitches rides on boats and has great adventures. I've had him living on the evil captain's boat for the last three books. He keeps the captain from doing anything too wicked. But the neat part is that the captain doesn't even know Rodin exists. See, the captain has this fancy brass bed. But all the big brass curlicues are hollow brass pipe. That's where Rodin lives. And hides all his possessions.

"A little rat's home because that's all a little rat needs," Charlie sang out in a brave falsetto. This time I was pretty

sure he was in character. At least he wasn't roaring and flinging his arms around, just tilting his head and wiggling his nose
ever so slightly. "A muslin pouch of herbs for a bed, and the
captain's missing sash for a sheet. And a sachet from a long-
lost love for his pillow."

"So just how does a rat keep a captain from doing evil
deeds?" Wayne asked.

I shot a quick glance Wayne's way. Was he really curious
or was there something hidden in these rat tales that he thought
was really about Sid Semling? But nothing showed in
Wayne's face.

"Oh, all kinds of ways," Charlie answered cheerfully. "Re-
moving the powder from the captain's musket. Rodin does that
all the time." Charlie chuckled and wiggled his nose a little
more. "Chewing up the documents that bind his deckhands
into servitude. Stealing keys for prisoners."

"Must make the captain angry," Wayne said quietly.

"That's what's so neat. See the captain never knows it's
Rodin. Rodin's like Zorro. And Robin Hood. And the Lone
Ranger. He comes and goes and helps the people who need
it, but no one ever knows that he's the real hero. The only
person on the whole boat that even knows of Rodin's existence
at all is the cook. And he just thinks Rodin's a common rat.
But he likes him anyway, so he leaves out food for him."

Charlie didn't look miserable anymore. He wasn't wringing
his hands together. He wasn't staring into space. His face was
animated with a big, goofy smile, and his voice was clear and
easy. Rodin Rodent's ship was obviously where Charlie
Hirsch's soul resided.

"In the one I'm writing now, the evil captain has taken over
another ship. This ship's captain is a woman. Captain Penelope
Page. Captain Page is a courageous and ingenious woman. She
sails a tiny ship for the spice trade, with male and female
deckhands . . ."

My head came up. The story was beginning to sound more interesting. Especially the surprising touch of feminism in Rodin's world.

". . . and a ship rat too. But Penelope knows her rat, knows her personally and cares for her. Rolanda Ratus." Charlie sighed and his eyes glazed over. "Rolanda's a brave rat, a female with silky brown fur, a scrap of red velvet for a cap, and a two-inch hat pin for a sword. And big brown eyes. Like no other rat that Rodin has ever known."

I wondered if Rolanda was Pam in disguise. Ratus Eroticus? And if she was, would Pam like being imagined as a rat, no matter how silky and brave?

"But the evil captain can't stand a woman being in charge of even so small a crew. So he rams her tiny ship and boards it, taking Captain Penelope Page and all her hands prisoners. And Rolanda too, unbeknownst to him. The evil captain wants Penelope's ship. And her crew. He tells her he'll kill her the next day if she won't agree to his terms. Then he ties her to a chair and leaves her to think it over. That's when Rodin and Rolanda meet. When they both come out of hiding in the same instant to chew the bonds from Penelope's hands and feet—"

The doorbell rang and I jumped in my seat. Damn. I was ready for the next installment.

"I'll get it," I said unenthusiastically.

Wayne didn't argue. Maybe he was waiting for the next installment too.

I didn't recognize the man standing on my front porch. Not at first. He was a short, sharp-nosed man with a beard and a clipboard in his hand.

"Hi, how are you this evening?" he began.

A solicitor.

"Have you seen my signs?" I demanded.

I had three of them. The first, a twelve-inch-long, red metal sign on the front fence reading, "NO SOLICITORS," ditto right above the doorbell, and my new homemade one thumbtacked to the middle of the front door which said in inch-high letters, "If you are a solicitor and you ring the bell you will just make me angry, not only at you but at your cause. Please don't ring the bell."

"Oh, but I'm not a solicitor," he assured me. "I'm here to help you save the environment—"

"You want to help me to save the environment personally?" I interrupted.

"Yes," he said enthusiastically. Then he shoved a sheaf of papers toward my face. "Did you know that the rate of—"

"By asking me to give you money for your cause," I continued as if he hadn't spoken.

"Well, yes," he agreed. "And you could also give your time. This period is crucial. Last week, more than forty thousand—"

"You *are* a solicitor," I concluded.

"Not really—"

"Yes, really. Now go away."

I started to shut the door, but I wasn't quick enough. He shoved his clipboard into the gap.

"You know, I came here on a weekday, a month ago," he told me. "And you said you worked during the day and that that's why you had all the 'no solicitors' signs up. And I understood completely. But this is Saturday night and you're not working—"

"I am working," I told him.

"No, you're not," he told me back.

"I'm working on a murder investigation at this very moment," I whispered at him.

"A murder?" he blurted, jerking his head back, his eyes widening in concern.

"Yes." I lowered my voice even further and bent my head forward conspiratorially. "A murder of a solicitor."

He lurched back a foot. I pressed my advantage and stepped forward, shortening the gap between us.

"Maybe you can help me," I suggested. "Do you know of any reason at all why someone would want to murder an un-invited solicitor?" I asked pleasantly.

He had turned and was down my front stairs in the time it would take to mouth the words, "a good cause."

"Tell all your friends!" I shouted after him hopefully.

When I rejoined Wayne and Charlie on the couch, Wayne was asking Charlie something about Sid Semling. What the hell had happened to Rodin, Rolanda, and Penelope? I opened my mouth to ask and then closed it again. Was Wayne investigating?

"Well, it was a shock to see him die that way," Charlie was saying. He looked down at his hands again. "A real shock. I didn't particularly like Sid, but still . . ."

His voice drifted off and his eyes took on that dazed puppy dog look again. Maybe I could feed him the Sid experience like a Rodin Rodent story and get him talking like he had before—

"I never have that kind of violence in my books," he assured us. "No one ever dies. Rodin always saves them."

"But didn't Sid need saving?" I asked softly.

He swiveled his head around, looking at me suspiciously.

I did my best to keep my face bland.

"Even the evil captain needs saving once in a while," Charlie finally conceded. Then he turned his head to stare back out into space.

"You know Sid and I were friends once," he added, surprising me with his return to reality. His voice went into high gear again. "We hung out a lot together. Or at least, Sid hung out with me. At the time I really thought he liked me. And I liked him. He could be fun. And he was nice to me. You know, doing me favors, introducing me to people as his friend. That's originally how I got into the group, remember?''

I nodded, though I didn't actually remember. I realized I barely remembered Charlie at all. Just a fairly quiet guy who hung around. And who eventually started going out with Pam.

''I figured out later the reason Sid hung out with me was because my parents were wealthy.'' Charlie blushed deeply. Was he ashamed of the wealth? ''And, um, sorta upper-class. At least my mother. She came from Mayflower stock and all. Her family wasn't all that happy with my father. See, he was Jewish. But still, a doctor. A wealthy and highly respected doctor. You wouldn't think that'd make a difference to a kid, would you though? But I think it made a difference to Sid for some reason. I'm not exactly sure why.

''Anyway, Sid kinda took me under his wing. Even told me how to dress. How to act with girls. He was nice to me. But—''

Charlie stopped as if someone had pulled his plug mid-sentence.

''But?'' Wayne prompted.

Charlie slammed his fist into his own calloused palm in answer. The couch shook with the impact. My stomach quivered uneasily.

''But there was always something in it for Sid,'' he rapped out. ''Sid never did anything if there wasn't something in it for Sid.'' Charlie took a few quick breaths and went on, his mouth still speeding.

''Like Sid didn't have a car. So we always drove mine. A Mustang. I think my father bought it for me so I could feel like a real, rootin'-tootin' American boy. The truth was I always just felt silly driving it. But Sid loved that Mustang. He loved to drive it. I even let him borrow it when I wasn't there.''

I nodded, remembering the car suddenly in full color. It had been a cherry-red convertible. And I remembered Sid's hands on the driver's wheel. Actually, I'd remembered it as Sid's car, not Charlie's.

"And I got Sid alcohol and cigarettes. Actually, I just raided my parents' house. They did a lot of entertaining. There was always stuff around. But the thing Sid really seemed to want was for me to take him to my parents' club, to introduce him to the people there. My parents' kind of people. And I was glad to. He was my friend."

Charlie shook his head and his voice slowed a little.

"See, there was something weird about Sid's parents. I can't really explain. They had money. His father owned a local bottling company. And it wasn't just that his parents didn't have class, though they didn't. They dressed all wrong and talked all wrong. At least for my parents' crowd. But it was something weirder. Sid's dad was always pissed at him, always giving him a hard time. And Sid's mom cried a lot. But both Mr. and Mrs. Semling tried to act happy to see me whenever I came over. It was all so strange. I sometimes wondered if Sid was my friend because his father ordered it."

"But why would Sid's father order it?" I asked.

Charlie shook his head again, this time in puzzlement.

"I don't know. And I've tried to figure it out over the years. I even thought about writing a short story about the whole thing. Because here was Sid, this intrinsically popular kid with unpopular parents. And here was me, this intrinsically unpopular kid with popular parents—"

"Not that unpopular," I reminded him. Someone had to. Obviously Rodin Rodent wasn't giving this guy enough lessons in self-worth. "Pam certainly liked you."

He smiled softly.

"Sid did help me with Pam," Charlie said quietly. "He told her what a great guy I was. And he convinced me she liked me too. But Pam and I never talked. I guess we were both too shy. And then one evening, the three of us went out to the beach in the Mustang, and Sid just left us there. Drove right off. So Pam and I had to talk. God, it seemed like we were there for years before Sid came back. And Sid was right, she did like me. I was in heaven.'' He sighed. "We were in heaven.''

Heaven didn't seem to have lasted though. Charlie frowned again.

"But then Sid kept wanting more stuff from me. My father found out I was letting Sid drive the Mustang without me, and he said I couldn't let Sid do that anymore. When I told Sid, he tried to blackmail me. He told me he'd tell Pam I was having sex with another girl if I didn't let him keep driving the car. I couldn't believe it. I would have never made love to anyone else. I was in love with Pam. I told Sid I couldn't disobey my father. And Sid did what he said he would. He told Pam this long story about all the girls I'd been with. Like Becky Burchell and Natalie Nusser. And a bunch of others.''

Charlie's body tensed. I waited for another explosion. But none came.

"Luckily, Pam was a very sensible girl,'' he said, his voice slower. But I could hear the vibration of the strain it took for him to keep the brakes on. "She just laughed at Sid and asked me what the deal was. I told her and she said I should stop hanging out with Sid.'' Charlie shook his head ruefully.

"Unfortunately, it wasn't that easy to stop hanging out with Sid. He was still pretending to be my friend. And oddly enough, I still believed him. Then the next thing he wanted was to date my sister. But she was a year older and definitely not interested. But Sid kept saying I could get him 'into her pants' if I really wanted to.''

Charlie wound his hands together tightly, his knuckles bulging.

"And then Pam got pregnant." Charlie's face reddened again, but I was pretty sure it was anger this time. I could even smell it in the bitter scent of his sweat now. "And I made the mistake of telling Sid. Sid treated it like a big joke, slapped me on the back. 'No college for you, ho-ho-ho.'"

I recognized the "ho-ho-ho." It was the evil captain's.

"And then he sat there grinning and told me either I got my sister to give him a 'roll in the hay,' or he'd tell everyone that Pam was pregnant. See, Pam and I wanted to at least keep it secret until we graduated. And neither of us had told our parents yet. We were still trying to figure out what to do. I pleaded with Sid. I told him there was no way I could get my sister to sleep with him, outside of drugging her and giving him the key to her room. He told me that sounded fine. It was like seeing Dr. Jekyll turn into Mr. Hyde. Because he was serious. I guess that was when I finally realized he'd never really liked me.

"I told him no. I had to. Pam and I talked it over. I couldn't sell him my sister, even if I wanted to. So Sid Semling told everyone he could think of that Pam was pregnant. He even made anonymous calls to both our parents. And everyone he didn't tell, his cousin, Elaine, did.

"Pam hated it, hated me. I hated myself then too, for getting her pregnant. And for letting myself believe that Sid Semling had been my friend."

"Did you kill Sid Semling?" Wayne asked quietly.

"What?" asked Charlie, his dreamy eyes focusing as if just awakening.

Actually, the question caught me off guard too. It shouldn't have though. If anyone had a motive, it was this man. But twenty-five years later?

"You must have wanted to kill him," Wayne added, his voice hypnotic.

But Charlie just shook his head.

"There wouldn't have been any use in it," he explained reasonably. "The harm was done. The tragedy was written. Sid just speeded things up a little."

"But then he started in on you in front of Pam again at the party," Wayne went on. "And cross-questioned you about Vietnam."

"That he did," Charlie agreed, sighing. "I think he still hated me after all these years. As if *I* had been the one to harm *him*. See, it's really weird, but I think in some way he was jealous of me still, because of my parents."

I wanted to ask Charlie if he even understood what Wayne was asking him. If he understood that we believed Sid was murdered that very day. But I couldn't find the words. Maybe my throat was too dry, and my mouth too sour, from Charlie's story.

And then the phone rang.

It was another solicitor. This confrontation didn't go as well as my last one. This solicitor got in the last word, asking me what I had against recycled umbrellas before hanging up. Actually, I don't have anything against recycled umbrellas. Or the environment. It just drives me crazy that a good cause is considered sufficient entitlement for invasion of privacy. But at least the umbrella call was a quick one.

When I got back to the couch, Charlie was mooning over Pam again.

"What if I never see her again?" he asked plaintively.

"Why don't you come to Aurora's tomorrow?" I suggested. "She's asking everyone who was at Sid's over for lunch. You gave her your card, didn't you?"

Charlie nodded. "Do you think Pam will come?" he asked.

I shrugged impatiently. How the hell would I know?

"Kate, Pam likes you," he said breathlessly. "Will you call her and see if she'll come?"

I stared at the man. No wonder he'd needed Sid's help

twenty-five years ago in setting up a meeting with Pam. But Charlie was a grown man now.

"Charlie, it's not up to me—" I began.

"It probably couldn't hurt," said a deeper voice from Charlie's other side.

I looked over at Wayne. Was this male bonding or what?

All right, so I ended up calling Pam. I told myself I just wanted to hear her voice after all that Charlie had told me. To hear her as the strong, happy, vital woman she was now.

The minute I dialed the phone, Charlie stood up and started looking around the living room, as if seeing it for the first time.

"Nice place," I heard him tell Wayne. "You take good care of your plants."

Maybe he had some social skills after all.

"Mind if I play a game of pinball?" he asked just as Pam's voice came on the line.

"Hi, this is Kate, Kate Jasper," I announced awkwardly, feeling all the more foolish in my mission once I had Pam on the phone.

"Oh, Kate, I'm so glad you called!" she yelled in my ear and I relaxed a little. "I needed to talk to someone about Sid." Didn't we all? I thought. Maybe Aurora's posttrauma lunch wasn't such a bad idea after all. "Wasn't it just awful? I guess it took a while for it to sink in that he's really dead . . ."

I identified the happy pinging and chiming of Hayburners being played from behind me without turning around. Different pinball machines have different sounds, whole different personalities.

". . . wasn't the greatest guy in the whole world, but he was Sid. Such a kidder, so full of life. *Por Dios*, he was only forty-three. And then to die that way of a heart attack. . . ."

Did Pam really think Sid had only suffered a heart attack? Didn't she realize he was electrocuted? The queasy feeling in my stomach told me I didn't even want to ask her that question. Not now.

"Did Aurora call you about lunch tomorrow?" I asked her instead.

"Yeah," she told me. "I gave her a tentative yes. I think it will be good for all of us." She paused, then asked softly, "Kate, do you think Charlie will be going?"

I couldn't stifle the laughter that burst out of my mouth and into the phone receiver.

But Pam just laughed with me, as if she knew Charlie was behind me playing pinball.

"Listen, I'm sure Charlie will be going," I told her. Then I added hastily, "I've gotten psychic over the last twenty-five years."

She didn't even question the explanation. Instead she suggested we get together for a late lunch on Monday at a new Nepalese restaurant in San Francisco. I agreed. I had a lot of things I wanted to ask Pam. Or didn't want to ask Pam. But I needed to ask them anyway.

C.C. began yowling at me the minute I got off the phone. Dinner was late. I trotted into the kitchen guiltily, and was scooping up Friskies Senior when I heard a new sound coming from the living room.

It took me a moment to identify it. It was the sound of a pinball machine jamming.

SEVEN

꩜

I dropped the open can of Friskies Senior onto the floor. A pinball machine was jamming. In a flash, I saw Charlie Hirsch being electrocuted in my mind.

As I ran to the living room, I considered my options, one per gasping breath. Grab him by the shoulders and pull him off Hayburners and risk electrocution myself. Or crawl around under the machine where all the old boxes of gag gifts were stored to find the plug to yank from the socket. Or just knock him off the machine with one quick push.

By the time I got to Hayburners, my body had decided for me. I turned and swept my arm against Charlie's chest in a tai chi move that sent him reeling from the machine. Luckily, Wayne was there to catch Charlie in his arms before the man actually hit the floor.

"Are you all right?" I demanded anxiously, still gasping.

"You hit me," Charlie whispered. His dreamy eyes were wide with what looked like fear.

"But you were—"

I stopped mid-sentence, listening more closely to Hayburners. It wasn't making the dramatic grating sound that Hot Flash had when it'd blown. It was a more subtle sound, a more common sound. The sound of a jammed thumper-bumper. I turned and looked at the machine and could even see the bumper that was stuck in the down position, buzzing angrily.

Damn.

I turned the machine off, then on again, as my heartbeat decelerated. It was an easy repair that worked. The thumper-bumper wasn't jammed anymore. And, of course, no one had been electrocuted.

"Sorry," I said to Charlie. "But after Sid today, I thought you were—"

I left the sentence unfinished when I noticed the blood leaving his face. Had he just figured it out?

"The machine's fine now," I assured him. "You can play another game if you want to."

"No, thank you," he said carefully, looking over his shoulder toward the front door.

But when he turned his head back, his eyes were more determined.

"Did you talk to Pam?" he asked.

"Yeah," I told him, feeling my own lips curve into a smile. "And she's probably coming tomorrow."

"Really?" he breathed, all fear gone from his eyes now.

"Really," I told him. "And Charlie, she asked if you were coming too."

His mouth gaped open for a moment as his face colored from white to rose-red. Then he said, "Wow."

That was pretty much it for his conversational abilities from that point on. We eventually guided him out the doorway. And even with our help, he managed to bash himself on the doorjamb. It didn't seem to phase him though. He made it to his gardening truck without further damage, waved goodbye with a goofy smile, and then took off, merrily rattling the rakes and shovels tied to the truck's sides as he went.

"So," I said to Wayne, once the truck was gone from sight. "Do you think Charlie's crazy?"

"No," Wayne answered, with a hint of a smile. "Just a writer." I had a feeling that smile was because Wayne was a fledgling writer himself. And then I allowed myself a moment to be thankful Wayne wrote adult short stories, not children's adventures.

"And here I thought Charlie was quiet," I added ruefully.

"Maybe he is," Wayne replied. "I think it's his characters who are the talkative ones. Rodin Rodent. Charlie as a remembered young man. Though Charlie himself? Charlie today?" He shrugged eloquently. Beautifully. It's amazing how really beautiful a homely man can be.

I sighed and stepped closer, putting my arms around him.

"Now where were we?" I whispered.

"Here, I think," he whispered back and then his mouth was on mine again.

C.C. was meowing loudly for food the next morning despite the fact that she'd eaten the full can of Friskies I'd left on the floor the night before. Or maybe her friends had. Neither Wayne nor I had remembered to shut the cat door for the night. And C.C. wasn't the only one demanding attention. My answering machine was full of calls.

Mark wanted to know if we were going to Aurora's. And so did Elaine. And Aurora wanted to know if we could bring something vegetarian for the potluck. Mark and Aurora were easy. Yes, and yes.

But Elaine wanted more. She wanted to talk. Not on the phone, not at the Kanicks', but at her house.

I could hear Wayne in the kitchen, whipping up something for the potluck as I listened to Elaine on the telephone. He'd started cooking once the conversation began sounding complicated. I was glad. There was one thing about living with a restaurateur. He could, and did, cook a lot better than I. Whatever he made would be good.

"There're some things I've gotta tell you," Elaine insisted over the sound of something sizzling on the stove. "Things I've found out that might be important—"

"So tell me now," I tried again.

"No," she whispered. "Not on the phone."

Who'd she think was listening in? The FBI? C.C.? For all I knew maybe she was worried about Martians. I didn't know this woman very well. Especially after twenty-five years.

"Look," she went on, louder. "I'm right here in Gravendale. Not that far from the Kanicks'. You can stop in on the way." She paused and her voice lowered again. "Then we can talk."

"I suppose," I said, still considering. Now I heard the blender whirring from the kitchen. A whiff of something, soy sauce maybe, teased my nose. If anyone knew Sid Semling well, it was his cousin Elaine. She might have some interesting things to say about him. Very interesting things. And I wondered just what it was that she had found out.

"Wayne's coming with me if I do," I added finally.

There was a long pause, then she asked, "Does he really have to?"

"Elaine, what is your problem—" I began, exasperated.

"Okay, okay," she conceded before I could get into it. Then she gave me a long series of directions to get to her house, telling me—ordering me—to get there an hour before we were due at the Kanicks'.

"We're at the top of a long driveway," she finished up. "But don't drive up the driveway. Park at the bottom on the street and walk up. Or else you'll block the garage."

"All right," I agreed peevishly, thinking that Elaine's visit and Aurora's lunch pretty much took care of Sunday as a day of rest and relaxation.

"Thanks, Kate," Elaine offered, and the unexpected warmth of gratitude in her voice surprised me into a moment of liking her. And wondering if she really had found out something important.

A couple of hours later, we were on the road.

"So what's in the salad?" I asked Wayne as I steered my Toyota toward Gravendale past rolling straw-brown hills brightened by bursts of shining green oak trees.

"Chinese vegetable salad," he answered. "Lettuce, shredded carrots, bean sprouts, broccoli, and a bunch of other veggies. Plus pine nuts and rice sticks and tofu."

"And ginger and soy," I said. I'd been smelling it for the last half hour.

"In the dressing," he admitted, smiling. "Hungry?"

I nodded. And returned his smile. The straw-brown hills took me back to my childhood in Gravendale. Just the look of them and the scent (probably enough to give me allergies for a week) relaxed me into a spell of nostalgia. And the cows wandering on those hills loosened my mind even further. Black cows, brown cows, and black-and-white-spotted cows. I wanted to *moo*.

But as we got closer to the outskirts of the city, Gravendale didn't look much like I remembered it. There were warrens of condos and housing developments now. And even a couple of small shopping malls.

And then the outskirts gave way to downtown Gravendale. At least there was no McDonald's there. Though there was a pink brick drive-in restaurant that advertised "the finest in automotive dining." I noted a vegetarian restaurant too, an art gallery, a few boutiques and, to my relief, a grocery, a hardware, and a drug store that probably weren't but might have been there twenty-five years ago.

Elaine's house was way out on the other side of downtown Gravendale, the undeveloped side. The houses out here were spread over full-acre lots and more, and the lots were separated by great stands of trees. Mostly oak, but spruce, apple, and walnut were mixed in too. It was beautiful. And expensive-looking. If Elaine worked as a secretary, I wondered what her husband did for a living.

I parked on the street as ordered, and Wayne and I walked up the long tree-lined driveway. The trees blocked all view of the neighbors and muffled the sound. It would have been easy to believe we were alone in the country. Birds called, insects buzzed, and dogs barked, but most of the sound of traffic and human activity blended into a pleasant background hum. I put my arm around Wayne's waist and leaned into him, enjoying the momentary peace before we got to the house.

"Just on time," Elaine greeted us, opening the front door before I even pressed the buzzer. She was dressed today in a fitted, scroll front mauve jacket over matching linen pants, with matching platform pumps and silver jewelry. Oh, well. I'd worn my Mill Valley Library T-shirt and jeans for lunch at Aurora's.

"This is my husband, Ed," she added, pointing to a short, stocky man who nodded briefly at us. "He's in securities."

"Brandt Financial Group, Santa Rosa," he confirmed, sticking out his hand. That explained the expensive property, I decided. Probably the expensive clothing too.

"Glad to meet you," I muttered and grasped his hand. As he energetically shook mine, I introduced Wayne and myself, hoping Ed wasn't going to ask about our investment portfolio.

He didn't. Maybe it was a good thing I'd worn the T-shirt.

"And these are my kids," Elaine went on. "Dawn, Elyse, and Eddie Junior." She smiled down at three children, none of whom looked over ten.

All three glared back up. I could see the Semling genes in their small, squinting eyes. Meeting Mommy's friends wasn't apparently on the top of their list of favorite activities.

"Hi there," Wayne tried. "How old are—"

"Can we go now?" the biggest one demanded.

"Ed?" Elaine murmured with a jerk of her head upwards.

On cue, father and children disappeared up a long flight of stairs.

Elaine watched their ascent and didn't turn back to us until the sound of television floated back down the stairs. At least I hoped it was television. Or else there were cars screeching and people shouting and shots being fired on the upper floor of the house.

"Now we can talk," Elaine whispered.

I kept myself from screaming, "About what!" as she led us into a formal living room that was the size of my whole house. Or at least near to it. I didn't have a tape measure with me, so I couldn't be sure. Wayne and I took our places on an ivory brocade couch in a grouping set on an expanse of salmon-colored Aubusson carpet tucked into the left-hand corner of the room. Elaine swiveled her head around to look behind her, then pulled a matching Victorian chair closer to us before sitting down.

She stared at Wayne. Longer than was polite. As seconds became minutes, I felt blood beginning to pump into my face. Didn't she think he looked right on her fancy furniture? I stared back at her. As thin as she was, and with all the cosmetics she was wearing, she still bore an amazing resemblance to her cousin Sid with those broad cheekbones, the wide nose and wide mouth. And those small, calculating eyes.

"So talk," I said finally.

Her body jerked slightly, then she leaned back in her chair, clasping her hands together.

"Wayne," she said, her voice hushed and conspiratorial. "Where'd you know Sid from before?"

"Before the reunion?" he asked back, his brows lowering to half-mast.

She nodded.

"As far as I know, I'd never met your cousin before the reunion," he told her, brows lowering even further.

"What makes you think Wayne knew Sid before?" I demanded, any friendliness I had felt toward Elaine now completely evaporated.

"Someone told me," she whispered.

"Who?" I shot back.

"I don't exactly know," she admitted, pink coloring her cheeks. She crossed her arms and looked down at her expensive pumps. "I got an anonymous phone call last night—"

"An anonymous phone call!" I yelped.

"Shh," she warned, a finger to her lips. "I didn't tell Ed about it."

"Did you tell the police?" I asked.

She nodded, her cheeks flushing even pinker.

I glared at her. Great. Now the police would think Wayne was involved. The only person who had no connection to Sid Semling would be a prime suspect along with the rest of us. Only if the police were even considering murder, I reminded myself.

Elaine crossed her arms again and returned my look, her head tilted back defiantly.

"Anyway, it wasn't just about Wayne," she said defensively. "The person on the phone told me all kinds of stuff."

"Like what?" I asked in spite of myself. If the other tips were as good as the one about Wayne, they were probably useless. But I was still curious.

"That Natalie Nusser has AIDS," Elaine told me.

Even though I guessed it wasn't true, the statement pinched my diaphragm for a moment. I'd known two people who'd died of AIDS. I didn't know if my heart could take knowing any more.

"And that Jack owed Sid a lot of money," Elaine went on, bending forward in her chair eagerly. "And that Lillian's a bigamist. She has a husband she never divorced in Indonesia. And that Sid raped Becky our sophomore year.''

She leaned back in her chair, apparently finished with her secrets. There was a smug smile on her face. Now I remembered why I'd found it so hard to like Elaine in high school. It wasn't just that she liked to gossip. It was her unconcealed delight in other people's tragedies. A memory of the ecstatic expression that had been on her face when she'd told me Pam was pregnant all those years ago flashed in my mind. I shook it away, trying to shake away my dislike for Elaine at the same time. Somewhere in all of this there might be some truth, some truth that had some bearing on Sid Semling's death.

''Have you talked to anyone else?'' I asked. ''To see if any of this was true?''

''I called to talk to Jack,'' she answered, her smile gone now. ''But I got Lillian and she wouldn't even let him get on the phone. So I told her what I'd heard. I was giving her a chance, you know.'' She shook her head angrily. ''But the snotty witch got all bent out of shape. Told me none of it was true, and none of it was any of my business anyway.''

I found myself nodding in agreement. In agreement with Lillian, not Elaine.

''Can you believe it?'' Elaine said, apparently seeing solidarity in my nod.

I mumbled under my breath, hoping I sounded sympathetic.

''I thought about calling Natalie last night,'' Elaine went on. ''But I know her. She is one stuck-up woman. Do you know I visited her once at Nusser Networks—thought I'd check it out to see if she was the same Natalie Nusser I remembered—and she didn't say boo when I introduced myself.''

''Did you use your married name?'' I asked, wondering if Natalie had even recognized her.

"Yeah, but . . ." Elaine paused for a moment, catching on to the implication. "No, I'm sure she knew who I was. She was just too stuck-up to say so. Remember how stuck-up she was in high school. She thought she was so smart . . ."

That's because Natalie *was* smart, I thought. All A's would qualify if nothing else. But I kept the thought to myself.

". . . and all that time she was this big slut, sleeping with half the guys in our class—"

"Did you get that from an anonymous phone call too?" I couldn't resist asking.

"No, I didn't!" Elaine flared. "Sid told me so."

"Elaine?" Wayne intervened quietly.

"What?" she demanded, turning to him again, her face still angry.

"Can you give us an idea of what the voice on the phone sounded like last night?"

"Well," she said, pulling the word out reluctantly. Then she paused and pinched her brows together. Was she trying to remember?

"It was real weird," she told us finally. "Like maybe it was electronically altered. It didn't sound like anyone I recognized. You know, real *whooo-whooo-whooo.*"

The last part was a decent ghost imitation, but it didn't ring any bells with me either.

"Male or female?" Wayne tried again.

Elaine shook her head. "The police asked me all that stuff. But it was just too weird to tell."

"Well, thank you for letting me know what was said about me," Wayne told her.

I swallowed my own anger. It didn't taste good going down. But she had told Wayne. That was something.

"Yes, thank you, Elaine," I added, trying to keep my voice soft and understanding.

It worked.

"Listen, that's the thing, Kate," she offered, leaning forward in her chair. "You're not as snotty as the rest of them. And Sid. I really did love Sid." Her voice rose perilously as she said her cousin's name. Her eyes teared up too. Guilt stabbed me in the gut.

There probably wasn't anyone else in this world who had loved Sid as much as Elaine. She wasn't all malice. She was human. And she was hurting. I thought about putting my arm around her shoulders, but before I could get up, she started talking again, her voice low and tight. Grim.

"I want you to come to Sid's memorial service Tuesday," she told us. "And the other guys had better come too. All of them." She paused, squinting her small eyes and digging her manicured nails into the padded arms of her Victorian chair.

"Or else," she finished.

EIGHT

✦

"Or else what?" Wayne asked quietly. His brows were
pushed too low for me to read his eyes, but I could see the
intensity of his interest in the bulking of his shoulders.

"Or else they'll be sorry," Elaine replied just as quietly
and crossed her arms, bulking up her own shoulders. She stuck
out her face. "Real sorry."

Something tingled on the back of my neck. Was it my hair
standing up? I wouldn't want to be in Elaine's way if she
wanted me to be sorry, whatever she meant.

I opened my mouth to say I'd be at Sid's funeral, but one
of Elaine's children had something to say first. I hadn't heard
the girl's entrance through the living room door, but I could
certainly hear her once she was there.

"Eddie's being a moronic little ingrate and Daddy says—"
she began indignantly, her voice projecting across the vast
room. I wasn't sure if this was Dawn or Elyse, only that she
was the oldest girl.

"Listen to what your daddy says," Elaine instructed the girl
impatiently. She made shooing motions with her hands. "Now
get back upstairs."

The girl put her hands on her hips and glared fiercely. But
there was no real contest. She had probably learned the gesture

from the woman she was glaring at. Mother ignored daughter and finally the girl shuffled out of the room with a sigh worthy of Olivier. I predicted the girl would be an actress when she grew up.

"My kids have it so easy," Elaine confided once the girl was gone. "The best Montessori schools from the beginning. Personal computers for all of them, their own telephones, ballet lessons, karate lessons, whatever they want.

"Now with me and Sid it was different. We weren't spoiled. And we were both only children. That's one reason I had three kids. They'll never be lonely like Sid and I were."

She paused and looked my way.

"Cute kid," I offered into the silence. "All of your children are cute."

"And gifted," Elaine added, uncrossing her arms. "Dawn played the lead dinosaur in *Dino-Mites* this year. And there was a lot of competition—"

"Was that the one who just came in?" I asked.

Elaine nodded, confirming my actress theory. Sometimes I thought I was getting as psychic as my friend Barbara.

"Now Elyse is a star soccer player. And she's won first prize for her science projects two years in a row. And my Eddie is fluent in three languages already. And they're all musical."

Elaine paused again. I didn't know what to say. Did she want another compliment about her children?

"At least you and Sid had each other," Wayne put in.

"Did you know Sid and I were born three months apart?" Elaine demanded, bending forward eagerly.

Wayne and I shook our heads, feigning amazement at the coincidence.

Elaine nodded enthusiastically. "Listen," she ordered. "Our fathers were brothers, even partners in a bottling business for a while. Real close, you know. They bottled apple juice. It was a family business. A cannery. It's still going. Though Daddy sold it a long time ago. Uncle Simon, Sid's father, never did as well with the bottling plant after Daddy left. But Daddy couldn't handle Uncle Simon. Now I had my own problems with Daddy, but he was really a sweetheart underneath it all. Not Uncle Simon, though. He was a real s.o.b. through and through."

"A hard man?" Wayne prompted.

"Huh!" Elaine snorted. "Hard wouldn't cover it. He was a plain sadist. Beat Sid every day of his life. And not just hitting him, but at him all the time with his mouth for not being good enough. Always wanted Sid to be the best, but Sid just couldn't." She leaned back in her chair, her eyes out of focus. "Or maybe Sid just wouldn't. Maybe he had just unconsciously *refused* to be the best for his father after all that abuse. Sid was stubborn. Couldn't ever give in once he made up his mind. And Sid was smart. Smarter than people gave him credit for."

"Good with people," Wayne commented.

"Yeah," Elaine agreed, leaning forward again. It had been the right thing to say. "He was a great salesman. He just wasn't scholarship material. He never got great grades. God, he hated the smart kids. And the football stars."

"But why?" I asked.

"Because they were what his father would've wanted him to be," Elaine explained. "And what he couldn't be. Uncle Simon made him go out for football too, but he was never that good for all of his size. But what a joker." A smile touched her lips. "He did some great pranks on the other football guys, especially the star quarterback, do you remember him?"

I shook my head. Football hadn't been my thing.

"Guy named Gary." Elaine grinned broadly, looking all the more like Sid with those Sylvester the Cat cheekbones jutting out. "Man, Sid got him good. Gary was a real snot, thought he walked on water. But then this one time he really messed up, fumbled so bad he lost the whole game. The whole season. So Sid got the rest of the guys to strip him naked. Then they put girl's underwear on him, poured beer all over him, tied him up, and then drove him downtown and dumped him in front of the police station. It was a riot. Boy, was Gary embarrassed."

Elaine leaned back and laughed in memory.

I couldn't even squeeze out a responding chuckle. My neck was tingling again. And my stomach was queasy. Because Gary must have been a lot more than embarrassed. He must have been humiliated. And scared shitless. Or maybe football stars aren't subject to those kinds of feelings.

"What did the police do?" I asked softly.

"Oh, once they realized it was a prank, they let Gary go," Elaine said, shrugging. Then she pulled her lips back in that Sid/Sylvester grin again. "But first they gave Mr. Star Quarterback a grilling he never forgot. He was there over three hours, I heard."

If I'd been that guy, I could have killed Sid twenty-five years ago, I thought. Or twenty-five years later.

"Did Sid get in touch with Gary when he got back out here?" I asked.

"Uh-uh," Elaine said thoughtfully. "At least, I don't think so. They weren't really friends. I mean, Gary wasn't one of the gang. Anyway . . ." Her voice faltered.

Anyway, I decided, how could this Gary have electrocuted Sid if he didn't even know about the party? I needed to put some reins on my imagination.

"Listen," Elaine started up again. "Gary forgave Sid. He had to. Sid wasn't ever malicious. He just knew how to have fun."

"Just a prankster," I murmured, wondering just when pranks crossed the line into pure sadism.

"He did some other good ones on Gary though," Elaine told me, helping me to answer my own question. "Found a gay men's magazine in San Francisco and planted it in Gary's locker. No one ever knew but me. All the guys wondered about Gary from then on. And he found a little bottle of hair spray the same size as Gary's deodorant and switched the labels so Gary sprayed his armpits with hair spray. God, Sid was such a riot!

"Him and Robert and me did some good ones too. When we were real little, we'd just go downtown and stare up into the sky for a long time. Then crowds would form and stare up too. It was real funny 'cause there was nothing there."

I allowed myself a genuine smile. That one sounded harmless at least. And funny in a way.

"Or we'd go around to strange men saying, 'Daddy, Daddy, why'd you leave Mama?' I never quite understood it at the time, but did we get reactions! These weird old guys would get all uptight and run away. That was one Robert dreamt up." Elaine was relaxed now, lost in memory. At least for a while. Then her eyes came back into focus. "Still, Robert could be kinda stuck-up too. Always trying to outdo Sid with ideas. Though Sid didn't seem to mind."

"Was Sid in it with him on the fireworks?" I asked quickly.

"No," Elaine answered just as quickly, squinting her eyes at me. "That was Robert's show. Who told you that?"

"No one," I admitted, deep-sixing the Sid-gave-Robert-the-fireworks theory once and for all. "I just wondered."

"What did you and Sid think of the other guys in the gang?" Wayne asked before I could get myself into any more trouble.

"Well, he thought Charlie was an idiot," Elaine drawled in answer. "Charlie had everything, you know. Rich parents.

Smart in a way. But he was a complete dork. You wouldn't believe what Sid put up with to help that guy out. And for what? Then Charlie turns on him.''

I kept my expression sympathetic. That probably had been the way Sid had seen it. No more free car. No instant access to Charlie's sister. Complete betrayal.

"Now Jack was a different story," Elaine went on. "He wasn't dorky or stuck-up at all. And he really was a good musician. Remember, he was even in that rock 'n' roll band for a while.''

I did remember. Jack had been transformed when he played electric guitar, into someone completely and maniacally alive. And completely at odds with the quiet, good-natured kid he usually was.

"I even went out with Jack a few times,'' Elaine confided, her voice dropped to an almost inaudible whisper. "It was really cool, especially when he was playing in the band. But then he just seemed to give up. Gave up the band. Dropped out of college, I heard. I never knew what was going on with that guy. I still don't.'' She threw out her hands. "And now that snooty wife of his keeps him locked up like a prisoner or something. Sid was real good for him, coming back home and into Jack's life again. But try telling that witch about it.''

"When did Sid come back out?'' I asked.

"Oh, a couple of years ago. He sold hospital beds on the East Coast for a long time, but then he got laid off, so he came home.'' Elaine wrapped her arms around herself for a moment. "God, it was good to see him again. Letters just aren't the same. And he landed a job selling office furniture right off. He was good at it. But the company went bankrupt. The economy, you know.''

"How'd he get the job with Natalie?'' I pressed.

"I was the one who told him about Natalie,'' Elaine shot back, beaming. "Our company and hers are in competition on a lot of the same contracts. And, much as she's stuck-up and all, her company does do good work. But it needed a better sales department. Up till that time, I think Natalie was her own sales department. So I told Sid about her. And the next thing you know he's working for her. I told you he was a good salesman. He even sold himself to her—''

"I am so sick of watching TV I could just vomit," came a familiar voice through the living room door. Dawn, if I remembered correctly. "TV is sooo simplistic. Anyway, Daddy says it's almost time to go to Aunt Ursula's—''

"You and Daddy are going to Aunt Ursula's without me today," Elaine told Dawn as she looked down at her watch. "But you're right, it is time for us all to get going. I have to get to the Kanicks'."

"Who are the Kanicks?" asked a new voice, the little boy.

"None of your beeswax," Elaine replied, rising from her Victorian chair, looking for a moment like Queen Victoria herself for all her slenderness.

The boy blinked and turned away. His father did the same.

"That's okay," chimed in a third voice, the remaining girl, the youngest. "We're going to Aunt Ursula's. It'll be really fun."

"I'm sure you'll have a *fabulous* time with your aunt!" Elaine snapped. "She'll spoil you rotten as usual. Just remember who your mother is."

"She doesn't spoil us," Dawn informed her mother. "She merely teaches us to see the world in a different—''

Elaine put her hands on her hips and glared Dawn to a stop. I was impressed. I felt like practicing the move myself for future reference. But I knew I'd never be able to pull it off. Except maybe on Wayne . . .

"Elaine," Wayne offered diffidently. "Would you like a ride over to the Kanicks'?"

All eyes turned his way.

"No, no," Elaine replied breezily. She took her hands from her hips and ratcheted into gracious hostess mode. "I wouldn't want to put you to any trouble. But thank you so much for coming." She led us back to the front door and shook both of our hands, her children and husband forming a small parade behind her. "I'll follow you in a minute."

We were dismissed.

As the front door closed behind us, I could hear Elaine telling everyone to be good. I wondered if her husband was included in the order.

Once we got down the hill, I headed my Toyota back toward downtown Gravendale. Jack and his family lived in a house nearer to town than Elaine. One of the original Gravendale homes.

"Did I tell you that Jack and his family are living in the house that he grew up in?" I asked Wayne.

He shook his head. "I thought it was Aurora's house."

"Well, it was originally," I explained. "But now Aurora is living in some kind of experimental community. At least, I think that's what she said when she called to talk to me."

"Huh," Wayne muttered, his brows rising with interest.

"Wayne, why is it that everyone always has to talk to me?" I demanded abruptly. Irritation over my role as confidant had buzzed into my mind like a demented bee. Because this wasn't the first time this role had been demanded of me. "Aurora wants 'to talk.' Becky had 'to talk.' Charlie. Elaine. And Pam—"

"Because you're easy to talk to," he replied quietly, cutting me off mid-diatribe.

"I am?" That was a new one on me.

He turned to me, his vulnerable eyes amused and liquid with affection at the same time.

"You really listen," he assured me. "You're curious about

other people. And kind. And you probably were the same twenty-five years ago." He smiled. "It's your own fault."

"It is not," I objected. "I'm not kind. Well, sometimes I'm a pushover . . ."

"Co-dependent," Wayne muttered under his breath.

"But it's like I have this sign printed on my forehead that says 'tell me about it.' I swear. When I was living in the city and taking the bus to work, every single human being with a personal problem would sit next to me and tell me their story. I began to wonder if I looked like a therapist. A nun even told me she was afraid she was losing her vocation. And one day I got a wife talking about leaving her husband and the next day I got her husband. I was sure of it. They had the same kids and everything. At least no one ever confessed to any serious crimes. I'd started worrying about confidentiality—"

Wayne's laugh rumbled out, surprising me from the depths of my speech.

"I'm serious," I insisted, but I couldn't help smiling. In memory, it was kind of funny. Now that I didn't take the bus anymore.

Then Wayne took on a serious look himself. "Let me state something for the record," he announced. "I never knew Sid Semling before your high school reunion." He paused, then added, "To the best of my knowledge."

"You didn't have to tell me that," I objected. "It was enough to hear you tell Elaine." But even as I spoke, I knew I was glad he'd made the statement. I could feel it in the release of tension in my shoulders.

I would have hugged him to make my acceptance of his statement official, but my hands were on the steering wheel. And we were close to the Kanicks'. We passed onto a block with older houses on regular quarter-acre lots with well-trimmed lawns.

I recognized the Kanick house immediately. It was still

painted white with green shutters. Only the tree in front looked different. It was an old evergreen that had grown immensely wide but been kept trimmed short to the confines of the electric utility lines. It looked like a children's drawing of a tree, as broad as it was tall.

I pulled up to the curb and stared, thinking how strange it would be to still live in the house you grew up in. Would it be comforting? Or traumatizing?

"If both of Sid's parents are dead, who inherits?" Wayne asked, interrupting my thoughts.

"Elaine?" I said, taking my key from the ignition. And a whole new world of motive popped into my mind. The world of money. "But Elaine certainly looked like she had plenty of money and Sid—"

"Hey, Kate," a voice broke in from outside the car.

I saw Becky leaning down toward my open window. Her fragile face looked drawn and serious today.

"Sorry about last night," she murmured. "Jeez, I was stinking drunk and I busted in on you guys—"

"No problem," I lied and got out of the car. I would think about Elaine later.

Becky, Wayne, and I walked up the flagstone path to the Kanicks' house together, breathing in the scent of sweet alyssum that filled the gaps between the stones. And admiring the Shasta daisies and delphiniums bordering the yard, with the smaller petunias and nemesia nestled beneath them. A colorful and elegant arrangement. Someone clearly loved this yard and put work into it. Jack or Lillian? I wondered.

It was neither Jack nor Lillian who opened the front door, though, but Aurora Kanick. Aurora was wearing a rainbow-beaded vest over jeans and a white T-shirt today. No, she definitely wasn't Mrs. Cleaver anymore. Her eyes crinkled in greeting from beneath her oversized glasses as she led us into the living room.

The interior of the house didn't look anything like it had twenty-five years ago. The heaviness of mahogany and dark woven upholstery was gone. Teak and glass and stripes and bright florals were in their place. And wonderful curling bronze sculptures, some abstract, some formal busts. One wore a definite resemblance to Aurora.

"Did Lillian do—" I began, but Mark apparently didn't hear me.

"Take a seat, you guys," he interrupted benignly. "You're nearly the last of the litter to arrive."

So Wayne and I squeezed onto a navy-and-white-striped couch next to Natalie Nusser. She gave us a curt nod as Becky sat next to Jack and Lillian on the other couch. Their smiles seemed friendlier, but forced. Charlie and Pam sat next to each other in separate chairs that looked like they had come from the kitchen, carefully avoiding each other's faces, but bobbing their chins our way in tandem. Mark leaned back in a floral easy chair.

I was impressed. Aurora had done well. When Elaine arrived, we'd have pretty near the same group that had been at Sid's party. Except for D.V. And the Kanick children. And, of course, Sid.

"Same darn house," came Elaine's voice from the doorway. "Amazing."

We were all here.

Elaine and Aurora took the two remaining seats and Aurora began.

"A profound event has touched all of our lives," she told us, her voice crisp and resonant. There were some nods and murmurs of assent from the group. "A profound and troubling event. But if we act collectively today, it is possible that we can transform this event into something less troubling. In sharing our experience, we can overcome the pain."

I was nodding now too. It sounded great to me. She closed her eyes for a moment, took a breath, and went on.

"The first thing we must agree upon, however, is whether or not Sid Semling was murdered yesterday."

NINE

"You think Sid was murdered?" whispered Charlie.

Even for me, it was a shock to hear the proposition stated so baldly. But it was clearly more of a shock for some of the others. Especially Charlie. His dreamy eyes were wider than ever in his long, lean face as he stared at Aurora. Even his mouth was gaping open.

"Yes," Aurora answered deliberately, her own face as serene as Charlie's was shocked. "I do believe Sid Semling was murdered."

Lillian Kanick snorted loudly, shaking her head. I had a feeling she had already heard this proposal from her mother-in-law and rejected it.

"And quite possibly by someone in this room," Aurora continued unperturbed. "Pinball machines do not normally electrocute people. I spoke to an electrician, one of the members of my community, and he assured me it just plain doesn't happen. Not by accident."

"But God, I mean . . . I thought Sid might just have had a heart attack or something," Becky said softly.

Her tone held something like a plea in it that was reflected in the shape of her brows over her round blue eyes. She wanted it to be simple. She wanted it to all go away. I could tell that's what she wanted because the feeling part of me agreed with her absolutely.

"Electrocution probably *caused* Sid to have a heart attack," Mark put in. He was sitting up straight in the floral chair, his eyes intense in his round face now. "But he was electrocuted. I know. I worked on him, trying to revive him. And I saw—"

He put his arm in front of his face, stopping himself. I was just as glad. I didn't want to hear a description of Sid's body. Or of his burnt hands. I shivered, my mind unkindly providing the description Mark had so kindly spared us all. With matching pictures.

"I've meditated on this matter," Aurora went on. "And I truly believe the only way to restore emotional and spiritual harmony for each of us is to discover exactly what happened to Sid yesterday." Then she let her eyes move slowly around the group gathered in her former house. "Especially for the murderer. There can't be any peace for that person until the truth is told."

Her tone was so clear, so certain, I almost expected someone to confess. But what hope could she offer if someone did? She couldn't stop the course of the law.

My own gaze began to follow the path her eyes were taking around the group when a new thought stopped me. By playing the role of truth-seeker, Aurora had put herself out of the running as murderer in my mind. Had she played it that way on purpose? I jerked my head back, studying her face more closely. Aurora had to be at least sixty, but her elegant face was barely lined, and her eyes were radiant under her oversized glasses. Was her beauty the outer manifestation of her inner spiritual life? Not necessarily. And I reminded myself that neither age, beauty, nor spirituality equaled incapacity for violence. And that psychopaths were often described as charming and good-looking.

Mark opened his mouth to speak again. But Lillian beat him to it.

"Mom has a 'bug in her ear,' " she told us, the American idiom spoken carefully. "There are police officials involved already. I think we should just let them—"

"No way," Elaine interrupted. She wasn't yelling. She was hissing. Somehow I would have preferred yelling. "If someone here thinks they can get away with killing my cousin, just because—"

"I'm not saying let a murderer go," Lillian interrupted right back, "if there is a murderer. I'm just saying that the officials—"

Jack tapped his wife's arm softly and she stopped speaking instantly. It was then that I noticed the tears falling from beneath his black-rimmed glasses. He opened his mouth as if to say something, then closed it again, swinging his head back and forth slowly. With the beard and long hair, he could have been an old bear in pain.

And I wasn't the only one looking at him. We all were. Silent and staring. Elaine wasn't even hissing anymore as she squinted her eyes his way. Did she suspect Jack's tears were tears of confession? Did I?

Lillian's eyes were on Jack too, but hers were filled with concern. She stretched her small wiry arm around his shoulders and murmured something I couldn't hear.

I thought he was going to say something now, finally, but he just closed his eyes and began humming softly instead. The tune sounded like "Imagine." Was this the musical portion of our entertainment? Or was this how Jack dealt with distress?

Because Jack wasn't the only distressed person in the room. I could certainly see the distress on Elaine's face and in the tightness of her thin body as she dug her nails into the arms of her chair. I was glad I wasn't sitting next to her because I was pretty sure she was going to jump down someone's throat soon, Jack's behavior only acting as a convenient intermission.

And I could *feel* the distress emanating from Natalie sitting next to me. When she crossed her arms and shoved her body back against the cushions of the couch, the whole damn thing shook. I watched out of the corner of my eye as she pursed her lips and jerked her head over and over again, ruffling her short blow-dried hair with the violent movement. What the hell was that all about?

I felt like I'd gone back twenty years in time, working on the ward of a mental hospital again, watching my patients. We had some inappropriate crying, some inappropriate humming, and some repetitive head-jerking. Elaine was clawing her chair. Pam and Charlie were each sitting bolt upright, as if in catatonic stupors. And Becky was hugging herself and starting to rock. But unlike twenty years ago, this time I was one of the inmates.

I decided to speak up before I started pacing and muttering myself. If we were going to talk about murder, we were going to talk about murder.

"I don't believe Sid's death was an accident either," I announced. "I think someone rigged the machine—"

Becky stopped rocking to interrupt me. "But, but . . . I thought Sid rigged it, you know, to make jokes—"

"He did," Elaine told her. "He told me he was going to. That's all fine and dandy. He was gonna rig it to talk when people played it. A joke. A prank. But someone else rigged it to kill him." She leaned forward in her chair. The hiss of her voice lowered even further. "And whoever it is, they're gonna pay."

Now she looked around the group as Aurora had, but her expression was not serene. It reminded me of the look my cat had given me the day I had snatched the snake she was busy killing from her bloody claws. A look that had scared me far more than any look from a being less than a tenth of my size should have.

When Elaine's accusing gaze made it to Pam, Pam came out of her catatonic posture long enough to turn her lovely heart-shaped face to Charlie, her dark lustrous eyes touched with panic. Charlie clasped Pam's hand for a moment, then looked down in horror and dropped it like it was a nuclear potato. Then they both turned their eyes guiltily straight ahead again.

"So which one of you did it?" Elaine demanded, her voice louder now. "Which one of you killed my cousin?"

No one answered her.

"Don't think I won't figure it out," she warned. "You all think I'm stupid. You thought Sid was stupid too. Pretending to like him and laughing behind his back." She was crying now on top of everything else. She wiped the tears away with the back of her hand. "Well, Sid was laughing too. He knew lots. Plenty of secrets. He was as good as any of you—"

"Of course he was," Aurora put in softly. "Sid was a smart boy. I remember. And funny."

Elaine stopped as if slapped. Then she began to cry in earnest. "I'm sorry, Mrs. Kanick," she sobbed. "I know some of you liked Sid. It's just . . ." The rest of her words were lost in her tears.

"Elaine, I am sorry too," Lillian offered in her gently accented voice. "Sorry if you thought we didn't like Sid. I didn't know him very well, but he did seem like a . . . a charming man. And if he was murdered, his murderer must be found. I only wonder if it might truly have been an accident." She turned to me. "Kate, it was your machine . . ."

I felt every gaze shift toward me, weighing me. Remembering me. Remembering that Hot Flash was indeed my machine.

"I've thought about it, believe me," I told them briefly.

"And talked with an expert. An accident would be highly unlikely."

"But what if Sid did it himself, by mistake?" Lillian pressed.

"No," I answered after less than a minute's thought. It would have been too damn complicated to do by mistake. I just wished I could have said yes. I just wished I could have really believed that theory.

Because I could feel Natalie's eyes burning into me from my side. Burning me at the stake along with the others. Negligence, murder, I thought. Either would fit.

"If Sid rigged the machine for the jokes . . ." Mark began ponderously. He looked at Elaine and softened his voice. "Remember, this is just an idea. But if Sid rigged the machine, could he have rigged it to kill himself? Was he depressed about any—"

"No!" Elaine shouted, jumping from her chair. Her face was still wet with old tears. But her righteous fury had dammed any new ones. "No one's gonna get away with putting suicide on Sid. Or accident. Sid was *not* depressed. Or stupid. He was happy. He had a new job, a new place to live. And he was seeing his friends. Even when things were bad, Sid was never depressed. He was too alive to be depressed, too full of life." She slammed back into her chair and raked its arms with her fingernails. "But one of you killed him."

That about covered it, I thought. Accident, heart attack, suicide. Or homicide. And I was voting with Elaine.

"Perhaps we should table this discussion until we've had some time to think," suggested Aurora after a moment of silence that seemed to extend endlessly.

I turned to her. The woman had some nerve. Had she just wanted to see all of our reactions? Or was there more to come?

"And some time to have lunch," she added. "If everyone will bring their food to the kitchen who hasn't, I have plates and utensils set up. We can all dish up and come back here to eat.''

And by God, that's exactly what we did. Even Elaine. Everyone trooped out into the kitchen and filled their plates, some even exchanging small talk, and then we were back in the living room eating. Aurora had turned the group therapy/murder interrogation back into a friendly luncheon again.

Conversation was a bit awkward, but no more than at some slow parties I've been to, especially in the opening stages.

''Plenty more apple juice,'' Aurora assured Wayne as he gulped down his third glass. ''I brought a few gallons down from the Community. I can tell that you appreciate it. We press it ourselves from our own apples.''

''Really good,'' he offered quietly. ''Tart, not too sweet. So tell me about this community of yours.''

I took a bite of Wayne's Chinese vegetable salad. It tasted as good as it had smelled, sweet and hot, and crunchy with vegies, nuts, and rice sticks.

''Well, one of our members inherited acres and acres of apple orchards out in Lupton about the same time another one inherited enough money to turn some of those orchards into a community,'' she explained, putting down her plate. Her eyes shined brighter than ever now. ''*The* Community. Not a housing development, mind you, but a real experimental community designed with the environment in mind. And designed with the social environment in mind. All decisions are made collectively. We have day-care for young and old, our own playgrounds, a community dining hall, and our own tourist business. An inn, restaurant, and general store. You'd be surprised how many people want to vacation in a place where there are no McDonald's—''

''And more masseuses and masseurs per customer than anywhere else for miles,'' Lillian added.

Aurora laughed. ''That's true,'' she admitted. ''They come

in part to be pampered. But they support our programs too. We have our own sewage treatment, our own recycling program, and our own organically grown vegetables and fruit. And best of all, we've each helped build each other's houses, from pouring concrete to plumbing to sawing and hammering—''

"And electrical wiring," Wayne put in softly.

Aurora's smile dimmed for an instant, but only an instant. Then she laughed.

"And electrical wiring," she admitted with a wink, acknowledging his suspicions. Suspicions I was glad he had. Indulgence in apple juice was not dimming his perception any. "I've done my share. Though only under the direct supervision of our community electrician. Our houses are small but solid. And the wiring has to be done to code."

"Mom could do anything she put her mind to," Lillian told us. Were those words meant to be damning? I doubted it from the smile on Lillian's face. For once, her Asian features were relaxed in Buddha-like composure. "Mom has a . . . a . . .''— she waved her hands for a moment, trying to capture the words—"a 'green thumb' for learning new things. Jack and I have offered her a job at Karma-Kanick's, but she loves her bookstore too much."

"I didn't know you owned a bookstore," Pam said in surprise. She leaned forward eagerly. "That's wonderful. What kind?"

I was surprised to see a faint blush on Aurora's face as she answered. "Mostly metaphysical," she said. Was that what she was embarrassed about? Or maybe it was the capitalistic impudence to own her own store without collective input? "I carry some recovery books too. And self-help, personal growth, that kind of thing. And a few treasures to go along with the books themselves."

"I've always wanted to own my own bookstore," Pam said

dreamily. "My parents tell me I'm *loca*." She focused on Aurora more clearly. "If you don't mind, can I ask if you make a living from it?"

"Almost," Aurora answered with a graceful shrug. "Some months, it's as if everyone in Gravendale wants spiritual insights that can only be gleaned from my books." She chuckled. "Others, they're at the beach, and I'm working for less than minimum wage. But in the lean months, I offset my mortgage at the Community working at the general store, so the universe provides."

"That's how small American businesses can be," Lillian agreed. " 'Feast or famine.' We are very grateful for the steady business that Gravendale has given us."

She squeezed Jack's arm.

He grunted in agreement. He was looking better. And he wasn't crying anymore. Or humming. Maybe it's too hard to hum with your mouth full. For an unhappy guy, he seemed to have a good appetite.

"It's keeping on employees that's really problematic in these unpredictable economic times," Natalie burst out from my side. Her body was as tense as her voice, for all of her effort to be conversational. "I would never lay off my people no matter what the net gain. They have lives and families. But when the contracts get tight." She shrugged her shoulders forcefully, shaking the couch. "I worry about them. It's a responsibility."

"Lots of layoffs at the nonprofits right now too," Pam told us. "I'm not so sure of my own job at Wildspace. When people are worried about their jobs, donations get smaller. And my position as librarian isn't the most important. Fund-raising is. It has to be."

"When one door closes, another opens," Aurora assured her with a smile.

"That's easy to say," Natalie shot back. "But what would Pam do if she really got laid off?"

"I'm not sure," Pam answered for herself. She smiled sadly at Natalie as Charlie gazed on her with infinite sympathy. Would he pick up her hand again? No. He pulled his gaze away from her with an obvious effort as she went on. "I have a librarian's degree, but so do plenty of others." She threw up her hands. "Ay! The whole thing scares the hell out of me."

"It's very difficult," Natalie agreed. "So hard to do the right thing. I have one employee who I could afford to lose on the balance sheet, but her husband's really sick. If I laid her off, what kind of health care would he have? But still, if I had to choose another employee to lay off in her place, it would be like choosing a child to give away. Lose-lose, all the way."

"Well, no one's laying off at my place," Elaine contributed. At least she wasn't hissing. In fact, her voice was cheerful. And the look on her face was positively smug. "My boss is going like gangbusters. He's good. And he's in politics too. Knows all the right people."

For a moment, anger tightened Natalie's face. Then I remembered that Elaine's company was in competition with Natalie's. Did Elaine's boss's success mean layoffs at Natalie's business?

"Well, I'm not laying off either," Natalie said as if she'd heard my question. "Quite the contrary."

Elaine glared at Natalie now, no longer smug.

"I've got a partner in our veterinarian practice," Mark threw in quickly. Keep that conversational ball rolling. "So at least we share the major risk, but we do employ a receptionist and a bookkeeper. And I do feel responsible for the two pups. We've been lucky though. No matter how bad times are, people still have their pets. If not cats and dogs, then cobras and potbellied pigs. Good economy or bad economy.''

''And their gag gifts,'' I threw in. The unpredictable economy hadn't seemed to hurt my business. Just the opposite.

''So, Kate?'' Mark asked. ''How do you handle the employee question?''

''Well, I have two full-timers at Jest Gifts, Judy and Jean,'' I explained. ''And then I get seasonal help for the holidays. That way I never have to lay anyone off. And there's plenty of muscle for the sorting and lifting and—''

I stopped, suddenly struck by the image of Sid and Wayne lifting Hot Flash onto the bed of his truck. It took at least two people. Lifting a pinball machine isn't something one person can do alone. It's not all that easy for two. In fact, I'd helped shove a little myself despite my bad back. And if we'd helped Sid put it on the truck . . .

''So who helped Sid lift the pinball machine off the truck at his condo?'' I asked aloud.

TEN

My question might as well have been a gunshot. It stopped lunch in its conversational tracks just as effectively.

Elaine whipped her head around my way, new interest in her close-set eyes. And she wasn't the only one.

Everyone in the room was looking at me now. But no one was answering.

"Someone had to help Sid heave Hot Flash off the truck at his end," I tried to explain. Maybe they just didn't understand the question. "Wayne and I helped him get it on the truck at our end, but—"

"I assumed you lent Sid a hand with the machine at his condo too," Natalie interrupted from my left side. "It's your machine. You know how to set it up."

Oh, great. Ms. Spock had spoken, coolly and intelligently. Now probably everyone thought that hers was the logical conclusion.

"No, just on our end," I insisted, trying to keep my voice calm. I felt a drop of sweat trickle from beneath my T-shirt. I hoped it didn't show. Should I have kept the idea to myself? "Sid told us he had it handled on his end."

"Jack loaned Sid the truck," Lillian put in. "But Sid didn't ask us for any help. We assumed someone else had already offered.'' Her eyes were still on me.

Damn. I was glad I hadn't mentioned the second remote control theory yet. I'm sure Natalie would have let everyone know how easy that would have been for me to rig, my knowing pinball machines so well. I inched away from her on the couch.

"Kate and I helped Sid load the pinball machine on his truck," Wayne said quietly from my right side. "And that was it."

I gave his hand a little squeeze in lieu of the big hug I wanted to give him. Wayne's low quiet voice was a match for Natalie's cool one anytime. At least for me. I let myself settle back into the cushions of the couch next to Natalie. Two of us knew I didn't do it. Maybe three, if the murderer was in the room.

"Hand truck," Charlie muttered abruptly.

"What?" demanded Elaine, swiveling her head around his way now. At least she wasn't looking at me anymore.

"It doesn't necessarily take two people if you have a hand truck," Charlie explained, looking up at the ceiling as if for a second opinion.

I almost opened my mouth to ask if he'd ever moved a pinball machine. Because he was right. But how did he happen to know that? Now I was thinking like Natalie, I chided myself. It was a logical conclusion that anything that size could be moved by hand truck. Especially from a man who worked as a handyman.

"Or a friend," Aurora offered. "Did Sid have any other friends who might have helped him?"

That question set my mind off on a whole new tangent. Why was I so quick to assume the murderer must have been at the party? What if this unknown friend/enemy of Sid's, this X, helped Sid unload the machine and rigged it ahead of the party? But wouldn't *X* have had to have been at the party to actually set it off? Or could he or she have stood somewhere unseen beyond the condo, maybe behind the oak trees—

"Sid didn't have any real good buddies but Jack," Elaine answered Aurora, bringing my tangent to a standstill. She went on quickly. "Oh, he knew a lot of people. That's how Sid was. But he wasn't really that close to anyone."

"How about friends from work?" Mark suggested.

"Well, there were some guys he was friendly with when he was selling office furniture," Elaine answered, her voice taking on a sullen note as she tried to explain her popular cousin's friendless state. "But they all scattered after the company went bankrupt. And he wasn't at Natalie's really long enough to get close to the rest of the employees."

"What did Sid do for fun?" I asked, suddenly curious. A sociable guy like that, he must have done something on the weekends, on lonely evenings.

"Well," Elaine began. "He came over to visit me and my family a lot. And he went to the movies—"

"Bars," Jack put in unexpectedly. "And music clubs. And comedy clubs. He tried to talk me into going with him a few times, but I'm married and I think he wanted to . . ." He turned to his wife as his sentence petered out.

"To 'pick up' women," Lillian finished for him. She rolled her eyes. "Isn't that what they call it? Sid just wanted Jack to go with him for, for camouflage—"

"And for someone to talk to," Elaine protested, but her voice was losing steam. "Sid was lonely sometimes. He was friendly, but . . ." Her voice failed completely then and she sank back into her chair, crossing her arms. Was she going to cry again? I wouldn't blame her. Suddenly, Sid was sounding like a very lonely guy indeed.

What was it that Elaine had said about the loneliness of only children? I wondered how lonely she was too for a moment, even with her family and her job. I couldn't imagine her making friends any more easily than Sid did. Of the two, he'd been the outgoing one. And his life—

"Mrs. Kanick?" Becky said softly into the silence.

I turned to Becky, expecting a question about Sid, shocked once more by how haggard her fragile face looked after twenty-five years. I kept expecting her to look eighteen. And right now she looked closer to fifty. "Can I use your phone for a minute?" she asked instead.

She was looking at Aurora, but it was Lillian who answered her. That's right, there were technically two Mrs. Kanicks in the room. Or two Ms. Kanicks.

"Sure thing," Lillian said cheerfully. "There's a telephone in the kitchen on the counter. Touch-tone."

"I've been thinking," Pam announced tentatively as Becky stood and made her way to the kitchen. "If Sid really was murdered, it might have been someone else, someone who wasn't at the party." She paused for a moment.

I saw interest and relief buoy up a few heads. Not mine. I'd already given up my "X" theory. It was too damned complicated to electrocute someone with a second remote control anyway, much less hiding behind a tree. Too much chance of being seen. But Pam was always positive.

"Did Sid have any girlfriends?" she enquired politely.

Elaine shook her head.

"Was he ever married?" Mark asked a little less politely.

Elaine shook her head again.

"No kids?" he tried.

Another shake of the head. I was sure there were tears in Elaine's eyes now. I could see them.

"Where was Sid living before he moved back up to Gravendale?" I asked, hoping the specific question might divert those tears. I didn't want to see her cry again. I'd never make a good therapist. No matter how well I understand that crying is therapeutic, it always hurts my stomach to watch the process. Even in the movies.

"Sid lived in the city, San Francisco," she answered, her voice low. "In an apartment. I don't think he knew anyone real well there. It was a big place."

"How about enemies?" Mark demanded. "Did he tell you about any run-ins, any dogfights with anyone?"

Elaine shrugged. "Nothing important. People who cut him off on the road. Or women who didn't want to go home with him. Rude clerks. But no big deals. And Sid told me stuff. I would have known if there'd been a big deal."

As Elaine finished, Becky walked back in the room and sat back down by Lillian.

"Thanks," she whispered.

I looked around at the unhappy-looking group and asked myself what we'd accomplished. Had we managed to narrow Sid's death down to murder? And Sid's murderer down to someone in this room?

Then I wondered if there was any way to turn this back into a friendly luncheon again. I picked up a muffin and took a cautious nibble. It had molasses in it and maybe some allspice, I thought absently. I took a bigger bite.

"Elaine, may I ask a personal question?" Aurora said quietly. As if all her questions hadn't been personal. But Elaine was nodding and giving Aurora a look like you'd give your favorite aunt, the one who listened to you and gave you cookies. I wished I could be as smooth as Jack's mom when I grew up.

"Do you know who inherits now that Sid is gone?" Aurora pressed.

Ouch, that was personal! And interesting. I turned to Elaine eagerly. I'd have never had the nerve to ask directly.

Elaine blinked and sat up in her chair. Then she cocked her head. "I guess I do," she said slowly. "I don't think Sid had a will. Sid's parents are both dead. And my dad passed away too, last year. So, I'm probably the closest blood relative. I ought to be, anyway. Gee, I hadn't actually thought about it before.''

I believed her. Especially when a new calculating look narrowed her eyes.

''I don't think he had much though,'' she went on absently. ''His father was broke when he died. And Sid wasn't very good at saving, but . . .'' She paused, looking up to the side for a moment as if doing an inventory. ''But there were a few things. Maybe even insurance.''

Well, at least Aurora had managed to cheer Elaine up. That was more than I could claim.

''So what's Gravendale like these days?'' Pam asked conversationally.

''Very different than it was twenty-five years ago in many ways,'' Aurora answered. ''But very much the same in others.''

I heard a sigh of relief from someone in the group. For a moment, I'd thought it was my own. We were back to friendly conversation.

''Lots of these people they call 'yuppies,''' Lillian put in. ''But many of them are very nice. Good customers.''

''And lots of old hippies,'' Elaine added. ''You'd think they'd find somewhere else to go.'' A picture of Elaine with a headband and flowers in her hair came and left in my mind. ''And the worst thing is that some of the old bottling plants aren't even owned locally anymore. Canadians own the one down by . . .''

And so the conversation went for a while. Or maybe it could have been called an occasionally interrupted monologue. Gravendale meant a lot to Elaine.

Twenty-five years ago Gravendale had been known for its fruit orchards and canneries and bottling plants, as well as dairies and chicken farms. Elaine didn't mention that it'd been a bedroom community then too for the people who worked at the nearby university and hospital.

But today the old-time orchard owners and farmers were being overrun by the new custom wineries and condos. And the bottling plants were being bought by the Canadians and the Germans and God-knew-whatever-other-foreigners. And that Canadian plant was pouring its sewage into the creek waters—

"All of the bottling plants have been doing that for years," Mark managed to throw in. A brave man.

"It used to be safe," Elaine shot back. "When the people who owned the plants lived in Gravendale, they couldn't afford to mess up their own water, but now these foreigners just don't care."

"Well," Pam inserted quickly, rising from her chair, her half empty plate in her hand. "I hate to leave, but I really need to get back to the city. I have a date with a friend. So I'll have to say *hasta la próxima*. Till whenever. But thank you for arranging lunch, Aurora. And thank you for your hospitality, Lillian—"

"Wait a minute," Elaine ordered, rising from her chair too. She managed to keep her own plate in her left hand while shoving her right palm out in front of her like a traffic cop.

Pam stopped, leaning sideways as if to avoid an invisible force field. Or maybe not so invisible. Elaine's force seemed tangible as she stood and glared.

Charlie set his plate on the floor and rose from his chair to join the two women. Back straight, hands taut and nose twitching, he was Rodin Rodent in the flesh.

"Before anyone leaves, I gotta tell you about the memorial service for Sid," Elaine proclaimed, lowering her right hand, though not her voice. "It'll be on Tuesday."

"Oh, sure," Pam sighed, a look of relief on her face as she listed back to vertical.

Charlie relaxed into a stooped posture next to her.

"I'll give you each the details on the phone," Elaine went on. She squinted more fiercely. "And you'd all better come."

"I'll work it out with my supervisor," Pam promised in a burst and then turned to go.

"Um, Pam," Charlie murmured, looking up at the ceiling again as she turned back to him. "If you need a ride home, I'd be glad to, um, give you one."

"Oh," Pam replied, startled. Her hand darted up to her face as if by its own will. "I have my own car—"

"What a stupid question," Charlie muttered, smacking his palm with his fist. He shifted his gaze to his feet. "Of course you have your own car. How else would you have gotten here?"

"No, no," Pam assured him. "It wasn't a stupid question at all . . ."

I turned away. This was almost as painful as watching people crying.

Mark stood up and went to the kitchen as the two continued their muted conference.

"Well, I need to say adios too," he told us when he returned. "A lot of furry clients will need my assistance tomorrow. Mammal, bird, reptile, fish, insect. They're all people to me. Not to mention, paying customers." He sucked in his already flat belly and made his way to the door with a little wave over his shoulder. "See you later, alligators," he added and the door closed behind him.

Natalie didn't say anything funny when she made her escape, only her polite goodbyes.

Elaine didn't even bother with those. She glared at us all, snapped, "I'll see you all Tuesday," and was out the door on Natalie's heels.

When Becky stood up, I decided it was time for Wayne and me to leave too. I wanted to catch Becky and ask her about Elaine's rumor that Sid had raped her. I was pretty sure that she'd tell me the truth about it. And that would give me an idea if any of the rumors Elaine had heard by phone were true. Just because the one about Wayne was a lie didn't mean that they all were.

I tugged at Wayne's hand as I stood. He was up in an instant. I had a feeling he didn't want to stay here any longer than I did, not for all the good apple juice in Sonoma County. But at least he was courteous.

"Thank you for having us," he said with a nod in Aurora's direction and then in Lillian and Jack's. The etiquette was still a little confusing. Aurora had clearly hosted the event, but the house belonged to her son and daughter-in-law now. Then he gathered up our dishes and took them to the kitchen.

"Yeah, thanks," Becky and I said simultaneously.

We looked at each other and she giggled.

Charlie and Pam were still in their huddle, murmuring to each other anxiously, as I shook Aurora's hand and peered into her serene face, wondering what she had gleaned from today's luncheon. (And as I clasped Lillian's firm hand and Jack's looser one, wondering why he wasn't looking me in the eye.) So I left without saying goodbye to the two ex-spouses and hurried out the door with Wayne. Becky was just a little ahead of us.

"Let me talk to Becky alone for a minute," I whispered in Wayne's ear once we were following her down the flagstone path to our cars.

Wayne made a sound between a sigh and a groan, then shrugged his massive shoulders and went to wait in the Toyota.

"Becky," I caroled. "Wait up a minute."

She stopped where she stood on the sidewalk and turned to

look at me, her face sad and drawn. Then she tried on a lop-sided smile.

"Jeez, Kate," she trilled. "What now?"

I smiled back as I walked to her, trying to think of a diplomatic segue to the question of her rape.

"I was talking to Elaine—" I began.

"Lucky you," Becky put in, winking one blue eye.

That really made me smile. But only for a moment. I still had to know.

"Listen," I said finally. "Did Sid ever rape—"

"Did Sid ever rape who?" growled a familiar voice less than a foot behind me.

I whirled around, tempted to raise my knee to the groin that went with the voice. But, with an effort, I suppressed both the temptation and the knee, though not my own volume.

"Didn't I tell you not to sneak up on people like that?" I demanded loudly.

D.V. Vogel took a step backwards, hands up defensively. His baggy pants looked in danger of falling down.

"I just drove over to pick up my mom," he muttered with a jerk over his shoulder at the Fiat parked behind him.

I wrestled with a squabbling list of priorities. I wanted to ask Becky about the rape, but I couldn't with D.V. here. I wanted to give D.V. a lecture, but it was none of my business. And wasn't he fifteen years old anyway? What was he doing driving a car by himself? And I could see past D.V. to Wayne waiting for me in the Toyota. He looked like he was chuckling. I wanted to know what he thought was so funny.

In the end, I gave up the match, said goodbye, and marched back to the Toyota.

Wayne wasn't chuckling anymore by the time I climbed in. There wasn't even a smile on his face as I turned the key in the ignition. Wayne's a smart man. And he had a question for me as I pulled the car away from the curb.

"Has Jack Kanick ever been institutionalized?" he asked.

That was a good one.

"I don't know," I answered slowly.

Because, of course, Jack was classic. I'd worked in a mental hospital. I should have noticed. In fact, I had noticed. But everyone was acting nuts, so the impact hadn't been too great.

"Jack, Aurora, Lillian," Wayne muttered. "Three possible motives from one man's insanity."

Now that was food for thought. And I did think about it all the way home past the rolling hills of Sonoma County into the questionable civilization of Marin as Wayne and I rode silently for a while and then tried to talk about other things, cheery things. Nonhomicidal things.

We sniffed for cat spray when we got home. There was nothing new. But the message light on my answering machine was blinking.

I played the tape reluctantly. And heard the unedited story of yet one more crisis for Jest Gifts. My warehousewoman Judy had gone to work that day, Sunday or not, to make up for missing Friday and had noticed that two whole cases of obstetrician belly cups were missing. And a case of speculum earrings. They hadn't been stolen. I knew that. We'd find them. But probably after the OB-GYN convention was over.

The phone rang before I'd even finished playing the message. While Judy was still promising to seek and find.

It was my psychic friend, Barbara Chu.

"Are you all right?" she demanded.

Damn. I just hated it when she did that.

"I'm fine," I lied.

"Except that you're involved in something—"

The rest of her sentence was lost as I heard the clatter of the cat door opening.

A mammoth black cat came hurtling in like a furry bowling ball. He took one look at me and stopped in his tracks. Then his yellow eyes widened with panic.

ELEVEN

✧

"Out!" I screamed, dropping the receiver and searching around me for something to throw at the cat. Something deadly. I recognized the yellow color of his eyes. It was the color of urine. "Out, you . . . you rug molester!"

Mammal, bird, fish, reptile, insect, they were not all the same to me. I had caught one of the enemy. Blood lust heated my body.

The big black cat turned and ran. Not out the cat door though, where he might have been safe. But up my curtains, his claws making frantic ripping noises as he ascended.

My hand found a stapler to throw at him. But even as I lifted it, a saner self prevailed. Or maybe just a less homicidal one. I only wanted to scare the cat, not maim him. And I certainly didn't want to staple him to the curtains. I'd never get him down.

Water. That's what I needed. If he stayed up the curtains long enough maybe I could run a whole bucket full to pour on him. The thought gave my legs the energy to sprint to the kitchen.

Unfortunately, the plumbing was not as inspired as my legs were. I settled for filling a tall glass of water and ran back into the living room just in time to see Wayne with the cat in his arms, gently guiding him out the cat door.

"Wait, wait!" I yelled, waving the glass and splashing water all around me. "We've got to scare the pedinkle outa him so he'll never come back!"

"And you don't think you already have?" Wayne said, looking down at a wet stain on the rug near the curtains.

A wet stain that wasn't water.

"Do you think he'll come back?" I whispered.

Wayne looked into my eyes. "Would you?"

Would I? Fear was a good negative motivator. But revenge might be a stronger positive one. Especially when combined with territoriality.

C.C. walked up behind me and meowed plaintively. It was then that I remembered Barbara. I picked up the receiver, wondering if she'd still be on the other end.

She was.

"You've always had such a way with small animals," she commented. I could almost see the amusement in her very scrutable Asian eyes as she said it.

"Barbara!"

I could never tell if Barbara was really psychic or just intuitive. Probably anyone could have figured out I was engaged in cat battle listening to the dangling telephone.

"So anyway, kiddo," she went on. "I woke up this morning with the feeling that you've been in the presence of death again." She paused. "You can tell me I'm wrong," she added.

"No," I mumbled. I sat down in my comfy chair. C.C. immediately jumped in my lap and settled in to shred my thighs with a purr of satisfaction. "I can't tell you're wrong."

"Murder?" she asked softly.

"You tell me," I replied.

And then I waited. Barbara took these kinds of challenges seriously. I could picture her, leaning back in her own chair, her eyes closed, her face peaceful and expectant as she awaited an answer from wherever the hell it was she got her answers.

Maybe Barbara could help. It was always possible. Not that she ever had before. Not exactly. Barbara always knew things she couldn't possibly know. But never at the right time.

Wayne came in and began cleaning the wet spots on the carpet, both water and cat pedinkle. What a guy. Maybe I should give in and marry him in a formal ceremony. But Wayne's willingness to scrub carpets or not, I just knew I couldn't stomach the whole archaic ritual. Not again. Craig and I had even had flower girls at our wedding, for all the good it had done—

"Yes," Barbara intoned in a voice that sounded weirdly unlike her usual cheerful tone. "I do believe it was murder." Then her tone lightened again. "And don't worry, you and Wayne will work the wedding thing out."

I ignored her last comment.

"Listen," I put in anxiously. "Does Felix know I'm involved with this one?"

Felix Byrne was Barbara's pit bull reporter of a boyfriend. And if he found out that I'd been at the scene of a murder and hadn't bothered to tell him, I knew the process by which he would wring every detail of information from me would be as painful as unlicensed liposuction.

"He doesn't know yet," Barbara answered after another pause. "He would have bugged me about it by now if he did. But Jeez-Louise, you know Felix, he'll ferret it out soon. You'd better be ready."

Ferret, I thought. What a good description for Felix. Small and slender with dark soulful eyes. And always sniffing.

"Take care, kiddo," Barbara added. "You might be in some danger." Her voice dropped. "And Wayne too."

"Wayne?" I whispered, my heart pole-vaulting to my throat.

"Just a feeling." The line went silent once more as my pulse accelerated. Was she communing with her spirits? "Don't worry," she said finally. "I don't see any real damage in the future for either of you. Not anything permanent anyway. Everything's cool. You'll both be fine, I'm sure."

"But—"

"See you later, kiddo," she finished cheerfully.

And then she hung up.

Wayne was finished cleaning when I got off the phone. He stood, rag in hand, staring at me with a mournful expression on his kind, homely face.

"You're going to get involved in this murder, aren't you?" he accused quietly.

Was I? If Wayne was in danger, I wanted to know who the murderer was. How else could I protect him? And if the police didn't come up with an answer soon, maybe I could find out something on my own. Then my skin tightened with gooseflesh. What if sticking my nose in would just put Wayne in more danger? I shook away the question and the gooseflesh. Why was I listening to psychics anyway, even psychics who were my friends? Especially psychics who were my friends.

"I'm not sure if I'll get involved," I answered slowly.

"Nothing I can do will stop you anyway," Wayne growled, as if he hadn't heard my answer. "But please, Kate, be careful."

And then he turned away, his back and neck stiff with rejection.

"I have paperwork to do," he told me over a rigid shoulder.

"Well, so do I," I shot back.

This was nothing new. Both being self-employed, we did paperwork on Sunday afternoons and evenings fairly regularly. Usually in an atmosphere of companionable self-imposed drudgery. But not that Sunday. Papers were shuffled angrily, our evening meal was quiet and constrained, and our bedtime ritual was even worse. After a peck each on the cheek, we rolled over back to back and then crawled as far to the edges of our queen-size bed as possible. And I wasn't even sure if we were mad at each other about involvement in Sid's murder or about getting married. By the time my head hit the pillow, I told myself I didn't even care anymore. Of course, I was lying.

By seven o'clock Monday morning there was a new message on the answering machine. I was hoping it was from Judy telling me she'd found the boxes for the OB-GYN convention. We had to find them soon. The convention was less than two weeks away.

But the message wasn't from Jest Gifts. It was from the Gravendale Police Department. Wayne and I were requested to come in for an interview. At 9:45 a.m. Exactly.

Wayne and I looked at each other as the message played and then hugged each other convulsively. For a moment I blessed the Gravendale Police Department for bringing us closer together. But only for a moment. Because the Gravendale Police Department hadn't forgotten Sid Semling. And if they hadn't, we would never be able to either.

We ate and showered, asking each other what the Gravendale police thought. As if we could figure it out. And came up with the same damn answers we had come up with at lunch yesterday. Heart attack (they couldn't really buy that, could they?), accident (they couldn't really blame me, could they?), suicide (not really likely, but would they understand that?). Or, of course, homicide. I didn't want to talk to the police, no matter what their theory was. Nor did my stomach. It wasn't happy with its nine-grain toast and soy yogurt. Not happy at all.

Especially on the way to Gravendale. Wayne drove this time, his foot heavy on the Jaguar's gas pedal, rolling hills tumbling by in a nauseating blur. Cows churning into butter-milk.

Gravendale's Police Department was where it always had been, in one of the old red brick buildings near the library. Inside, the lobby was painted an institutional mold-green I hadn't seen since the first apartment I'd rented when I went away to college. A color I'd painted over within three days.

The uniformed policewoman behind the counter asked us to sit down and we did. The wooden benches we sat on had probably been there as long as the police station, scarred by years of carved initials and obscene communiqués. I wondered what kind of nerve it took to carve on a police station bench. Or what kind of stupidity. Then I wondered if the football player Sid had dressed in woman's undies twenty-five years ago had sat on this bench. I ran my hand along the wood, surprisingly smooth for all the carving. Maybe the football player's initials were inscribed here too.

"Ms. Jasper," the woman behind the counter announced. "Detective Sergeant Gonzales will see you now."

Wayne stood up with me. So did my queasy stomach.

"One at a time," the policewoman ordered, shaking her finger at Wayne. At least it wasn't a gun.

Wayne sat back down, his face a stone mask. I gave his shoulder a quick squeeze and then marched down the long dark hall the policewoman had indicated, pausing at Sergeant Detective Gonzales's office only long enough to knock on its frosted glass door and be commanded in.

Sergeant Gonzales's office didn't look anything like the lobby. The walls weren't green, to begin with. They were cream-colored. And there were framed art photos of dancers in motion on each side of his Daily Planner calendar. Not a wanted poster in sight. He motioned me to a seat in front of his desk. His very neat desk. Only a blotter, a few files, paper and pen. He looked good behind it with his dark, handsome features and Clark Gable mustache. Like an actor playing a policeman. Or maybe not a policeman. He was too good-looking. Maybe an actor playing a politician.

A young, red-haired officer sat next to the sergeant's neat desk, a notebook in hand. And a tape recorder.

"Glad you could come in and help us today, Ms. Jasper," Sergeant Gonzales began. Then he paused. "I'm sure you won't mind if we record this interview."

I shook my head. Not me. I didn't mind. No way. I had nothing to hide. Heh-heh.

"And of course you won't mind if we go through the Miranda formalities," he continued in a suave David Niven tone, the sort of tone suitable for asking if one preferred one's martinis shaken or stirred.

"Yeah, sure," I answered, hoping he couldn't hear the tremor in my voice. Miranda warnings at this stage?

It was the young, red-haired officer who actually asked me if I understood that I had a right to remain silent, that anything I said could be used in a court of law, that I had a right to an attorney, and all of the rest.

I said yes to everything and signed the form, feeling shaky as well as nauseated now. Then I waited for the sergeant to ask me a question.

He didn't. He just stared at me. If he was trying to make me nervous, he was succeeding. Was I supposed to blurt out something incriminating?

I looked at his two framed black-and-white photos instead. They both depicted dancers, dancers who looked like they were flying, four in a beautifully muscled midair collision in one shot, and four more with backs arched celestially in another. Beauty in motion.

"Lois Greenfield," I said, suddenly recognizing the photos.

"What?" Sergeant Gonzales demanded, his eyebrows jumping for a moment in his classic face.

This was obviously not a name he expected to hear.

"Lois Greenfield," I repeated, pointing to the photos behind him. "I saw her show in San Diego. She's a wonderful photographer, isn't she? I've never seen anyone else who could catch motion like that—"

"We're here to discuss Sid Semling's death," the sergeant snapped. Then he smoothed his tone down again. "As I'm sure you well know," he added.

"Oh," I murmured innocently. "I'm sorry."

Suddenly, my stomach was feeling much better. And I wasn't shaking anymore. Except with the adrenaline of triumph. Petty triumph.

"Is Hot Flash your pinball machine, Ms. Jasper?" the sergeant kicked off.

I nodded.

"Can you say 'yes' for the tape recorder?" the red-haired officer asked me.

I said "yes," and "yes" again to the repeated question, feeling not quite as triumphant as seconds before.

"You and Wayne Caruso assisted Sid Semling in loading this machine onto a truck borrowed by Mr. Semling from Jack and Lillian Kanick a few days before the day of the party?" Sergeant Gonzales pressed on.

I took a minute to take the question apart to its components and check, then finally nodded my head again.

Sergeant Gonzales tilted his head toward the tape recorder and raised his eyebrows.

"Yes, that's right," I verbalized loudly.

Like a skillful conductor, Detective Sergeant Gonzales took me minute by minute through the mechanics of the loading of the machine, the day of Sid's party, and the day of Aurora's luncheon without missing a beat. Someone had reported everything back. Except for the personalities involved. Somehow those vital personalities seemed missing from the recital. Who was the informer? I wondered. Elaine? Or Aurora? Or someone else entirely?

"Were there any personal disagreements at the party at Sid Semling's condo?" he asked after we had agreed to those mechanics.

I remembered Mark Myers's anger over Sid's HIV crack, and Pam and Sid's squabble over the Hispanic homeless. And Sid's attack on Charlie's livelihood. Not to mention D.V.'s reaction when Sid put his arm around Becky. Or Jack's lack of reaction when Sid put his arm around Lillian. Or Sid's Vietnam crack. Or—

"Nothing serious," I answered finally. "And I'll bet someone's already told you every single detail I could dredge up anyway." I thought that was a pretty clever deduction. I couldn't tell if the sergeant did. His regular features remained unchanged by my guess.

"I'd like to hear your version, Ms. Jasper," he insisted politely. Politely, but firmly.

So I gave him my version, remembering more as I talked. Aurora teasing Sid. Sid with his arm around Natalie. Sid squabbling with Elaine.

"As far as I can remember, Sid managed to offend everyone," I finally ended.

Gonzales nodded. I felt like telling him to say "yes" for the recorder. It would have been fun. Like carving my initials into the bench in the lobby. But I didn't.

"Listen," I tried instead, figuring it was my turn now. "Elaine Timmons told me about the anonymous phone call she received. Were any of the tips true? Because Wayne never met Sid before the reunion—"

"Why don't we let Mr. Caruso speak for himself on that particular question?" the sergeant suggested, and I felt a chill at the base of my spine.

"But—" I began.

"Ms. Jasper," he said, no change in the courteous inflection of his tone. "I played pinball machines in college. A thing like this doesn't happen by accident. We are assuming the machine was rigged."

Then he just stared at me some more.

"Sid rigged it to talk," I conceded. "I think by remote control. He showed me something in his pocket, something that looked like a garage door opener. But I don't think he rigged it to kill himself. At least, he didn't act like it . . ."

I looked up at the sergeant. I wanted a response. Even an unrecorded nod. He didn't give me one.

"So someone else must have had a second remote control," I added. "Right?"

Finally Detective Sergeant Gonzales responded. There was even a hint of emotion in his tone when he did.

He said, "A second remote control. That was very clever." He paused and bent forward ever so slightly. "So now we know how. All we need to know is why. Tell me, Ms. Jasper, why did you need to kill Sid Semling?"

TWELVE

✛

"Me!" I yelped. "What the hell are you talking about? I didn't need to kill Sid Semling!" A half a heartbeat later I added, "And I didn't kill him, either."

But Sergeant Gonzales didn't answer me. He was back to staring again. I felt the cool drizzle of sweat on my forehead and beneath my armpits. Even the palms of my hands and the backs of my knees had gone moist. Good, I told myself. Maybe that would cool me off so my heart would stop beating so fast. Maybe then I could breathe again. I needed air.

Because I had no idea how serious the sergeant was with his accusation. I looked hard, but saw no clues in his smooth, handsome face. Then I remembered the earlier Miranda warnings. I wished I hadn't. Because as that memory rose in my mind, my nine-grain toast and soy yogurt began to rise in my stomach.

I forced a long painful breath in and out. And willed breakfast back where it belonged.

How could I have been so stupid? I knew I shouldn't have told anyone about the second remote control idea. And who did I choose to tell? The policeman in charge of the murder investigation. Well, I'd wanted a response from the sergeant. And I'd gotten one.

"Look, this second remote control thing wasn't my idea," I told him. "It was my ex-husband's."

The sergeant's eyebrows rose. He leaned back in his executive chair with his arms crossed.

I went into babble mode. There was no use holding back now. There was nothing left to hide.

"Listen," I told him. "My ex-husband and I used to own a pinball machine business together. We took old machines and refurbished them and sold them for home use. He was more technical than I was. He's a computer programmer now. I was more the artist . . ."

Did his brows go up just a little higher? Somehow I had the feeling he didn't believe I was the less technical partner. Or maybe he was just trying to rattle me more. As if he had to. Now I understood just what Wayne had meant about scaring the cat enough already.

"Anyway," I went on. "The day Sid died I called my ex-husband—"

"His name, please?" the sergeant interrupted.

"Jasper," I complied, "Craig."

And immediately wished I hadn't brought him into it. Craig was my ex-husband and he could be a pain in the rear, but still—

"His address and phone number?" the sergeant asked.

I gave them to him reluctantly. At least Craig hadn't known Sid Semling. He couldn't be a suspect. I hoped.

"You were telling me about the day Sid Semling was killed," Sergeant Gonzales prompted me. "And how you called your ex-husband."

"Yeah," I admitted, trying to remember where I'd been. Rattled, that's where, but I went on anyway. "When we got home, I started thinking about Hot Flash. I could tell Sid had been electrocuted . . ."

I stopped myself that time. But too late. Was that another stupid thing to say?

The sergeant's face remained impassive. I repressed a sigh and went on.

"And I could tell that Sid's been electrocuted by my pinball machine. I couldn't believe it'd been an accident. But I wasn't sure. So I called a real expert, my ex-husband—"

Abruptly, the sergeant sat straight up and looked over my head, his eyes narrowing. What the hell had I said this time?

"So, Gonzales," a hearty voice boomed from behind me. I jumped in my seat. I'd never even heard the door open. "Found us our here murderess?"

I swiveled my head around and saw a barrel-chested, red-faced man standing over me, grinning. Simultaneously, I wondered who the hell this guy was and hoped that whoever he was, the grin meant he was joking.

"Chief Irick, Ms. Jasper," the sergeant introduced blandly. But the blandness of his voice didn't make it to his eyes. There was hatred there now. And it was directed toward the barrel-chested man. "Ms. Jasper, Chief Irick."

"Pretty cute for a murderess," observed Chief Irick, giving me his beefy hand to be shaken.

"I'm not a murderess," I snapped as I automatically shook his hand. I would have liked to have snapped his wrist too. But his hands were too big and strong. And damp on top of it.

"Just joking, little lady," the chief assured me. Then he turned his attention back to the sergeant. "About finished up in here?" he demanded.

I watched the sergeant's Adam's apple go up and down. What was he swallowing? A sigh? A shout? A homicidal urge of his own? Could Chief Irick see the hatred in his sergeant's eyes? Did Sergeant Gonzales know he could?

"I'm almost finished with Ms. Jasper," the sergeant answered evenly. "Then I'll be talking to Mr. Caruso."

"Well, finish up then," Irick ordered and sat down in the chair next to mine. Ugh. No good cop/bad cop here. Just a bad cop and an ickier one.

"Ms. Jasper," Sergeant Gonzales complied, his words coming more quickly now. "You have stated for the record that you did not kill Sid Semling. Is this a true statement?"

"It is," I replied, resisting the urge to cross my heart and hope to die.

"Do you have any theory as to how Mr. Semling might have been accidentally electrocuted by your machine?"

"Not a one," I replied briefly.

"Have you any reason to suspect anyone else of Sid Semling's murder?"

"Nope." This was getting a lot easier. It reminded me of my Girl Scouts' swearing-in ceremony a long time ago.

"Is there anything else you wish to tell us at this time?"

"No."

"Then you're free to go," he told me.

My legs had propelled me out of the chair and toward the door before my mind had even taken in the permission. Free! I was free!

"Don't leave town," Irick ordered just as my hand landed on the doorknob.

I looked over my shoulder to see if he was serious. He *was* grinning again. But that didn't mean it wasn't a real warning.

"Ms. Jasper," Sergeant Gonzales put in then. "I'm sorry if I didn't answer your earlier question. Yes, I think Lois Greenfield is a wonderful photographer."

Chief Irick's grin turned to a look of puzzlement, then sullen hostility.

"Yeah!" I agreed too loudly, the taste of freedom increasing both my enthusiasm and volume. "She's great!"

Then I got on out of there.

My brief feeling of complicity with Sergeant Gonzales faded the minute I closed the frosted glass door behind me. As much as I instinctively disliked Chief Irick, Sergeant Gonzales was the one who'd accused me of murder. Well, so had Irick actually. But he hadn't been serious. Or had he? Was I the official Gravendale Police Department's solution to the murder of Sid Semling?

My worries about myself transferred themselves to Wayne the instant I saw him heading down the dark hallway toward me. He must have been ordered to the sergeant's office the minute they let me go. When Wayne and I met midway, I scanned the hall to make sure no one was looking, then wrapped myself around him in an unshakable hug. He'd need it, I told myself as he returned my embrace tightly. Not only was it his turn to be grilled, he was going to get both Detective Sergeant Gonzales and Chief Irick for the job.

The wooden bench in the lobby felt even less comfortable than it had before as I sat and waited for Wayne. I was beginning to understand the urge to carve one's initials. And wishing I'd brought a book to read. I thought of making small talk with the policewoman behind the counter. *So, do you guys really think I did it?* That kind of thing. But then a worse idea occurred to me. What if they thought Wayne and I were in on it together?

Wayne had helped load the machine. Elaine had passed along the rumor that Wayne knew Sid before. And Wayne was so damned homely, people always thought the worst of him. If they thought I did it, why not make it a doubleheader?

By the time Wayne came back down the dark hallway, I had our separate prison cells pictured right on down to the hungry rats and the larger, more disgusting roommates. Formal marriage, informal marriage, what did it matter? I just wanted a joint cell with my sweetie.

Wayne's face was set in stone until we got to the car.

And we were a good ten minutes hurtling down the road before he finally spoke. Not that *I* wasted any time. I'd been jabbering all the way, spewing out theories about suspects and motives and methods as fast as they came into my head. If it wasn't one of us, it had to be someone else.

"They think we did it," he finally growled when I paused for a breath.

"What did they say exactly?" I demanded.

"Sergeant Gonzales asked me why I killed Sid Semling."

"He asked me the same thing," I told him. Maybe this was good news. Maybe Sergeant Gonzales asked everyone if they had killed Sid Semling. He'd probably ask Chief Irick if he had a chance of conviction.

Wayne's brows lowered angrily. "Then he asked if we did it together," he added, his deep voice up an octave. "Kate, can they really believe that?"

Neither of us had an answer by the time we'd returned home.

Wayne and I were barely in the house long enough to sniff for cat spray before Wayne had to turn around and go to work.

"Be careful," he told me at the door. My neck stiffened. Was that an order? "I love you," he added softly and I relaxed . . . as much as I could relax anyway, having been recently accused of murder.

I closed the door behind him and went straight to my desk. No genies had taken care of my stacks of Jest Gifts paperwork in my absence. But then again, no cats had sprayed the towering piles either. I counted myself lucky and called in at the Jest Gifts warehouse.

Judy told me she'd found the obstetrician belly cups and the speculum earrings. Jean had put them under a table the Friday Judy had been gone. So they wouldn't get lost.

"Pretty funny, huh?" Judy giggled.

I didn't argue. A few hours lost employee time was a lot funnier than murder. And Judy was a good employee. So was Jean when she wasn't hiding our products.

June was a fairly quiet time for Jest Gifts. I was always working on new designs, and the paperwork was endless, but at least holiday madness wasn't fully upon us yet. I was pushing paper about forty hours a week and designing the rest of the time. And counting myself lucky. I had a friend whose vision of hell was eternal food preparation. She had a family of five. My infernal vision was eternal paperwork.

I picked up a stack of ledgers. It was time to begin preparing the figures for my quarterly financial statements. Something I would never ever consider bothering with if my accountant, and more importantly my banker (who ever so cautiously extended me a puny but often lifesaving line of credit), hadn't insisted. But as I ran my pencil down columns of figures, my mind inevitably drifted back to Sid Semling.

It didn't take long before I broke the pencil lead and decided that was a perfectly good reason to go look for high school yearbooks.

I found them on the top shelf of a nine-foot bookcase, next to a how-to-do-your-own-divorce handbook I'd bought in self-defense when Craig had started proceedings. Marriage, divorce, they'd be forever linked in my mind. I shook off the thought and carried my Gravendale High senior yearbook to my comfy chair to read. C.C. climbed up the back of the chair as if it were a mini-Matterhorn and then perched on my shoulder to help.

"Look," I told her. "There's Patty Innes, she was my best friend. 'National Thespians, Player's Guild, *Our Town*, *Taming of the Shrew*, *The Panama Game*.' She's a gastroenterologist on the East Coast now. Put herself through medical school as an actress in TV ads."

C.C. sniffed, unimpressed, and delicately nibbled her armpit.

"Think I should call her?"

C.C. jumped off my shoulder onto the yearbook. I shoved her under it and flipped a page.

"There's Jack," I went on. " 'Band, Music Club.' " I kept flipping. "And Mark Myers, no extracurricular activities. He's sure better looking now than he was then. And Natalie Nusser. Wow, look at all this stuff: 'Astronomical Society, Chess Club, Computer Math Club, Finance Board, National Merit Finalist.' And here's Pam, 'Esperanto Club, Library Club—' "

I stood up, dropping the yearbook, but not C.C., whose claws held her securely onto my thighs for a few extra instants before she descended at her own leisurely pace.

"Lunch with Pam!" I yelped. Those claws hurt. "I was supposed to have lunch with Pam."

C.C. stalked away as I looked at my watch. Twelve-thirty. Luckily, Pam and I had decided on a relatively late lunch. I could still probably make it by one as promised.

As I rushed out the door I picked up the stack of business cards I'd collected at Sid's party. Maybe I'd check out a few people on the way back from lunch. Wayne's concerned face rose up like a ghost on the windshield as I turned the key in the Toyota's ignition. Forget it, I assured him mentally. No one's going to kill me at their place of business. Anyway, I rationalized further, visiting without Wayne would keep him out of danger. Then I popped gravel, tearing out of the driveway.

The Nepalese restaurant that Pam had recommended was actually a Nepalese-Tibetan-Indian restaurant with an unpronounceable name located in the Richmond district of San Francisco. I got there exactly at one o'clock. Pam literally came running in the door a couple of minutes later. She looked good in a belted burgundy tunic over black leggings as her heavy breathing animated her substantial curves.

"I took a bus from downtown," she told me, still panting. She threw up her hands. "It broke down about a zillion blocks away. But I cleared an extra hour at work, so everything's cool." Then she grinned. "Let's eat."

We ordered vegetarian specials from a waitress who looked like she might have been of Nepalese ancestry. Or maybe Indian. Or South American or Italian for that matter. Then I casually asked Pam whether she'd seen much of Sid before the reunion.

"I was waiting for you to ask," she told me with a wink. "And the answer is very little."

"But you did see him?" I prodded, my pulse ratcheting up a notch.

"Yeah, I ran into Sid in the lobby at Wildspace over a year ago. You know, where I work. He was selling office furniture. Or trying to sell office furniture. I don't think Wildspace bought any. It wasn't an environmentally friendly line. Lots of teak, for one thing. And you know, teak—"

"And Sid?" I interrupted gently. I didn't want to get lost in a lecture about environmentally correct furniture.

"And Sid acted like I was his long-lost buddy," Pam answered, her large brown eyes widening even larger. "It was kinda sad, like he didn't have many friends. Or maybe he was just trying to get laid. You know Sid."

I nodded automatically, all the time thinking just how little I had known Sid Semling. And not just in the intervening years between high school and the reunion.

"We had lunch together a couple of times. Then he started pressuring me to have dinner." She threw up her hands. "Well, I was pretty sure I knew what dinner would mean to Sid, so I told him no. Numerous times. And finally, he stopped bugging me—"

Pam stopped as a waitress laid a plate of homemade flat bread on our table. I grabbed a piece and bit in. It was whole wheat and herbed. Not as good as Wayne's, but good. Pam took a bite too and continued talking.

"Boy, was I relieved," she mumbled through her mouthful. "Sid can be pretty intense." She closed her eyes for a moment. "*Could* be, I should say. Anyway, I wouldn't have minded the continued friendship. But anything more than that, forget it." She swallowed, then said more clearly, "Sid just wasn't my type."

"How about Charlie?" I asked. I just couldn't resist.

Pam's brown skin pinkened to a lovely shade of terra-cotta in answer.

"Oh, Kate," she sighed. "That's really what I wanted to talk to you about. You know Charlie and I had to, well, had to get married way back when. And then I miscarried." I nodded, feeling a little guilty at just how much I did know from Charlie. "It was all my fault, but I blamed Charlie . . ."

God, I wished Charlie could hear this. She shook her head slowly before going on.

"And then we split up. And I didn't see him for close to twenty-five years. And then . . ." Her lustrous brown eyes went out of focus.

"And then, what?" I prompted loudly.

Her focus snapped back. She bent forward over the table and peered into my face.

"Kate, do you believe in love at first sight?" she demanded.

"No," I answered. Her head jerked back. "But I do believe in love at second sight with a twenty-five-year intermission," I added quickly.

There was no stopping her after that. All she could talk about was Charlie. How he made her feel just to look at him. Just to think about him. How she had misjudged him before. But how she was afraid of a relationship now, especially with someone with no career track. Charlie was a handyman. He lived in some little house on someone else's property, which was fine with her, but what if she got laid off at Wildspace? Would they just be poor and angry with each other again? And anyway, what if the attraction was all on her side? What if he was just embarrassed by her attention?

"Am I completely *loca*?" she asked finally.

"No," I answered firmly. "He obviously adores you too. I can tell." And boy, would I have told if it hadn't been for my feeling that Charlie's words to me about Pam must have been meant in confidence. "You're both crazy about each other. Go for it."

"But—"

"Don't intellectualize your way out of it," I advised, remembering the same advice having been given to me some years before. As long as he isn't a murderer, I added silently to myself. And then wondered if I should be giving out advice before we'd established that point.

"Okay, okay," she whispered, a goofy smile on her face again. "Enough about Charlie."

"Then tell me more about Sid," I ordered.

"Oh, poor Sid," Pam complied. "He was harmless but he always drove me nuts. He always wanted something—"

"Sex," I put in.

We both laughed.

"Especially sex," she agreed. "But he really wanted everything. Attention. Favors. You name it. And he could be so obnoxious. And racist. All that *mierda* about Mexicans." She threw up her arms.

"He made you angry," I observed cautiously.

"But not enough to rig a pinball machine," she shot back instantly.

THIRTEEN

✢

"*Por dios*, Kate!" Pam admonished, her voice seeming unnaturally loud over the buzz of restaurant noise. She shook her finger across the table at me, her lustrous brown eyes narrowed with anger now. "I know you're checking everyone out, but you don't have to be so weasely about it. If you have a question, just ask."

I shrunk into my seat. My lungs shrunk with me, making breathing difficult. I wondered just what color my hot face was. I hadn't been weasely, had I? Just, well, subtle. At least that's what I'd been trying for.

"Excuse me," came a quiet voice from my side. It was our waitress with our vegetarian specials.

Pam sighed and leaned back in her chair as the waitress set out our plates quietly and cautiously, looking neither of us in the eye. I wondered just how much she had heard of our conversation. Or was Pam's expression and shaking finger alone enough to inhibit her?

"As if I don't have enough problems," Pam went on once the waitress was gone. She crossed her arms over her formidable chest. "The police are on my case too. I have an appointment with them this evening. I have to leave work early and drive all the way to Gravendale.'' She paused and looked me in the eye. "And no, I did not kill Sid Semling.''

I was glad to hear the direct denial. So glad, I hurried to make amends. By way of unrequested and most likely ill-considered confessions.

"Wayne and I have already been grilled by the Gravendale police,'' I confided in a whisper. "And they accused both of us of murdering Sid.''

All the anger went out of Pam's eyes. Now they widened with concern.

"But why you, Kate?'' she asked. "You don't even have a motive.'' She paused, peering even more intently at me. "Do you?''

"No,'' I snapped, annoyed. Now she was doing it. All right, she wasn't being weasely, but all the same. "I just own the pinball machine in question. A previously harmless piece of entertainment equipment, now a murder weapon. Unfortunately, that may be a simple enough solution for the Gravendale Police Department.''

Pam shook her head, then looked down at her plate and seemed to forget about murder.

"Yum,'' she said cheerfully. "The baked eggplant with onions, *sabroso*.'' She kissed her fingertips to complete her sentence. "Even the basmati rice is special. And the chutney—''

"Pam,'' I said, keeping my eyes off my plate and on my duty. "I don't want to be weasely, but I do want to ask people more questions. Not just you, but everyone. See, if the police want to pin this thing on Wayne and me, I have to do what I can to figure it out myself.''

Pam took a bite of eggplant and nodded solemnly. The muscles in my chest relaxed.

"So, about motive,'' I began enthusiastically. Then I stopped. How was I going to get into this without spilling the beans about Charlie spilling the beans? Pam chewed and stared at me, awaiting the next installment. Maybe it would help their relationship if I let her know what he'd said, I told myself, conning my own conscience. And Charlie hadn't specifically asked me to keep our talk in confidence, I remembered. I opened my mouth again.

"Charlie came to talk to me and Wayne on Saturday night. He filled us in on . . ." How to put it? I looked down at my plate in distraction. The food did look good. And the aromas that drifted up to my nostrils were doing their job, filling my mouth with saliva.

"What did he tell you?" Pam prompted impatiently.

I jerked my head back up and shot out the words fast in an attempt to bypass any self-censure synapses. "He told us how Sid tried to blackmail him, and then how Sid spread the news about your pregnancy all over Gravendale."

Pam's face colored again, but a slightly different shade. Embarrassment was represented in the mix, but so was anger.

"And did he mention how Sid informed me that Charlie was sleeping with half the girls at school, including you?" she fired back evenly.

I flinched at her tone but answered, "He didn't say Sid had included me."

"Listen, Kate," Pam pressed on, holding the edges of our small table. "That was twenty-five years ago. I was pissed at Sid. But I was more pissed at myself. And at Charlie. Getting pregnant. God, *estúpida!*"

Then she flung out her open hands as if trying to grasp the right words.

"But what Sid did, it was just, just icing on the cake. Or icing on the morning sickness maybe." She managed a little laugh. "Ugh, I wish I hadn't said that. But you know what I mean. Sid's rumor-mongering couldn't, and didn't, make the situation a whole lot worse than it already was."

I nodded, hoping she would go on. Because she just about had me convinced.

"And I wouldn't know how to rig a pinball machine anyway," she finished up. Bingo. I was convinced.

"Who would know?" I demanded, glad to be on to somebody other than Pam. Now I could breathe again.

"Well . . ." She looked up at the ceiling for a moment. "Jack's a mechanic. So is Lillian, isn't she? And Natalie does some kind of computer programming—"

"And Charlie's a handyman," I threw in without thinking.

"Kate!" she objected, her palms slapping on the table on either side of her plate. "You know Charlie. Charlie couldn't even conceive of murder. Much less carry it out."

"But could Rodin Rodent?" I murmured, mostly to myself.

"No," Pam answered seriously. "I went and got a couple of Rodin Rodent books from the public library yesterday. Rodin never hurts anyone. He saves them."

Then suddenly her whole face softened. "What else did Charlie say about me?" she asked in a whisper.

"He thinks everything that happened twenty-five years ago was his fault," I told her. "And," I added happily, "he thinks he's in love with you."

Pam's skin flushed to terra-cotta again. There was a soft little smile on her full lips, and her big lustrous eyes were out of focus. She was lovely, a woman in love. A woman to be loved.

"Oh," she sighed after a moment.

When her eyes finally refocused, she looked at me as if she had just noticed me.

"Kate, you're not eating," she reprimanded. "Eat! I'm the one who shouldn't be eating, not with all these pounds on me. I—"

"You're beautiful," I interrupted. "And curvy and luscious—"

"Oh, cut it out." She turned her head and waved a hand by the side of her face.

"I won't," I insisted. "I get so tired of big, beautiful people putting themselves down. If you're so damned unattractive, then why is Charlie in love with you?"

"Okay, okay," she capitulated, her lips curving into a tilted smile. "I'm big and I'm beautiful."

Satisfied, I speared a piece of eggplant and brought it to my lips.

"To some people," she muttered under her breath.

I pretended not to hear the amendment and took a bite of the eggplant. Pam was right about one thing. The food was great here. The eggplant and onions tasted roasted, even barbecued, instead of stewed. And the chutney had to be homemade. I could taste peaches and pears as well as the usual mangoes in the spicy mix. Even the basmati rice was subtly flavored and bright saffron yellow.

We ate for a while without talking, listening to the clank of plates and hum of other conversations in the restaurant, then spent the rest of our time sipping herbal tea and gossiping about the people we'd known at Gravendale High. Sip. Gossip. Sip. Gossip. Pam was the one who brought up Sid again.

"You know, even after he drilled the peepholes in the girls' dressing room, I still liked him," she confessed with a self-deprecating shake of the head.

"Damn," I said. For those of us whose breasts had barely sprouted, that trick had seemed especially humiliating. "I'd forgotten that one. Whose swimming pool was it?"

"Charlie's parents'," she answered, chuckling. "Of course. You should have seen Charlie scouting around for wood putty, scared to death his parents would find out. But the thing was, it was hard to get mad at Sid because he was so vulnerable underneath all that need for attention. And he *was* Charlie's friend." She leaned across the table, her face serious. "I know

Charlie doesn't believe it, but I think Sid really did like Charlie. Liked him a lot. He could be a big brother to Charlie. It was when Charlie started rebelling against Sid's authority that the friendship started eroding. And Sid was jealous of Charlie's relationship with me, even though he helped kick-start it.''

I nodded and took another sip of honey-sweetened tea. Pam was smart about people. She was probably right.

''All our relationships were incredibly fragile,'' I put in, remembering a fight I'd had with my best friend Patty that had lasted for months. I couldn't even remember what had started it. Just the sick feeling in my stomach I'd had all the way through it. ''Painful too.''

''That's because we were all so weird,'' Pam concluded brusquely. ''I still haven't figured out if it was just our group, or if everyone is strange at that age.''

''Remember how Becky used to drink codeine cough syrup from a brown bag during lunch?'' I reminisced. ''She had a refillable prescription and her parents' charge account at the local druggist. She refilled it every week.'' I'd admired the trick in those days, thought it an incredibly clever way to get high without spending any money. Now, all I could think was drug/alcohol problem.

''And Natalie's dorky clothes?'' Pam threw in.

''And Elaine as a hippie,'' I added. ''Remember when they sent her home for having a skirt shorter than the feathers in her headband?''

''*Ay, Dios Mío,*'' Pam said, her hand over her heart as she laughed. ''You know, that *muchacha* was already a racist even when she was a hippie. She wouldn't date my brother because he was Mexican.''

I shook my head and took another sweet sip of tea. That sounded like Elaine.

"Now, Charlie didn't have a racist bone in his body," she added, her eyes glossing over.

Fifteen minutes later of Charlie-this and Charlie-that, I walked Pam to the bus stop to see her off. I wrapped my arms around her luxurious body in a tight hug, glad we knew each other again. And wondering if we would resume our friendship once the murder was solved. "Not if she's the murderer," someone in my mind shouted from the back row. But I ignored the heckler. I didn't want it to be Pam. I liked her too much. "What if it's Charlie?" the heckler added.

"*Hasta la proxima*, Kate," Pam said quickly as a Muni bus lurched up to the curb.

I waited till she was on board and the bus had lumbered away, exhaling exhaust, then walked slowly back to my car, pawing through my purse for my stack of business cards as I went. I was already away from my desk. Maybe the next thing I'd do was go and talk to some of the people who'd been mentioned in Elaine's anonymous phone call.

Rebecca Vogel, Attorney at Law, was on the top of the stack. Perfect. I studied the address, then looked up just in time to sidestep an elderly man limping along directly in my path.

Becky was right here in the city, albeit all the way downtown. But at least her son wouldn't be at her office. I hoped. I didn't want to mention the alleged rape anywhere near D.V. Actually, I didn't want to mention much of anything anywhere near D.V. The kid spooked me.

I found a pay phone on the next block and called Harvey, Payne, and Putnam, studying incomprehensible graffiti as the switchboard placed my call. Unfortunately, Becky wasn't in her office any more than D.V. was. I suspected she might actually have been present physically. But in her secretary's words, she was "unavailable for the rest of the afternoon."

I hung up and looked at my other cards.

Who else? According to the phone caller, Jack had owed Sid money. Lillian was a bigamist. And Natalie Nusser had AIDS.

Karma-Kanick Auto Repair was in Gravendale. Natalie Nusser's office was in Santa Rosa. It was a toss-up which would take longer to get to. But I felt pulled toward Gravendale.

I got in my car and drove without even phoning, thinking about Jack Kanick as I traveled over the Golden Gate Bridge, long past Mill Valley and into the rolling brown hills of Sonoma. He'd been a nice kid. Quiet, musical. Crazy?

Would I have even recognized crazy at that age? I still didn't have an answer by the time I parked in front of Karma-Kanick Auto Repair in downtown Gravendale.

The whole front of the Kanicks' auto shop was open, its corrugated doors rolled up to the beams. The walls were red brick and lined with metal shelves filled with cans and boxes and car parts I'd never be able to identify. I peered in and saw Lillian, wiry in her blue overalls, standing and pointing like a conductor in the din of air-powered drills, hydraulic lifts, revving, grinding, and shouting. Three men in the same color overalls were responding to her directions, but none of them looked like Jack.

I walked in hesitantly, resisting the urge to plug my fingers in my ears, smelling oil, gas, and rubber. And something burning. Maybe I should have made up something wrong with my car. Not that I really had to. There was plenty wrong with my Toyota. But did I really want to leave it in Gravendale?

"Lillian," I shouted, just as she disappeared under an old Lincoln Continental.

"Can I help you?" a man yelled from my side.

I added sweat to my inventory of smells as I turned toward the man, a tall, painfully thin man who was looking down at me with a pleasant smile on his long face.

"Is Jack here?" I yelled back.

He shook his head. "Lillian is though," he said and pointed. Lillian reappeared from underneath the Lincoln as if conjured up by his gesture. She saw me the same time I saw her. There was no welcoming smile on her face.

As I walked toward her, she crossed her wiry arms over her chest. I had a feeling it wouldn't be enough to say I was in the neighborhood and thought I'd drop in. No more weaseling, I told myself.

"I wanted to talk to you about Sid Semling," I blurted out loudly and directly.

"I didn't really know Sid," she replied just as directly. Only her volume was normal. I could just make out her words. "He was just a big, obnoxious American. A 'playboy,' isn't that the word? Always playing, never serious. I have noticed many Americans are like this."

"What country are you from originally?" I asked, glad for the hint of a conversational opening.

For a moment I thought she might not answer. Then she said, "Indonesia, but my parents are Chinese-Indonesian." I could hear her better now, but she wasn't telling me much.

"So what's Indonesia like?" I tried again.

She shrugged. "Some parts are beautiful, some are awful, just like anyplace else."

"Did you meet Jack there?" I pressed.

She shook her head.

"Listen," I pushed on. "I heard the rumor that you were married before in Indonesia—"

"Did you get that from Elaine?" she shouted. It figured. Just when my ears had gotten used to the din, she finally got her volume up. She straightened her spine and curled her hands into fists at her sides.

"It is a complete lie," she went on. "But when you are not born in America, people will believe anything about you. And,

146   JAQUELINE GIRDNER

how they say, 'when someone throws mud, it sticks.' Well, it won't stick to me. Anyone can check if they want. I've never been married before.''

"Oh, I believe you," I assured her, backpedaling fast. And I did. "The same person who told that lie told lies about Wayne too."

Her fists uncurled slowly.

As they did, I remembered Sid saying Lillian reminded him of a Vietnamese girl he knew. Sid, the ugly American again. Or was there some connection? I wasn't about to ask now though.

"Listen," I began over again. "I'm sure you want this thing figured out just as much as I—"

"Lillian, phone call!" someone shouted.

Lillian stepped past me without a word and strode to the phone on the brick wall at the back of the shop. I followed her casually.

"Karma-Kanick," she announced. Then her eyes widened. "Jack?" she said.

I turned my head away politely and strained my ears to compensate as she listened to whatever Jack was saying, but of course I couldn't hear his voice. I probably couldn't have heard it even without the overpowering din of the auto shop. But I sure wished I could. Because he seemed to be doing a lot of talking.

"No, Jack," Lillian said firmly after what seemed like at least ten minutes. "No. Don't say those things. Everything is good now, remember? 'Coming up roses.' Everything is all right now.''

FOURTEEN

Lillian went silent again, the phone still pressed to her ear.

Just what did "all right now" mean? All right, now that Sid was dead? No, not necessarily, I told myself. It could mean a lot of things. All right now that the back screen had been repaired, for instance. Or all right now that the kids' colds were better. Or . . . It could mean anything.

An air-powered drill started up a few feet behind us, taking bolts off a tire. The sound reminded me of a dentist's drill. A great big dentist's drill. But there was no antiseptic smell here. Only grease and rubber and all kinds of smells that a dentist's office wouldn't have allowed. My queasy stomach wasn't sure whether dentist office smells or auto shop smells were worse.

And it wasn't just the smell. It was the vibrations that were getting to me. Not the psychic ones, but the mechanical ones from all the machinery pumping and lifting and drilling and grinding. And the frustration.

What the hell was Jack saying to Lillian now?

"Jack, remember I have much love for you," Lillian told him after a few more minutes went by. She sighed and turned her head, noticing that I was a foot away from her for the first time.

She aimed a glare my way that could have drilled concrete. I took the hint, walking off a yard or so to watch a Volkswagen van go up on a hydraulic lift. That didn't help my queasy stomach any. And now that Lillian was finally doing the talking, I was too far away to hear her except in little pieces.

I caught ". . . call Mom?" in a moment of relative silence. And later, "to sing," and "the children." And a final "good-bye," as she hung up the phone.

I let her come to me, acting acutely casual. If I'd turned around to face her she'd have known I'd been listening to her farewell to Jack. I was pretty sure she knew anyway, but just in case . . .

"Kate," she said softly from behind me.

I turned now, hoping for an explanation of what I'd overheard, but resisting the urge to ask. Eavesdroppers don't have interrogation rights.

"Jack is home with the kids today," she told me.

I nodded, wanting more, mentally willing her to tell me more.

"He's having a difficult time now. 'In the dumps,' I guess you'd say . . ." Her words tapered off as if she'd just noticed who she was talking to.

Then she pulled her head back and glared again. For some reason, it just made me want to talk to her more.

"I'd sure like to see your sculpture," I ad-libbed frantically.

"My sculpture?" She tilted her face, the glare receding slightly.

"That was your stuff at your house, wasn't it?" I pressed on. "All that beautiful bronze curling stuff and the busts?"

She nodded, the glare almost completely gone now from her small pretty face.

"I work from the back room here," she told me. Her tone was quiet, almost shy now. She lifted her hands gently, as if in denial. "It's not like a gallery, only a workshop." She paused. "A studio," she corrected herself.

"I'd love to see it," I insisted.

Lillian led me through a door in the back of the auto shop and it was like beaming onto another planet. I could still hear the racket of the auto shop behind us. But the visuals were magic.

The back room was clearly an addition with its white plasterboard walls and high, skylighted ceilings. It was lined with workbenches. And tools. And art. That's where the magic came in.

There were yard-long strips of bronze curved into forms that suggested, but weren't quite recognizable, shapes from nature. And I saw a few tiny pieces on another bench that looked like jewelry.

But what I loved were the busts. They were mostly of women. Real women with wrinkles and ringlets and Afros and jowls and scars. With beads hanging from their bronze ears and glass marbles for eyes. Those marbles brought them alive. Or maybe it was the detail work. The spirit of each woman was as clear as if she were telling her own story. I knew this one was a proud warrior, that one an intellect, and this one a performer, definitely a performer with a sly wink in her marble eye. Lillian was good.

Only a few of the busts were in bronze though. There were a few stone carvings of a more traditional type. But the majority of the busts were made of plaster. And the plaster ones were stacked everywhere, underneath workbenches, on top of workbenches, on chairs, and on the floor.

"Wow," I whispered finally. "They're incredible."

Lillian's lips curved into a little smile. Then she tilted her face away. Embarrassed?

"They're so real," I added. "Are they from real people?"

"I do busts of the socially prominent—you call these 'socialites' I think—on commission. But most of these are faces I've passed on the street, faces I couldn't forget. They burn into my mind like . . . like music.''

I nodded. I wouldn't forget them either. Not now.

"You've made them immortal," I said. And I meant it.

A faint blush touched her skin. She turned her face even further away now. Was it the praise that embarrassed her, I wondered, or her exposed passion for her own work.

"I sculpt the busts first in plaster," she told me brusquely, jerking her face in the direction of the biggest workbench. "Then I have them cast in bronze at the foundry."

She pointed up at the free-form pieces. "The abstract pieces I weld myself. I have sold some to banks, hospitals, institutions—institutions don't want anything representational. And I sell a little jewelry, here and there." She paused and sighed. "But it's the women I love doing. I am 'into' the women."

I understood her completely. Though I worried that her love for American idioms might get her in trouble someday.

"I like the women best too," I agreed. "They have personality, soul—"

"Yes," she interrupted eagerly. "I see this woman on the street." She pointed at the proud-faced one. "And I want to capture her soul. Why is she so confident? What does she have in her soul to make her so?"

I left some fifteen minutes later, so overwhelmed by the art and the conversation that I'd almost forgotten my purpose in bringing up the sculpture in the first place. It had been an excuse to ask more questions about Jack.

"What does Jack think of your work?" I asked as we passed through the magic door back into the din of the auto shop.

"He loves them. He sees in them what he feels in his music. The same 'vibes,' he says. I think that's why he first fell in love with me. And I with him. The American expressions are so wonderful, 'falling in love.' I did feel like I was falling. Especially when I heard his music . . ." Suddenly something pinched her small pretty face, something unhappy. "He is a very talented man."

"Does he still play?" I asked.

"Sometimes," she said, then shook her head as if she had said enough.

I let it go.

I grabbed her hand impulsively, her calloused sculptor's hand.

"Thank you for letting me see your work," I told her. "And let me know when you have gallery exhibitions. I'm not rich enough to buy, but I have friends." And I have Wayne, I thought. Maybe he could set her up a show in the gallery of one of his restaurants. But I didn't want to promise anything until I talked to him.

She nodded, blushing again faintly.

I left her then and sat in my car, my curiosity wrestling with my conscience. Jack Kanick was at home, not more than a few blocks away. And I wanted to talk to him. Badly. But a bond had been forged between Lillian and myself through her work. Would she feel I'd betrayed that bond if I visited Jack? I could always tell her first that I was going to. No. I shook my head. That would never work. She would just ask me not to. She was clearly protecting Jack from outsiders. In the end, that realization was the deciding factor that allowed my curiosity to win. Why was she protecting Jack from outsiders? I had to know.

I walked up the flagstone path to the Kanicks' house alone this time, taking the steps slowly enough to admire the beautifully landscaped yard and breathe in the scent of sweet alyssum before I knocked on the door.

A small girl, maybe eight years old, with a serious Eurasian face opened the front door and peered out into the light. What was her name? Lark, that was it.

"Are you a solicitor?" she enquired gravely.

I snorted involuntarily. It was better than laughing hysterically. Because technically I was. I was here to solicit information from Jack. But I didn't tell the girl that.

"No," I lied instead. "I'm Kate Jasper, an old friend of your father's." I also decided not to remind her we'd met at Sid's party. That had to be too traumatic a subject to bring up to a child. It had certainly been too traumatic to bring up to most of the adults involved. Including myself.

The girl was still staring at me.

"Is your father in?" I prompted.

"Daddy!" the girl shouted loud enough to back me up a step. I wondered how many of her formative years had been spent down at the auto shop. Learning to speak over the sound of hydraulic lifts and pumps and drills.

It seemed to take forever for Jack to get to the front door. I could hear his shambling steps before I spotted him. Finally, I saw his head looming over Lark's, one hand up shielding his eyes from the sun.

When Jack showed me into the house I saw why he was shielding his eyes. The Kanicks' living room was darker than the day before, the curtains closed and the lights shut off. I could hear Roberta Flack singing "Killing Me Softly With His Song" somewhere in the background. I squinted up into Jack's face. It looked much the same in the gloom, hidden beneath its beard and black-rimmed glasses. This close to him I caught a whiff of acrid sweat. Not the smell of the need to bathe, but the smell of distress. But what kind of distress?

"Do you want me to stay, Daddy?" Lark asked from behind us.

"No," he murmured gently. "That's okay, honey. You can

go fool around with your brother. Or draw. You have plenty of paper?''

Lark nodded quickly, then walked off, turning and looking once more over her shoulder as Jack motioned me to sit on the same navy-and-white-striped couch I'd sat on the day before. She was still worried about him. You could see it in her eyes. But she left the room as requested while Jack slowly lowered his tall, skinny body onto the couch across from mine.

I tried to think of what to say. At least he hadn't questioned my presence here. Nor had he welcomed me. I wasn't even sure if he recognized me. He'd shown me in without a word. And now he was staring just above my head, as if there was someone else perched there. I resisted the urge to look up to see if there was.

"So, how are you doing, Jack?" I tried.

"Okay," he replied, his voice a low mumble, his shoulders slumped.

He brought his eyes down, and they seemed to register me for a moment.

"Kate," he said, his volume normal. "Kate Koffenburger."

I flinched in spite of the relief of his recognition. God, I hated that name. But I didn't correct him. I wasn't here to remind him of my name change.

"Listen, Jack," I said, remembering what I *was* here for. "I wanted to talk to you about Sid."

He closed his eyes for a moment, then opened them again.

"Sid," he repeated dully.

"You were one of Sid's best friends," I told him cheerily. I wasn't sure if this was true. But I was pretty sure at this point he was one of Sid's *only* friends. "What was Sid really like?"

"Oh." His eyelids lowered for another moment. And another. I was just about to prompt him again when the lids finally rolled back up.

"Sid was really cool," he told me, his eyes rambling around the room as his voice rambled around the octaves. "Like always planning stuff. Tricks and goofy stuff. A real wild man sometimes. The court jester of Gravendale High." Jack hummed a little and his shoulders straightened ever so slightly. The Beach Boys? Something from the past, the deep past. "Dug music too, though he didn't talk about it much. Music . . ."

"You were buddies?" I asked when I realized he had rambled off into silence again.

"Yeah, buddies," he repeated. "Sid was a good buddy. Always goofin' on people. Making them laugh."

"And making them angry?"

Jack's eyes landed on me again, clear for a moment behind the thick glasses. He shrugged, then looked away.

It was time to come back to the present.

"So Sid looked you up when he returned to the area a couple of years ago?" I prodded.

"Yeah," Jack agreed. He started humming something that sounded an awful lot like "Mack the Knife." But maybe it was my imagination.

"And was he the same old Sid?" I pressed.

"Same old Sid," Jack repeated. "Older, but still funny. And scamming. Always scamming."

"Did you know there's a rumor going around that you owed Sid money?" I asked.

Jack's brows went up for a moment above his glasses. A smile touched his lips. "That'd be a turnaround," he said. And then the smile was gone.

"Well, the police have heard the rumor," I warned him. "You might want to tell them it isn't true."

Jack shrugged, then his shoulders slumped even further. I had a feeling I'd lost him.

"There's a rumor that Lillian was—" I began, then

changed my mind. He didn't need to hear about that one. Lillian already had. He didn't seem interested anyway.

"How'd you feel when Sid put his arm around Lillian?" I asked instead.

He shrugged once more, but at least he talked. "None of my business," he told me. "Lillian's a damn strong woman. She can take care of herself. Doesn't need a knight in shining armor jumping in to defend her." He paused and I thought I'd lost him again, but then he went on. "She's a damn good woman too." Tears formed in his eyes. "Don't know why she puts up with me. I can't get it together anymore. I'm useless—"

"Daddy?" a voice asked from behind us.

I jumped in my chair. But it was only Lark.

"Yeah, hon," he replied quietly. "You need something?"

"No," she answered earnestly. "Do you?"

"Just a hug," he told her, stretching a smile onto his haggard face.

She crawled into his lap and put her little arms around his neck. He squeezed her gently and she jumped off again. My own eyes were getting a little misty now. Just who was taking care of whom around here?

"Househusband," he commented as Lark left the room again. "One thing I can still do. Cook, garden, take care of the kids."

I nodded. That was the most positive thing he'd said yet. And it was good to know he was responsible for the color and symmetry of the front yard. For some reason I couldn't imagine a man that put that much care into daisies and delphiniums and petunias as a murderer.

"All the rest," he went on. "It's gone. Just like Sid. Gone." Tears were in his eyes again. "And Robert. Remember Robert? Gone too. Everyone gone but me." The tears were flowing down from beneath his glasses now, soaking into his beard. His voice was thick with emotion.

"Their lives are over. Gone. Mine's gone too. I'm dead, but I'm still standing upright. Too stupid to lie down." He put his face in his hands. "I can't do anything. Nothing means anything . . ." His words dribbled off into a chasm of tears.

"Oh, God, I'm sorry, Jack," I murmured. I wanted to put my arm around his shoulders, but I wasn't sure if it would help. All I knew was that he was in pain. And all the time I wanted to help, I kept wondering if this was the pain of a guilty man, garden or no garden.

At one time I would have known how to handle him. But I wasn't working in a mental hospital now. I didn't know his history. And there was no one to call for medication. He might be suicidal. He might be violent. He might be a murderer.

"Jack," I tried. "Is there someone I should call? Is there—"

I heard the front door open and turned around in relief, expecting to see Lillian.

But it was Aurora Kanick who came striding through the door, her usually serene face tight with determination. She saw me and nodded briskly in my direction, but her attention was all on Jack. I might have been another chair.

"Remember what is written on your heart, Jack," she commanded, her deep, calm voice crisp. "Remember it now."

Jack's head jerked up as if she had yanked it. Even his eyeballs moved behind his glasses, rolling so high in their sockets they almost disappeared.

She had his attention. She had mine. A chill of recognition crawled up my spine. Hadn't she used those exact words before? I searched my memory and found them. She'd told Jack the same thing at Sid's party. After Sid had been electrocuted.

"You know you have the resources to heal yourself in your heart," she went on, her voice slowing, less crisp now, more hypnotic. "When I reach out and touch your shoulder, you'll remember something pleasant." She paused. "Maybe something amusing or pleasurable." Then she reached out and touched Jack's shoulder.

His face relaxed into a near smile, his eyes unfocused.

"Now, Jack," she pressed on, quietly and firmly. "I want you to keep those good feelings as we deal with the unpleasant ones. Do you think you can do that?"

He nodded his head slowly. I could see the struggle in his face to obey as the sadness came up again. Tears were still coming from his eyes as his head moved up and down.

"Jack, is there someone inside you who could deal with these unpleasant feelings?"

"Yes." The word came out uncertainly, thick with tears.

"Someone who could even find pleasure in experiencing the unpleasant feelings and overcoming them?"

He nodded again, a little more confidently.

"Is that person sitting over in that chair?" she asked, pointing at the flowered easy chair that sat at the end of the couches.

"Yes," he stated. His eyes focused on the chair.

"Who is he?" Aurora asked.

"Super-Jack," her son told her.

Super-Jack? I rubbed my arms, cold in the gloom of the dark living room. This was too weird. But I said nothing. Because it was working.

"Can you see him clearly now?" Aurora asked and paused. Jack moved his head up and down, his eyes never leaving the flowered chair.

"Can you hear him?" Aurora asked so softly I could barely hear her. And then, "How would it feel to be him?"

"Good," Jack said.

"Jack, you can move now." Aurora's voice took on volume. "Go over now and sit in that chair. Become Super-Jack."

Jack got up from the couch and stepped over to the flowered chair. The minute he sat down he began to change. His shoulders straightened. Light came into his eyes. And he started to sing. Beautifully. A song I'd never heard before. He was a different man. Super-Jack. The hair went up on the back of my neck. Could Super-Jack kill?

Jack was still singing as Aurora turned to me. There was no serenity in Aurora's face now. And certainly no friendliness. Only determination. And anger.

Fifteen

⊤

"Wait for me outside," Aurora ordered brusquely. "I'll meet you at your car in a few minutes."

I obeyed her command instantly, fleeing the Kanick house with only one last look over my shoulder at the glaring mother and her singing son. Maybe Aurora had me mesmerized too.

Unfortunately, the promised "few minutes" became fifteen, and then twenty, as I sat in my oven of a Toyota. The only air-conditioning the car had ever offered me before was the rush of air through open windows as I drove. And I wasn't driving now.

On the other hand, I had all the more time to wonder about Jack Kanick as I sweated in the front seat. And Super-Jack. Was one or the other a murderer? Jack was certainly acting crazier than anyone else who had been there the day that Sid died. But did that mean anything? There were all kinds of crazy: crazy-deluded, crazy-mean, crazy-catatonic, and crazy-frenzied. Just for starters. Not to mention crazy-psychopathic. But one thing was for sure. Jack was out of control. I thought of the tears soaking into his beard. And his words. What had he said? "Dead, but still standing—"

The rap on my car window was as good as a goose. I jumped in my seat and thought about adding a new category.

Crazy-nervous? Then I told myself to cut it out and rolled down my window.

Aurora Kanick was peering down at me. I looked back up into her eyes through the transparent expanse of her oversized glasses. At least I could see friendliness there again. And serenity. Her eyes had that soft but alert look certain Buddhist monks' and Carmelite nuns' eyes have, the look that says they've seen it all and it doesn't hurt anymore. But I'd seen Aurora's eyes narrowed in anger. If only for a moment. And that made me doubt her serenity altogether. Did monks and nuns have their moments of pique too, their moments of rage?

"Kate," Aurora said, her voice as deep and quiet and calm as ever. "I apologize for my bad manners. When Jack is in pain, I seem to lose my center."

I could only nod. I was still processing her mood change. And her words. If you lose your center, do you ever kill people?

"I know you must have some questions," she went on kindly. "Would you like to share some tea and I'll answer them? I left Cassandra in charge of the store for the next hour or so anyway."

"That'd be great!" I answered enthusiastically. My baked brain was coming back to life with a buzz. I wiped the sweat off my forehead. Someone wanted to talk to me! What a change. Tea it was.

The Honeybuns Teahouse was only a few blocks away, so Aurora and I walked, chatting about the mild June weather, and the old houses and newer businesses that we passed. It was good to be out of my oven of a car. And even better to be away from the murk of the Kanicks' living room. I let the summer breeze caress my face as Aurora's gentle voice caressed my ears all the way to the teahouse.

It wasn't until we'd sat down and ordered peppermint tea for me and chamomile for Aurora (as if Aurora needed to be any more relaxed) that I felt I could begin with the questions she had offered to answer.

I took a big breath and asked, "What's wrong with Jack?"

"Jack is out of touch with the joy in his heart," Aurora replied easily. Something in my chest sank. Was she going to answer all my questions with New Age no-speak? Because I knew from experience that this form of speech could be as content-free as a politician's.

She must have seen the look in my eye.

She added quickly, "A doctor would say 'severe manic-depression with suicidal tendencies,' but I believe what my son really suffers from is a great overwhelming despair." She leaned forward, her eyes earnest. "When Jack is overwhelmed by that despair, everything else vanishes. It's as if a wall comes up that blocks love and light and play. That blocks harmony and music, anything that really matters."

"How long has he been this way?" I whispered, sobered by her description, now that her words were all too full of content.

"The despair comes and goes in bouts," she told me. She brought the palms of her hands together gently as if in prayer. "Most of the time he's in touch with the experience of joy and the pleasures of everyday life. He really is a kind and playful man. A vibrant man. But every once in a while—sometimes months will go by without a problem, sometimes years—he loses himself in the despair." She shook her head slowly, looking down at her empty setting on the table. "Sometimes I wonder if the bouts are actually necessary to his ultimate healing, if I shouldn't interfere. But he's in so much pain."

I nodded my agreement. I'd seen the pain. I wouldn't be able to let that go by in someone I loved.

"And the alternatives are worse," she added in a murmur. "Medication. Hospitalization."

Poor Aurora. Suddenly I found myself pitying the woman whose serenity and spirit I'd been so envious of before. What would it be like to be mother to a son like Jack? But then, a little voice niggled, what if it was something in the way she'd brought Jack up that caused him these mid-life bouts of depression in the first place? Neglect? Or even abuse? No, I told the voice. I just couldn't look at Aurora and believe that. And anyway, I remembered her as she had been twenty-five years ago, the mother whose house all the kids had loved to visit. She'd been perfect, kind and interested in us, one and all. Not that that proved anything, the voice reminded me.

Aurora looked back up from the table. "I will not be negative," she stated, her voice calm and firm again. "Everyone has cycles of joy and despair. They're what life's about. Jack's are just more intense than most."

"What did you do to bring him out of it today?" I demanded. Because whatever it was, it seemed to work better than medication or hospitalization. My patients of twenty-five years ago could have used a dose of Aurora's magic.

"Just some techniques I've picked up," she replied. "You've got to remember I own a metaphysical bookstore." She tilted her head and smiled, her skin pinkening ever so slightly. "I've probably read every pop-metaphysical-self-help-recovery book ever written. But the wisdom in each book really boils down to one thing. Each one of us has the power in his or her own heart to heal. What I did with Jack was to simply access that source of power. Jack's own inner source of healing power."

It'd looked a little more complicated than that to me. More like magic. Or witchcraft, I thought, remembering Super-Jack. But I didn't have the proper vocabulary to ask Aurora for details.

"Was that his own song he sang?" I asked instead.

"Yes," she answered, a lilt of pleasure raising the pitch of her usually deep voice. Her eyes sparkled. Metaphysical mama or not, she was clearly as proud of her son's music as his ability to heal himself.

"The melody was really beautiful," I told her sincerely, remembering what Lillian had said about the corresponding "vibes" of Jack's music and her sculpture. Both were powerfully evocative, that much was for sure. "Has Jack ever tried to sell his work?"

"Not very hard," Aurora shot back with a wry look. "Lillian got very energetic and sent out some of his tapes one time, and for a while Windham Hill seemed interested in producing a collection. But Jack let it slip." She put her palms together again. "I need to remember that Jack's music is a very personal resource for him. In his good times he's able to channel the pain he feels directly into his music. And the joy for that matter. But as far as sharing the experience with others . . ." She shrugged. "He just isn't as skilled at marketing himself as he is at making music."

"Too bad," I put in. "It's a loss to the rest of us."

Aurora lifted her hands gently in a gesture of resignation, then said briskly, "It's enough that he's alive right now. And coping by using various techniques. When he gets better, then . . ." She let her hands fly up like freed birds. "Only the goddess knows."

I had a feeling she was reassuring herself as much as me.

"Does he hum and sing to himself to fight his depression?" I guessed.

"Yes," Aurora said, nodding eagerly. "He thought up that technique himself. It's his trigger to fight the worst of the despair."

I wasn't about to tell her, but it didn't seem to be working very well as far as I could see. On the other hand, maybe he'd be even worse without the humming and singing. I shivered. I didn't like to think of him worse.

"Lillian and I work with him when we can," Aurora went on. "Pulling him through the bad times. And then suddenly he's himself again, laughing, singing, loving. He has so much love within him. Even in his bad spells, he never loses his kind nature."

Which brought me back to thinking of Jack as a murderer.

"Is this recent depression related to Sid's death?" I prodded.

"I don't believe so," Aurora answered slowly, frowning as she thought. "Jack's gotten worse, but the despair was already enveloping him before Sid's death."

"How soon before?" I asked eagerly. Maybe too eagerly. Aurora was an astute woman, not a "perma-twink" as my ex-husband termed those poor souls who searched for spiritual and emotional meaning at every New Age seminar that came around the pyramid. No, Aurora seemed truly wise, not naively expectant. And certainly not stupid.

"Jack had been upset for about a month or so," she said, looking me straight in the eye. "And no, Sid wasn't the cause of this current bout to the best of my knowledge. Remember, Kate, Sid's been back for two years. And he actually seemed to cheer Jack up, to get him in touch with his playful side." She paused and looked back down at the table. "But I have wondered if the high school reunion itself could have triggered this bout."

I thought about that for a second. And about all the feelings the reunion had stirred up in me. Feelings of inadequacy and painful self-consciousness. For Jack—

"Here's your tea," our waitress announced cheerfully, interrupting my thoughts as she plopped a tray down on the table and began distributing the goodies. "And almond cookies. No white sugar."

No white sugar. Only lots of honey and fat, I guessed, and ever so delicately snatched a sample from the china plate. One crunch confirmed my guess. Nothing that tasted this good could be completely sin-free. I was just glad it wasn't labeled. As I chewed, I decided to change my interrogative approach.

"Funny how some people liked Sid so much and some couldn't stand him," I put out for comment.

"Jack liked Sid," Aurora assured me, nibbling on her own cookie. "Maybe it was because they were such complete opposites. Sid, funny and playful but completely insensitive. Jack, kind and intense but oversensitive." She put down her cookie and took a sip of unsweetened tea before going on. "Lillian is the one who had a hard time accepting Sid. But she tried for Jack's sake. The kids disliked Sid though. Intensely. Odd, because Sid was so much like a child himself." She frowned at her tea. "Children can see things sometimes, things the rest of us can't."

"Jack takes care of the kids?" I asked. I tried to keep my tone neutral. But the whole thing worried me. Jack might not be crazy enough to murder, but was he sane enough to watch over two young children?

"Don't worry about the children," Aurora answered quickly, as if she'd immediately divined my concern. Owning that metaphysical bookshop might have given her psychic abilities for all I knew. "No matter what state Jack is in, he never forgets the children. Or ceases to love them. Lillian and I used to worry. But he's never forgotten to feed them, never failed to come to their rescue for scraped knees and sibling spats, never had a day he didn't share art or music projects with them." She shrugged. "I don't fully understand it myself, but the children seem outside the wall of Jack's despair. They center his energy and love."

I wasn't convinced. I'd seen Lark's concern for her father. What would it do to a child to see her father cry like that?

"And I believe the children have actually been made more compassionate by their experience with their troubled father," she added. Damn. Maybe she really was psychic. "All families are dysfunctional in their own way. At least in Jack's case he sincerely loves his children." She lifted her hands gently. "Lark and Josh are vibrant, happy, intelligent, and caring little beings. That's all the proof I need."

I took a casual sip of my tea, waiting for my hot cheeks to cool down. Aurora didn't need to prove anything to me. The whole thing was none of my business. And she was probably right about the children.

She nodded as if she had heard my thought and went on.

"And then there's Lillian," she said, leaning back in her chair with an unfocused smile on her face. "Lillian is truly the perfect soul mate for Jack, his exact counterpoint. She not only runs Karma-Kanick, but she creates sculpture of . . . of a completely magical quality."

I bobbed my head up and down earnestly. "I saw her sculpture at her workshop today," I told Aurora.

Her eyes widened with surprise. Maybe she wasn't psychic after all, I decided smugly.

"The bronze busts are my favorite," I added and took another sip of tea, peppermint clearing my sinuses.

"Lillian is an incredible woman," Aurora went on. "She's Chinese-Indonesian. Did you know that native Indonesians discriminate against those of Chinese ancestry?"

I shook my head. I wasn't even sure where Indonesia was. And I didn't know if this conversation would ever lead back to Jack, much less to Sid's murder.

"They just aren't thinking globally yet," Aurora told me, shaking her head. "They even have quotas so not too many Chinese-Indonesians can go to school or have government jobs. But this discrimination was what ultimately brought Lillian to the United States, so I can't complain. It was serendipity at work. Her aunt, a farseeing woman, sent Lillian to art school here." Aurora threw up her hands. "As if Lillian needed an art degree. Everything she needs for her art comes from her heart. But the education did help her English. Lillian wants very badly to speak English correctly, not like some of her Chinese-Indonesian friends who settle for pidgin. Not Lillian.'' Aurora's voice was deep with affection. Then she smiled. ''Though Lillian does get her idioms a little confused sometimes. She loves American expressions.''

''You're very proud of her,'' I said after a moment.

''Yes,'' Aurora agreed quietly. ''I am. She's the daughter of my heart. I couldn't ask the universe for more.''

We each took another simultaneous sip of tea. And I tried to think if anything Aurora had told me about Lillian held a clue to Sid Semling's murder. Not a thing, I decided. Tea and cookies aside, I was no further now than I had been when we'd stepped through the door of the teahouse. Except for the guess that Aurora had a real store of wisdom beneath her metaphysical exterior.

''Listen, Aurora,'' I plunged in finally. ''What can you tell me about Sid Semling? We were all just kids then. Did you see something in him that we didn't?''

''Ah, Sid,'' she whispered sadly. ''Did you know his father beat him?''

I nodded.

''And beat his poor mother, Shirley, too,'' she added. Now that I hadn't known. What a miserable family life Sid must have had. ''That kind of abuse is something that karma is supposed to explain, but . . .'' Aurora's voice faltered for a moment in doubt, then came back to life.

''Sid was capable of great cruelty, but unconscious of it. He hated instead of loved. Hated the people that could do what he couldn't, the football stars, the smart kids, the good-looking ones. And he was mediocre. He didn't have to be, but he wasted all his energy in hating. I worried about him even back then.

"But then I worried about a lot of you kids. Becky with her drug problems. And Mark, fearing his sexual identity so strongly. I used to worry he might kill himself. And Elaine. Her father wasn't much more advanced than Sid's—no matter however much she defended him. And her mother was a walking Barbie doll. And poor Natalie. Her mother died young—I can't remember what of—and her father drank, drank himself to death eventually. And Pam's and Charlie's parents, so different but so identical in their parental attitudes, one minute doting, the next absolutely refusing to forgive their children for being imperfect human beings."

She shook her head and then suddenly smiled across the table at me.

"And you, Kate, with that wild boyfriend of yours," she added. "What an ego he had. No thought for anyone but himself. I used to have to pinch myself to keep from telling you that you deserved better." A silvery little laugh ascended from her mouth.

I didn't need a mirror to see the color that filled my face. And I had thought Ken was so cool. But once Aurora mentioned it, I began to remember little things. Like the time—

"Now I can see that each of you has your own karma," Aurora went on, sober once more. "No one else can work out your issues for you. But it was painful to watch back then."

Her eyes were misty now, lost in the past. Was she thinking of all of us? Or of one very troubled boy? Her own boy.

"Who did it?" I asked her in a whisper.

Her eyes cleared immediately. She looked straight back at me.

"I don't know," she answered crisply. "I've tried every technique I know to reach a higher consciousness, but nothing has worked. I've meditated on the question. I've asked my inner self. I've even put in a bid for a private eye spirit guide," she said diffidently. I wasn't sure if she was joking or not. "But I get no answer."

"Oh," I mumbled. So much for metaphysics.

"Except for one," she added softly. Her eyes went out of focus as she spoke. Her already low voice sank even lower. "Whoever killed Sid Semling was someone he hurt on a deep, deep level. Someone who never forgave. Someone who still hates."

The hair went up on the back of my neck. Aurora may have been joking about spirit guides, but that voice didn't sound like her at all. It sounded like someone else, maybe the someone who never forgave. Maybe the someone who still hated.

"Who—" I began again.

"Oh, goddess, look at the time," Aurora cut in, her voice her own again, her eyes turned toward her wristwatch. "I've got to get back to the store. Cassandra must be going mad with the afternoon rush."

How very appropriate for Cassandra, I thought in frustration. But Aurora was already on her feet, dropping some bills on the table and pressing another business card into my hand.

"Come see me at the store," she ordered, and then she turned and was gone in a whoosh of lavender cotton.

It didn't take me long to finish my tea. And the plate of cookies. Then I walked slowly back to my car, thinking how much I liked Aurora. That was the problem. I liked everyone. Pam, Lillian, Aurora. Even Jack, for the kindness he kept intact for his children's sake despite his overwhelming despair.

Well, not everyone, I admitted to myself. I didn't like Elaine very much. And Becky wasn't acting very lovable lately either. And Natalie . . . I pulled Natalie's card out of my stack. "Natalie Nusser, Nusser Networks."

Her office was in Santa Rosa, not far away. I looked at my own watch. It was four o'clock. I could get there before five easily and check the last rumor. Was Natalie HIV positive? Probably not. A diagnosis like that might explain why she was so uptight, but so would a lot of things. Like a guilty conscience, for one.

And I was interested in Natalie anyway. She had been Sid Semling's boss. She of all people had spent time with him before his death, probably eight hours a day.

I'd need a map to get there, I decided. I hurried the rest of the way to my car, got in on the passenger's side, opened the glove compartment, and slid my hand into its depths.

But I never touched the Santa Rosa map. Instead I touched something fuzzy and vibrating. I jerked my fingers back, but the thing came along with my hand in a purple buzzing blur. My heart was jumping too as I tried to get away. But now the thing was in my lap, its fuzzy legs kicking as it tried to right itself.

I closed my eyes and waited for it to explode.

Sixteen

✦

But, of course, windup toys aren't built to explode.

I held my breath for an instant, then slowly opened one eye. I saw a two-inch-long fuzzy purple gremlin, complete with a white plastic leer, orange eyes, and a windup knob on its side. And, of course, purple kicking legs. Though the legs seemed to be jerking a little slower than before, the loud buzzing sounded more like a weaker clicking now.

I couldn't even say just why I'd expected the gremlin to explode. Somehow it had seemed logical in that instant of panic. Electrocution by pinball machine, car bomb by windup toy. Right.

I let out my breath, opened my other eye, and snatched the thing up off my lap. It wasn't even a very cuddly windup toy. Its purple fuzz felt stiff and coarse. But at least its legs were barely moving now. They were certainly moving slower than my heart was. I set the gremlin on the dashboard and watched as it took one little step and fell over exhausted, its work done, having scared the sense right out of me.

I picked it up again and looked it in the face. Sid, I thought. It even looked like him with the close together orange eyes and the big white leer. It had to be one of his jokes. What had he done, wound it up and jammed it in so it wouldn't start buzzing until I opened the glove compartment? Or did it have a more sinister meaning? Could it have been from the murderer? Then I noticed a flash of white on my lap. It was a little white card with a handwritten message: "Greetings from Sid Semling." Case closed. Now if I could just get my pulse to slow back down.

I picked up the gremlin and rolled down the window, ready to throw it out, something I should have done when it first landed in my lap, I realized. But I couldn't do it. It was, after all, all that was left of Sid. Sid was dead, long live the purple gremlin. I got out my Santa Rosa map, stuck the gremlin back in the glove compartment, and was on my way to Nusser Networks two minutes later.

Nusser Networks was housed in a low-slung building on the outskirts of Santa Rosa between a chiropodist and an accountant's.

I opened the see-through door uneasily. I had already spotted the receptionist through the glass. She was a formidable-looking woman with short-cropped gray hair who, by the expression on her face, was not happy with whomever she was speaking to over the phone.

"No, tomorrow is not good enough," she was saying as I stepped into the room. "I don't care what time it is. Today or not at all!"

Then she slammed the receiver down hard and looked up at me from behind her teak desk.

"Do you have an appointment?" she demanded.

"Uh, no—" I began.

"What are you selling?" she asked with a sigh.

I felt my mouth fall open for a second before I regained the use of it.

"I'm not selling anything—"

"Right," she interrupted. "And you don't represent a good

cause? Or have some little gadget that we just can't do without? Or need a job at a computer firm?''

I shook my head no all three times, wondering if I had bad solicitor karma now.

"Then what are you here for?" she finally finished.

"I'm a friend of Natalie Nusser," I put in quickly. "I was nearby so I thought I'd drop in."

The receptionist squinted at me for a full minute and then demanded, "Name?"

"Kate Jasper," I told her, resisting the urge to salute.

She picked up the receiver again, pushed a button, and turned away from me as she spoke. But I could still hear her.

"There's a woman named Kate Jasper out here, claims to know you," she said. Then she paused. "Oh," "I suppose," and "okay" followed shortly after.

She turned back to me as she put down the receiver.

"Sorry about that," she said, her voice and face softening into that of a friendly human being. "You wouldn't believe how many solicitors have been here today."

"Oh, yes, I would," I assured her earnestly.

We were still exchanging solicitor stories when Natalie Nusser came walking down the hall a few minutes later.

Natalie looked good in her business suit, navy pin-striped with a rose-colored blouse. In fact, she really was an attractive woman, slender with full breasts and a plain but pretty face. But the awkwardness of her movements robbed her of the grace that might have made her seem beautiful at first glance. Her jerking gait as she walked toward me was the same she'd had as a teenager. Though the tension I saw in her face as she came closer was new. It stretched her pretty eyes and mouth into narrow, severe contours.

"Kate?" she said brusquely, a question in her voice as she stuck out her hand to be shaken.

I shook her hand firmly and answered just as brusquely, hoping for some rapport, "Thought we could talk about Sid."

Her face tightened even further. I hoped her day hadn't been as bad as her receptionist's had.

"I can give you a few minutes," she finally answered. "Why don't you come back to my office?"

So I followed her past a few cubicles corralled off by gray room dividers to a room with a sliding glass door. I could hear the sound of computer keys being tapped as we walked and one low voice on the phone to someone who sounded suspiciously like a sweetie, not a business contact.

And then we were sitting in Natalie's office in identical gray-padded office chairs on opposite sides of her wide and crowded desk, the sliding glass door closed and shutting out the sound of the rest of the office. It was time to talk. And I didn't know exactly how to start. For a moment, I wondered how anyone could even suspect me of being a solicitor, I was so lousy at opening lines.

"So, this is your own company," I began, smiling so hard my lips felt stiff.

Natalie nodded curtly, pursing her own lips.

"Nusser Networks," I pressed on cheerily. "Computers?"

"Computer networks," she clarified.

"Oh, like connecting computers together?" I hazarded.

"I specialize in secure network communications," she told me. "Are you interested in our services?"

"No, no," I answered, shaking my head and waving my hand and wondering why the hell I'd ever even brought up her business in the first place. I was beginning to sweat. "I was just curious."

She bent forward abruptly and glared at me. "You're not in the computer business yourself, are you?" she demanded.

"Not at all," I answered, my voice too high. I squirmed in the padded chair and sweated some more. Did she think I was here to steal company secrets? "Gag gifts," I added desperately. "Shark earrings for lawyers, mugs with twisted spines for chiropractors, 'uh-huh' ties for psychologists—"

"Oh, that's right," she murmured and leaned back in her chair, her tense face relaxing a quarter of a muscle. "I'd forgotten."

"I didn't mean to pry," I assured her. "I was just wondering."

"No, no," she assured me back with a quick twitch of her hand. "Sorry to be so secretive, but our clients are confidential, some are even classified. And you know how careful you have to be as a woman in business. You have to go that extra mile. Especially in the arena of confidentiality."

I nodded knowingly. Though I hadn't actually run into many confidentiality problems in my gag gift business.

"You know the stereotypes," she went on, clasping her hands together so tightly her knuckles were mottled red and white. "Women aren't as smart as men. Or as politically savvy. We're too governed by our emotions, too talkative." Her eyes darted around the office angrily as her voice grew louder. "I have to fight like hell for my contracts. Technically, no one can beat Nusser Networks, but I have to prove myself again and again every damn time."

Maybe her day hadn't gone any better than her receptionist's, I thought as I watched her talk.

"It looks like you're doing well though," I offered tentatively.

She focused in on me again.

"You'd better believe we are," she replied. "We have to be. Nusser Networks' continued existence is nonnegotiable as far as I'm concerned. I have to keep the company viable. Not just for myself, but for my employees. What are they going to do if I go under?" She grabbed a pen and pounded it on a pad of paper. "One of my employees' husband has cancer.

Do you know what a difference the right medical coverage means?''

I shook my head, enthralled by her intensity. No wonder she was successful. She had the energy to fuel a rocket ship, more than enough for a computer company.

"Well, I know," she told me, her eyes fierce. "I saw my mother die of leukemia on the county ward. That's not going to happen to one of my people. Not if I can help it.''

I nodded earnestly. I believed her. Then I started wondering if it was the receptionist whose husband was dying of cancer. Somehow, I hoped not. I opened my mouth to ask, but I wasn't quick enough.

"All this fuss over Sid Semling's death," Natalie was saying. "At least he went fast. That's merciful compared to a drawn-out illness.''

"I guess so," I agreed slowly, slowly because now I was remembering one of the reasons I'd come here. To ask Natalie about the rumor that she was HIV positive. Suddenly, the idea didn't seem so ridiculous anymore. Was that why Natalie was so concerned about illness?

"There are some terrible rumors going around," I led in. "About the people who were there when Sid died.''

Natalie's eyes widened in question.

"Natalie," I blurted out. "Are you HIV positive?''

"Good Lord, no," she replied, her skin turning the identical rose color of her blouse.

"Just a rumor," I assured her, feeling my own face heating up. "A false one like the rest.''

"Well, I can disprove that one easily enough," she said briskly. "I was tested for insurance purposes earlier this year. All Nusser Networks employees are.''

I put up my hand. That was enough proof for me.

"You might want to tell the police that," I advised her as

an afterthought. "The person who heard these rumors passed them all on to the Gravendale Police Department."

Natalie's cheeks got even rosier. I thought for a moment about strangling Elaine myself. Why the hell had she passed on the rumors? And who had called her with them in the first place? I shook my head. It was time to pull one foot out of my mouth and insert the other.

"I really came to get some feedback from you about Sid," I told Natalie. "You were his employer. You must have known him about as well as anyone—"

"Not really," she disagreed before I'd even finished. She sat back in her chair, clasping her hands together again. "Sid had only been on board a relatively short time. I'd done my own sales and marketing up until very recently. But the company seemed poised for expansion, ready for a full-time sales-man."

"Didn't Sid say he'd just lined up a big government contract?" I asked, just remembering.

Natalie glared and then I remembered something else, Natalie's feelings about confidentiality. I wondered why Sid hadn't. Time to change the subject again. But I was running out of feet to put in my mouth. Might as well go for the big question.

"You're a smart woman," I began, figuring a little flattery couldn't hurt the proud owner of Nusser Networks. "Who do you think murdered Sid Semling?"

"Are we sure he was murdered?" Natalie returned coolly. So much for the flattery.

"I think so," I answered, feeling like a school kid with the wrong answer as I tried to keep my voice firm.

"Have accident and suicide been ruled out?" she pressed.

"You knew Sid," I objected. "Sid would never kill himself." But even as I said it I knew I wasn't one hundred percent sure. Probably the effect of being around all those mathematically certain computers. Then another thought surged up into my mind. "Sid wasn't sick, was he?" I asked.

"He had a bad heart," she answered.

"But you don't kill yourself over a bad heart," I insisted. I'd been thinking cancer, AIDS, leukemia, all the sad possibilities we'd been discussing.

Natalie shrugged. "Well, I certainly wouldn't," she said. "But I wouldn't presume to speak for Sid." She crossed her arms over her chest. I was losing her. "In any case, I'm not convinced that Sid's death wasn't an accident. A man with a bad heart playing a faulty pinball machine."

"Hot Flash was not faulty!" I answered a little too quickly and a little too loudly. Actually, a lot too loudly. My pulse wasn't quite racing, but it was jogging. I took a deep breath to slow it down.

This was ridiculous. Sid had been murdered. The police knew it. I knew it. My ex-husband knew it. Aurora knew it.

Another approach, I decided. For some reason Natalie's refusal to see Sid's death as a murder made me all the more tenacious.

"Just pretend for a moment that Sid was murdered," I began.

"Hypothesize?"

"Yeah," I said eagerly. Maybe this was how you got through to these science types. "Hypothesize. If Sid were murdered, can you think of any reason why?"

Natalie's eyes flickered, but again she just shrugged her shoulders.

"Any idea who?"

Another shrug answered that one.

I stared at her across her crowded desk. She stared back at me.

"Maybe something from the past," she finally said softly,

surprising me. She looked down at her desk, as if embarrassed by her own untested hypothesis.

The past. Right. But what? Who?

"Who was he closest to then?" I asked, thinking aloud. "Elaine for sure. But who else?"

"Robert Weiss," she answered quickly.

"And Robert blew himself up with fireworks," I said. "Could someone else have bought the fireworks—"

"No," Natalie shot back, flushing. "And don't start *that* old rumor flying again. The police investigated at the time of the event. Robert bought those fireworks himself."

I knew she was right. Robert bought the fireworks. He set them up himself. And they exploded. No one else rigged them. Robert's death was an accident as much as Sid's was murder. Still . . .

"But what if someone thought that—"

"Listen, Kate," Natalie interrupted. "I'm running a business here. I have urgent priorities. Is there anything else you have to ask that really can't wait until another time?"

"No," I sighed, slinking out of my padded chair, suddenly embarrassed for taking so much of her time. She was right. She was running a business, and I was interrupting her.

But as I turned to leave, I changed my mind. "I mean yes," I amended, turning back. "Can I take a peek at Sid's desk?"

Natalie's eyes narrowed even further. Annoyance or something else? Suspicion maybe. I couldn't tell. But I wanted to take a look at the place where he'd worked. I wondered if the police had already looked, but I wasn't about to ask Natalie. I had a feeling I'd used up my allotment of questions.

"If you must," she agreed after a few taps on her desk with her pen. "I'll show you."

She popped out of her chair and led me out the sliding glass door and down the hall to one of the gray cubicles across the way. She didn't waste any time getting there. I had to walk double time to catch up with her jerking stride.

But there wasn't a lot to see once we got to Sid's cubicle. A couple of jokes were pinned to the gray wall. One showed a preacher saying, "Aren't you tired of being a poor sinner?" and a drunk replying, "Yeah, but I just can't seem to get rich." The other one was pornographic. The requisite computer monitor and keyboard sat on top of the desk next to a pen and notebook with a few doodles. I studied the doodles. "Uncle Sam," was the clearest, and "$ $ $!!!!," and a scribble that looked like an attempt at a naked lady.

"Can I look in the drawers?" I asked softly.

Natalie raised her eyebrows and jerked her hands in the air, but she didn't say no. I took the combination as a go-ahead and rifled the drawers as she watched. Not that there was much to find there either. Pencils, pens, paper clips, and Post-its in the top drawer. A stapler and Scotch tape in the second. The only interesting thing was in the bottom drawer, a printed list of companies, contact people, and phone numbers with penciled-in check marks by a few of them. I peeked at it quickly, then said, "Confidential?" and replaced it before Natalie had a chance to do it for me.

That was it, besides another gray padded chair. I guessed Natalie was right. Sid hadn't worked there too long. Or too hard, from the looks of it.

Natalie hustled me down the hall to the reception area after that. If she'd had security guards, I'm sure they would have done the honors for her. The look that she exchanged with her receptionist when we got there told me that my status as a future visitor was probably below that of solicitor now.

"So," I said as Natalie turned to go back down the hall. "Elaine works for a computer company in town too." Natalie turned back to me and jerked her head up and down impatiently.

"And?" she prompted.

"Oh, I just thought you'd be interested."

She didn't answer. I guessed she wasn't interested. But I just couldn't seem to stop my mouth. Something about Natalie cried out to be tweaked. To be pushed. Maybe it was the way she pushed first. I couldn't put my finger on it. Was it her brusqueness that brought out the bulldog in me? Or her inherent correctness? I wondered how much tweaking Sid had pulled on her. Probably not much if she was his boss. On the other hand . . .

"Have you opened your glove compartment lately?" I asked.

"What are you talking about now?" she demanded.

"I opened mine today," I hurried to explain. "And a big furry windup toy came flying out. Courtesy of Sid. I think he put it in during the party. Just thought I'd warn you."

"That sounds like Sid," she snapped, clearly exasperated. Whether at me or at Sid, I wasn't sure. Well, actually I was pretty sure it was me.

I said a quick goodbye and left on the dot of five. With Natalie and her receptionist glaring after me.

It was a long drive back home at rush hour. I had plenty of time to think. About Pam. About Jack and Lillian and Aurora. And about Natalie. If the murderer could have been identified by stress levels, then I'd certainly have pointed to Natalie. That woman was wound tighter than Sid's purple gremlin had been. But she'd probably been uptight all her life. And even if Jack didn't have her exact kind of tension, he was certainly further out of control in his own fashion. And what did anyone's stress and control levels have to do with it anyway?

I clenched my hands on the steering wheel as a Volkswagen bug cut in front of me. I was running a business too. And I'd wasted the whole day talking to people, most of whom didn't want to talk to me. And for what? Nothing.

I was tired, frustrated, and sweaty by the time I parked my car in my driveway. C.C. was yowling, and the message light on my answering machine was flashing as I opened my front door.

I played back my messages first, to the background of C.C.'s loud objections.

The first one was from my ex-husband, Craig. There was a mixture of nervousness and excitement in his voice. The Gravendale police had called to check up on his opinion of Hot Flash's potential as a murder machine. He just wanted me to know.

The second voice was unrecognizable. It sounded metallic and flat. Electronically altered? But its words were clear enough.

"Stop snooping," it said. "Now. Or it won't be just you who'll get hurt. It'll be your boyfriend. Shall I list the ten ways he could die? All by accident?" There was a pause, then the voice went on, "Or can you think of ten ways on your own?"

SEVENTEEN

Unfortunately, I was one hundred percent capable of thinking of ten ways that Wayne could die. And I did, right then as the answering machine tape wound on with another call from a roofing company. Accidental poisoning, car crash, fall. . . . The acidic dread in my stomach churned its way into my chest as postmortem pictures flashed across the synapses of my brain.

But who had left the message? Now my mind was churning along with my body. Natalie? She'd certainly been angry with me when I'd left. But she didn't have to leave an anonymous threat to let me know that. Aurora's serene face appeared before me as I thought of the hypnotic quality of the last line. "Or can you think of ten ways on your own?" A little suggestibility trick she'd picked up from one of her pop psychology manuals?

It had to be someone I'd talked to today. Or did it? Pam might have called Charlie and told him I was snooping. Elaine could have called anyone I'd spoken to today and gotten the information. Or Becky. Or Mark—

I heard the sound of the front door opening and whirled around, adrenaline pumping.

But it was just Wayne who came through the doorway. No

monster. No murderer. Just someone I loved more than anyone else in the world. I watched his kind, homely face as he walked toward me and suddenly remembered Barbara's warning that Wayne might be in danger. Should I let him hear the words on the tape? I had less than a second to decide.

My hand shaking, I punched the rewind button, burying the tape's message forever. I told myself I could let Wayne know about the threat later if I had to. But I didn't want him to press a button and hear those ugly words by accident.

"Kate?" said Wayne, a look of concern on his face.

I rushed him before he could ask me what was wrong and wrapped my arms around his solid body, breathing in his scent like it was pure oxygen. I wanted to hold on to him forever. Whoever had left the message knew my priorities. I couldn't even imagine a world without Wayne. And even if I could, I wouldn't.

Eventually, I had to release Wayne from my impassioned grip. Even a man who loved hugs as much as he did might have become suspicious after a fifteen-minute embrace.

"So, how's it going?" I asked inanely as I let him go.

"Fine," he replied, tilting his head to the side, his brows lowering to half-mast. "Are you okay—"

"Gonna cook me dinner?" I demanded. "I'm starving."

"Sure," he answered, a hint of a smile battling with the suspicion that still lingered on his face. Wayne loved to feed me almost as much as he loved to make love to me. Almost. "Feel like minestrone?"

"*Sí* and *buona sera*," I replied, using up my scant Italian, if it even was Italian, and thinking that indeed I did feel like minestrone, with all the different theories, anxieties, and impressions stirring in the cauldron of my brain. If they'd have been vegetables, I'd have been soup for sure.

I followed Wayne into the kitchen where he opened the refrigerator and began pulling out whatever he could find there. Wayne's minestrone was different every time he made it, but always good. He gave me the job of opening a couple cans of pinto beans as he began chopping vegetables and herbs. Each to his or her own skills.

"Eat lunch with Pam?" he asked with affected nonchalance as he diced a bulb of fennel.

"Uh-huh," I answered, lost in thought. If Wayne was in danger, maybe I should follow him around for the next couple of days. A bodyguard for a former bodyguard? Would he notice?

"And?" he prompted, flashing me a look over his muscular shoulder, suspicion in his voice again.

So I told him all about my lunch with Pam, playing up her feelings for Charlie and playing down my questions about murder as he combined the beans, garlic, homemade broth, and massive fistfuls of vegetables in a big pot. He handed me some mustard greens to chop, and I gave him the short version about visiting Lillian at Karma-Kanick.

"Her bronze busts are incredible," I finished up. "Do you think you could fit them in your gallery?"

Wayne turned slowly away from the bubbling pot on the stove and looked me full in the face.

"You visited Lillian at her shop?" he asked, his voice as low as his eyebrows.

"There were people all around," I defended myself. "It was perfectly safe."

He sighed and turned back to the stove, giving the soup a long, deep stir with his wooden spoon, then adding more vegetables in silence. He didn't say anything more either as he pulled his leftover homemade bread from the refrigerator and heated it in the microwave. Or as he put the finishing touches on the soup.

It was in that silence, filled only with the aromas of garlic and herbs and bread, that I decided not to tell Wayne about

my visit to Jack. Or Aurora. Or Natalie. Or about the an-
swering machine message. And I decided to stop snooping.
Nothing was worth any danger to Wayne. Nothing. Why did
I care who killed Sid Semling? I was done with it.

We ate a dinner that was probably delicious, but I could
barely taste it. And we talked off and on. We talked about
food and an interview of Maya Angelou that Wayne had heard
on the radio coming home. Then we talked a little about gardening. And trimming our fruit trees this year. We didn't quite
get to talking about the weather.

The one thing we didn't discuss was Sid's murder. I could
tell by the abstraction in his voice that Wayne was as much
on automatic pilot as I was. We might as well have been
speaking Italian. Or Mandarin, or Hindi, for that matter. I
wasn't exactly sure what Wayne was really thinking about.
But I knew what was on my mind. Murder was dangerous.
How could I have forgotten?

I didn't talk to anyone even remotely connected with Sid
Semling's death for the rest of the evening. Or the next morning. Instead, I worked diligently on Jest Gifts like a good little
sole proprietor. But I had to answer the phone when Elaine
called to make sure Wayne and I would be at the memorial
service for Sid that afternoon. And I told her we'd go. For
sure. The fierceness of her tone as she insisted that everyone
had to come to the service convinced me that it might have
been more dangerous to refuse her invitation than to accept.
And attending a memorial service was not the same thing as
snooping. Right? Luckily, Wayne concurred when I called him
to tell him I'd agreed to go. For both of us.

Wayne came home an hour later and we climbed into my
Toyota to make the trip to the old Sonoma winery where the
memorial service was going to take place. Apparently, the
winery was owned by one of Elaine's in-laws and the exten-

sive grounds were often rented for company picnics and weddings. And funerals.

When we got there, I could see why. The winery operations were housed in modest, almost shabby, wooden buildings, but the grounds themselves were glorious in the afternoon sun. Spacious lawns extended beyond the modest buildings with scattered oak trees, picnic tables, and even a small pond complete with ducks to exude a picture of rural bliss. Rows of folding chairs and a podium had been set up on a sparkling patch of lawn near the pond. The picnic tables were filled with food and drink. I saw Elaine's husband, Ed, busily arranging a tray of what looked like cheese wedges as we got out of our car in the nearby parking lot. I took a deep breath and looked at my watch. We were still fifteen minutes early for the ceremony.

Wayne nudged me gently and pointed his head toward the other side of the tables. I turned my own head and saw Elaine there, dressed in black. But her clothing was party-black not funeral-black. Her silk dress was cut low down the spine and short at the hem. Her black stockings glittered with gold threads, and her black stiletto heels were complete with big gold bows that matched her bracelets and layers of necklaces. I wondered if the stiletto heels were sinking into the lawn at the same time as I compared my own black cotton turtleneck and ChiPants, the best I could do on short notice.

I also spotted Becky, standing nearby in a modest black suit and low heels. And Pam and Charlie sitting next to each other in the first row of folding chairs. Charlie was in a black turtleneck too. That made us a set, but somehow I still didn't think the two of us were making the proper funereal fashion statement.

"Been to too many of these damn things lately," a voice murmured from behind us.

I didn't leap out of my shoes, but my shoulders hopped.

Damn, I was jumpy. I turned and saw Mark Myers, somber in his black suit.

"Setting's gorgeous though," Wayne offered quietly.

Mark surveyed the scene. I could tell when his eyes lighted on the ducks. His face softened into a little smile.

"Don't get many waterfowl in the office," he commented. "Well-groomed feathers. Don't look overfed either."

For a moment I was disconcerted. Waterfowl in the office? Then I remembered that Mark was a veterinarian. In that suit I'd taken him for a lawyer. Or maybe an undertaker.

Mark started whistling something that sounded suspiciously like "Be Kind to Our Web-Footed Friends" as I tried to think of something socially acceptable to say.

Natalie Nusser joined us before I could.

"Kate," she greeted us brusquely. "Mark. Wayne."

She seemed to have forgotten yesterday's pique for the occasion. But she still looked tense, her lips pursed and her hands clasped behind her military fashion.

The four of us stood for a short but infinite space of time without speaking until Natalie looked at her watch.

"Time to join the others," she said and strode toward the gathering by the pond.

We followed her jerking steps without hesitation, ending up scattered behind the folding chairs. Natalie was a natural born leader. No wonder her employees appreciated her.

As we arrived, I noticed how few mourners there really were assembled for Sid's memorial. We still had a few minutes to go, but there couldn't have been more than a dozen people present that I didn't recognize. A handful of elderly men and women. A few more a little younger. Were these Sid's relatives? I wondered. Or were there some of his friends scattered among them? Had Sid had any other friends?

Elaine's three children sat in the last two rows of folding chairs, gathered around a short, stocky woman whose face reminded me of Ed Timmons. His sister? She held an open book in her lap as she spoke to the children.

"If everyone is sitting on a table, is it still a table?" I heard her ask. "Or is it now a chair?"

"Or maybe a couch?" Dawn offered seriously.

"Very good," the woman commented as Elyse giggled at the thought. Eddie Junior tilted his head professorially.

"So, it's the perception and belief about the nature of the object that really defines it," the woman went on.

All three children nodded solemnly. She had their interest completely. At that very moment, I was sure each of them had forgotten just why they were sitting in the folding chairs near a duck pond. I just wished I could join them. In mind as well as body.

"Aunt Ursula . . ." Dawn began.

"Gad, Kate," a new voice hailed me.

I turned to see Becky, standing, leaning a little, in front of me. Her fragile face was close to mine, her blue eyes already tear-filled.

"Poor ol' Sid," she muttered, and I caught the bouquet of alcohol on her breath.

Poor old Becky, I thought back. And I pulled her into my arms for a quick hug. As I let her go, I peered into her face. She had too many damn wrinkles there for her age. And too many broken blood vessels. I knew it was none of my business, but I wanted to take care of her in that moment, to pull her back to sobriety if I couldn't bring her back to her youth. She had been so alive twenty-five years ago, so full of mischief. But then, so had Sid. Pretty soon my eyes would be filled with premature tears too, I decided, and turned my face away. Just in time to see Aurora and Jack arrive.

Jack was humming as he shambled along beside Aurora, his head down and swinging to his own melody. At least it wasn't "Be Kind to Our Web-Footed Friends." It sounded more like

"Good Night, Irene." In fact I was sure of the tune for once because Jack's hum was loud today, loud enough to record. Aurora looked as serene as always by his side in a flowing purple pants suit.

Could this woman have left me a threatening message? She enclosed me *and* the question in a solid hug before I even had time to consider it. Then she turned to hug Wayne. And Mark. I wondered if she'd have the guts to tackle Natalie. But I never found out. She had just taken Becky into her arms when Elaine arrived.

"I knew you'd all come," Elaine said, surveying us slowly, one by one. Her voice was not particularly welcoming. Nor was her smile. There was more triumph evident in its curve then cordiality. And then even the smile evaporated.

"Where's Lillian?" she demanded.

"Lillian had to mind the shop," Aurora answered quietly.

Elaine opened her mouth as if she was going to demand that Lillian be produced that instant, then clamped it shut again and glared at us for a few heartbeats.

"This is for Sid," she told us finally and spun on her stiletto heels to walk up to the podium, golden threads glinting off the black of her stockings in the sunlight. The warm June sunlight.

I was already beginning to sweat under my black turtleneck. There was no shade by the pond and the afternoon sun was beating down, doing its best for the occasion.

When Elaine reached the podium, she turned, grabbed its sides, and spoke. Loudly.

"It's time to begin," she announced. "Please take a seat if you haven't." Her voice held a tone of friendliness it hadn't before. But maybe that was for the benefit of the relatives who had assembled for the memorial.

I scrambled to sit down in the second row next to Wayne. The folding chair I chose was metal and sizzling hot. I could feel its brand on the back of my knees all the way through my ChiPants. I was just glad I wasn't wearing a skirt.

"We're all here to remember Sid Semling," Elaine told us. She paused and pointedly turned her head to gaze at the little table that sat next to the podium. There was only one thing on that table, a brass urn in the classic Greek shape.

My heart gave a little jump in recognition. Sid's ashes were in that urn. They had to be. My imagination traveled from his electrocution through his cremation and to the sizzling chair beneath my bottom. The trip wasn't a pleasant one. I could have used some Dramamine.

"Sid Semling was my cousin," Elaine said, still looking at the urn. "I could almost say he was my brother. I loved him. A lot. Some people didn't understand Sid." She glared for a moment before moving on. "But when you did, you couldn't help but love him. And I know there are some of you out there who did love him."

I hoped so, for Sid's sake. Maybe some of those elderly relatives had loved Sid. Maybe Jack had. I wanted to look Jack's way suddenly, as if I'd be able to see if he'd loved Sid, but Jack was sitting behind me. So I kept my eyes on Sid's ashes along with Elaine as she introduced a tall, red-haired woman in a long, flowered dress and a large, black-brimmed hat who had seemed to appear out of nowhere.

My pulse sped up. Was this woman Sid's secret lover? A long-lost love? She looked the right age. And she was beautiful enough for the part with her milky white skin and bright green eyes.

"This is Anna May Price," Elaine told us brusquely. "And she will sing for Sid today." And then the romantic balloon burst. This was no long-lost love. This was a hired singer.

But disappointment turned to appreciation when the woman began to sing, "Amazing grace, how sweet the sound . . ."

Her voice was as pure as her sparkling green eyes. And

filled with every nuance of sadness and longing that "Amazing Grace" is capable of eliciting. I felt unexpected tears in my eyes. Tears for Sid, and tears for a vague religious yearning that I'm rarely aware of except through music. And I wasn't the only one who was moved. I could hear sniffles all around me, even sobs. And a harmonic humming that could only have been Jack's from behind me.

When Anna May brought the song to its last sweet note, I would have bet there wasn't a dry eye in the house. She gave a little bow to the audience and then bowed toward the table with the brass urn before walking away and out of sight. Amazing grace indeed.

I brushed off my hot legs and prepared to stand. This was the perfect end for Sid's memorial. But it wasn't the end.

Elaine's husband, Ed, was up at the podium next with another welcome for our small crowd and a rambling series of recollections of his brother-in-law. "A real funny guy," seemed to be the common thread of his stories. Then, mercifully, his words came to an end.

The next mourner up to bat was an elderly man of a stocky build who introduced himself as Sid's great-uncle, Steven Semling.

"That kid, Sid, was a great joker," he told us. "A real Semling. Told me a great one the last time I saw him."

I settled back into my hot seat, my sweaty turtleneck sticking to my shoulders. I had a feeling we were in for a joke, and I was pretty sure it was going to be longer than "Amazing Grace."

"See, seems there's this old guy who meets an old friend after a lot of years," Sid's great-uncle began with a wink. "Guy says, 'So, how's your wife, Mabel?' 'Oh, Mabel,' the friend replies. 'She died.' 'Too bad,' the guy says. 'What of?' 'Poison,' his friend says. 'Poison, that's terrible!' the guy says. 'Did you ever remarry?' 'Oh, yeah, Alice. But she died too.'

'How?' asks the old guy. 'Poison too,' his friend tells him.''
Sid's great-uncle clasped his chest in a great show of shock
here.

'' 'No! That's terrible. Well I guess that must have turned
you against marriage.' 'Nope,' the friend says. 'I married me
a woman named Helen after that.' 'She still alive?' asked the
old guy, hopeful-like. 'Nope, died of gunshot wounds.' ''

Sid's great-uncle paused and surveyed the audience now. I
had a feeling the punch line was coming.

'' 'Gunshot wounds?' the old guy said. 'How the heck did
she die of gunshot wounds?' 'Well,' his friend whispered, 'Helen wouldn't take the poison.' ''

Then Sid's great-uncle slapped his leg and began to laugh
hysterically. Jack joined in from behind us, only his hysteria
sounded more like the medical kind. Oddly enough, I found
Sid's great-uncle's story touching in its own way. I would
have bet it was just the kind of story Sid would have told at
a memorial service. Even at the memorial of a man who had
been murdered.

A couple of other relatives got up and spoke after that. Most
of them dwelt on Sid's childhood antics and sense of humor.
Some of them talked about other funny members of the family
too. By the time they were through I had sweated completely
through my black turtleneck and through the back of the thighs
of my ChiPants.

Then Elaine looked out at the rest of us and asked if we
had any remembrances we'd like to share.

After a long uncomfortable silence, Mark finally stood up
and told us that Sid was ''outgoing, funny, and always glad
to meet new people.''

But that wasn't enough for Elaine.

''Natalie?'' she demanded as Mark took his seat again.
''You were Sid's boss. You must have something to say.''

But Natalie wouldn't take the bait. She shook her head. Elaine glowered.

Natalie glared back.

Elaine glowered even more fiercely. And won.

Natalie rose, jerking out of her chair with all the grace of a badly designed robot. "Sid was a good salesman," she offered tersely. "Sid was a determined man. He never gave up until he got what he wanted."

Then she sat back down, dropping into her seat like a cannonball. She was the only one who hadn't mentioned Sid was funny. Maybe she'd never noticed.

Finally, it seemed that even Elaine had heard enough.

"Anna May!" she called out.

And then the lovely woman with the red hair and black-brimmed hat appeared once more, walking up the path from around the other side of the pond. When she got to the podium, she nodded at the urn on the little table and began to sing again.

This time, the song was "Just a Closer Walk with Thee." Another tearjerker. But I was just too hot to cry anymore by then, though I did do my best to imagine Sid walking with God in whatever form God took as Anna May's pure voice soared above us into the bright sunlight.

Once Anna May was finished, Elaine asked us to join in a silent prayer for Sid. I lowered my head and did my agnostic best, offering my sincere wish that Sid might find peace and light. And joy. And maybe even laughter. It couldn't hurt to try.

I had just raised my head again when I heard a shout coming from the podium. No, coming from the table with the brass urn on it.

"Help!" it bellowed. "Help! Let me outa this urn! Whoa, I really made an ash of myself this time!"

EIGHTEEN

✦

I jumped up out of my folding chair, barely hearing the crash as it fell over behind me. Sid. That was Sid calling from the urn!

"Help!" the voice from the urn shouted again.

In the same instant, I heard a startled yelp from my right side and felt Wayne rise on my left. And then the shouts and cries from all around us.

My pulse beat as erratically as the bedlam that surrounded us. But seconds later, it began to slow as I realized Sid's voice was just a prank. One more obnoxious prank.

"At least I lost weight!" the voice went on, still bellowing. "Would you believe I can fit in this little tiny urn?"

Damn Sid and his stupid pranks, I thought. And then the sweaty little hairs on the back of my neck went up. Sid was dead. But Sid was still playing pranks.

No, not Sid. I shook the thought out of my head violently. That was impossible. But if not Sid, then—I scanned the gathering quickly, glancing at Wayne's face first to see if he was all right. His halfway-lowered brows told me he was puzzled but not panicked. Rare in this crowd. I looked to the front row, but I couldn't see Pam's and Charlie's faces, only their backs. Pam's arms were waving a mile a minute though. Charlie placed one tentative hand on her runaway shoulder as I turned to my right. Natalie stood next to me, her face white and slack-mouthed with shock. Mark didn't look a whole lot better on her other side. And Becky had closed her eyes and was holding her hands over her ears.

I swiveled my head around and saw Jack and Aurora, each with identical looks of perplexity on their faces. Even in the bedlam, I found their reactions interesting. The person in the crowd most likely to be voted insane seemed to be as calm as the person most likely to be voted sane. Assuming serenity equaled sanity.

"Actually, it ain't so bad in here! I think I've *urned* a little respect . . ."

Finally, I jerked my head in the direction the voice was coming from. To the table by the podium. Where Elaine Timmons nee Semling was standing. And then asked myself why I'd even bothered to look anywhere else. Of course it was Elaine who'd done this. I could even see the smug little smile tugging at her lips as she tried to keep her expression somber. This was Elaine's tribute to her cousin, to her beloved almost-brother.

I smiled a little myself in that moment of recognition. Because the voice from the urn really was the perfect memorial for Sid. Far more fitting than "Amazing Grace" or "Just a Closer Walk with Thee."

"In all *urn-estness*, I must say that I appreciate your coming to see me today . . ."

And then I even recognized the voice. It was Elaine's husband Ed's voice. Despite the volume of its bellowing, Ed Timmons's voice lacked the richness and timbre that came from a man of Sid's size. A man who *had* been Sid's size, I corrected myself sadly.

I reached behind me and picked up my half-flattened chair and bent it back into shape again. Most of the assembled mourners had begun to quiet down by now. Yelps and cries had been replaced by frantic conversations, some whispered, some aloud, as people tried to explain the trick to one another. I sat down, feeling a lot cooler than I had before in my sweat-soaked clothes, thankful that acute shock is chilling among other things.

"Hee-hee-hee!" Sid's great-uncle laughed nearby, slapping his leg. "That was a good one, Sid."

I took another glance at Wayne, whose face was about as readable as rock now, and gave his hand a quick squeeze. He squeezed back without blinking and resumed his own seat.

And then Ed's imitation of Sid's voice was abruptly gone. And Elaine's voice was back.

"You know Sid wouldn't pass out of this world without one final prank," she told us, at the podium again. A full smile stretched all the way to her broad cheekbones now.

There were some murmurs of assent from the crowd. As well as a few angry comments from the unamused. And more than one "humph."

"So say goodbye to Sid," Elaine went on, unfazed. "And then stand up and enjoy some of the great food that Aunt Lenore and Uncle Marty were good enough to provide today."

Elaine's smile faltered then as she added, "In the memory of one heck of a funny guy, Sid Semling."

There went my appetite. Because, for all the pranks, Sid was still dead. But I stood up and mingled even though I didn't feel like eating. Mingling was not snooping. And I was still curious, appetite or no appetite.

As I suspected, the people in the crowd that I hadn't rec-ognized were mostly Sid's and Elaine's relatives with a couple of Elaine's friends thrown in for good measure. Ed introduced me to his sister, Ursula, the woman I had seen with his chil-dren earlier. Ursula shook my hand briskly, then turned to Ed.

"I'm taking the children for a walk," she told him. Then

she took his shoulders in her strong hands and gave him a little shake. Clearly, she was an *older* sister. "Bad, bad taste," she scolded him, but there was a hint of laughter in the shape of her eyes. "But then humor is relative."

With that, she winked and released him, walking off with his children.

"The kids knew all about the joke," Ed assured me as we watched Ursula lead them laughing down the path that led around the duck pond.

"It was your voice, wasn't it?" I asked, hoping I wasn't being too nosy. And knowing I was. "How'd you set it up?"

"A little tape recorder under the table," Ed admitted, blushing. "A friend of mine thought it up. All Elaine had to do was hit the switch while everyone's heads were bowed."

"No remote control?" I asked.

Ed shook his head, his eyes widening a little.

It was a question I had to ask. Because if it had been remote control, it would have been the same MO as the pinball machine pranks. For whatever that would have proved. I repressed a sigh. The remote control idea had probably been Sid's in the first place. The same MO wouldn't have proved anything anyway.

I was just reminding myself not to snoop anymore when Pam walked up to me and grabbed my arm.

"Kate!" she hissed in my ear. "You have to take a walk with me."

I looked around me and saw Wayne safe, talking with Aurora. I just hoped taking a walk with Pam didn't look like snooping to anyone.

But nobody seemed interested in us anyway, so I let Pam drag me up a grassy slope to one of the old oak trees, talking the whole time.

". . . So Charlie called me and asked if he could pick me up and bring me to the memorial, and I said yes, but then when I hung up I realized he had to drive all the way down to my place just to drive all the way back up here.'' I took a deep breath for both of us. Pam didn't seem to be able to stop long enough to breathe, she was talking so fast. ''And then on the way up here he tells me when his father died, he inherited his estate.'' She paused for one short second, then pulled me toward her so that our faces were inches apart. ''Kate,'' she breathed. ''He's worth close to a million dollars.''

''Charlie?'' I said, unbelieving.

''Yes, Charlie!'' Pam yelped and let me go. ''*Por Dios*, he lives in this handyman's cottage on his friends' property and does grounds keeping for them because that's what he's always done. Not for the money at all. And he writes his Rodin Rat stories. But he's rich—''

''But that's great!'' I told her. ''Now you don't have to worry about being laid off or about supporting him or—''

''That's what Charlie said,'' she interrupted. ''He said now that he's met me again, he'd move anywhere I wanted, that we could live off the royalties from his books and the interest on his father's money. But . . . but, I feel like such a gold digger. The inheritance isn't my money, Kate. I didn't earn it—''

''Nor did he,'' I reminded her.

''That's what he said!''

''Listen,'' I told her, leading her back down the slope. ''This is almost like what happened to Wayne and me. Wayne inherited a big estate too, but we live in my little house and split the expenses. He could live in a mansion if he wanted. But he doesn't want to. The only real money he ever spent was on his mother. And I keep on with Jest Gifts because I want to.''

''Really?'' Her liquid brown eyes widened.

"Don't you want to keep working as a librarian?" I demanded.

"Well, of course. Wildspace is one of the few organizations that's really—"

"Then just keep on doing it," I told her. "And pick a place to live somewhere between the two of you. Or just stay at your place."

I gave her a great big smile, remembering worrying about all the same things. Damn, it felt good to be able to pass on my experience, real experience that might actually help her. Unless Charlie was a murderer, of course. There was always that possibility.

"But date for a while and live apart till you're sure," I amended quickly. "That's what we did." At least "dating" was a good euphemism for what Wayne and I had done. Almost every night. But I was pretty sure Pam got the point.

She nodded her head, her eyes still wide open.

"It'll be perfect," I promised her, just hoping I wasn't lying.

"Ay, Kate, *muchas gracias*!" she cried and pulled me into a hug that almost smothered me. She was a big and beautiful woman all right, all the way around.

Once I caught my breath, Pam and I walked back to the crowd, arm in arm. I looked over at Charlie who was standing with Anna May, the woman who had sung "Amazing Grace" and "Just a Closer Walk with Thee," but Charlie's eyes were on Pam. And they were sparkling. I would have bet mine were too. Love really was grand. As long as neither of the lovers were murderers, anyway.

We were almost to Wayne and Aurora when I heard Aurora's clear, deep voice chime out.

". . . And it was so good to see Kate yesterday," she was telling Wayne. "And as far as her talking with Jack, I think she might actually have been helpful in unlocking the abundance of joy Jack holds within his heart.'' She reached out to put a wrinkled hand on her son's arm. Jack did look pretty good. He was humming, his eyes focused. But Wayne. All I could see of my sweetie was his back, but the sudden stiffness in his neck and shoulders said it all. Damn. I never had told him about meeting Aurora yesterday. Or Jack. Or Natalie for that matter.

''You know,'' Aurora continued, ''sometimes the most fantastic miracles can arise from events that look disastrous at face value.'' I hoped she was right as she turned to give Jack a small embrace.

Wayne took Aurora's momentary distraction as an opportunity to jerk his head around and aim a quick glare my way, before turning back just as quickly. My whole body flinched in guilt. And then I wondered how he'd even known I was behind him.

''It's really true, what the masters say,'' Aurora went on serenely as she released her son from her embrace. ''Transformation is always possible.''

I slapped an inane smile on my face and pulled Pam the other way, wondering what I would say to Wayne when we finally discussed the matter. If we ever did discuss the matter. My legs felt weak as we drifted over to where Natalie and Mark were talking. Actually, to where Natalie was talking.

''People die,'' she was saying, her usual brusque voice tight with something that sounded like more than just sadness. Was it fear? Or maybe even anger? ''There's no net gain. There's no net loss. People just die! That's just the way it is!''

Another conversation I didn't feel like joining in. I looked at Pam. She looked back at me. And we abruptly executed an about-face and walked the other way. And saw Becky and Charlie heading toward us.

''Talk to him,'' I whispered when Charlie reached us, giving Pam a little push. ''Just talk to him.''

Pam gave me a kiss on the cheek and left with Charlie, walking toward the duck pond. They weren't holding hands, but their bodies were so close, it would have been hard to slide a ruler between them.

"Are they a couple again?" Becky asked me softly.

"I hope so!" I answered with all my heart.

"I hope so too," Becky murmured. "There ought to be some happiness for someone out of all of this, this . . ."

I swiveled my head back her way as she began to cry.

"Oh, Kate," she sobbed, grabbing my arms. "I'm so sorry."

"About what?" I asked impatiently. And then realized that this was my chance. I looked around us. There was no one within ten feet.

"Becky," I whispered. "Did Sid rape you in high school?"

Her head bobbed up, and she dropped my arms. She gazed at me, her wet blue eyes wide with surprise.

"What?" she demanded and leaned back precariously.

I reached out an arm to steady her. She grabbed it and pulled herself forward again.

"Did Sid rape you in high school?" I repeated.

She stared at me for a moment more and then began to giggle, her eyes still wet with tears. I wondered how much alcohol had played a part in the spread Aunt Lenore and Uncle Marty had provided.

"Sid never had to rape me," Becky declared, forgoing even a hint of a whisper now. I glanced around stealthily, but no one seemed to be listening. "You know how Sid could talk. Talk, talk, talk. He could have talked his way into a nunnery. Hell, he's probably talking his way into heaven right now. Well, he just talked me right into, well . . . you know." She winked one wet blue eye largely. "Course, we were awful stoned at the time." Then she giggled again, leaning into me. "Awful stoned."

I felt a hand on my shoulder. I figured it was Becky's son, D.V., again. I hadn't seen him at the memorial, but he always seemed to turn up whenever I was talking to his mother. Well, at least the hand was gentler than before. Maybe he was learning. I turned, without raising my knee this time. Only it wasn't D.V. behind me. It was Wayne.

My heart did a double flip in my chest. I looked up into Wayne's eyes, searching for forgiveness. But all I saw was eyebrows.

"Walk," was what he said.

"Sure," was what I said back, untangling myself from Becky's grip gently. When Wayne got down to one-syllable sentences, he was upset.

"Are you all right, Becky?" I asked, but Becky had already turned and was waving over her shoulder as she staggered over toward Mark and Natalie. That would be an interesting conversation, I decided. If she ever got there.

I put my arm into the crook of Wayne's bigger one and we began to walk away from the crowd, toward the hills. But before we had gone five feet, I felt a tug on my other arm.

What was it, tug on Kate day? I thought as I turned.

"Kate!" Elaine hissed. "I have to talk to you."

"So talk," I advised, trying to control my irritation as I scanned the remaining mourners and wondered how clandestine this meeting looked to whomever had threatened Wayne's life. I felt like screaming out that I wasn't snooping. For all the good it would have done.

"Privately," Elaine whispered, jerking her head in a furtive over-the-shoulder sweep. "At my house in an hour."

"I really can't," I began. "There's no reason for me to—"

"We'll be there," Wayne cut in.

"But—" But what? I looked up at his granite features. Was I going to tell him I'd stopped investigating because someone had threatened his life? And I hadn't bothered to tell him about it?

"Please?" Elaine said, looking at me again, looking into my eyes.

"Oh, all right," I gave in without grace. It was two against one. And maybe, just maybe, no one else would know.

"One hour," Elaine repeated, her words imperious now that I'd agreed. Then she turned on her stiletto heels and strode back to the main party.

Wayne took my arm gently in his. At least he didn't tug on it.

"If you're going to talk to these people, I'm going to be with you," he stated quietly and began to walk again. No, not to walk. To march. Up a steep green hill. With me marching double time to keep up.

And that was all he said until we reached the top of the hill a half an hour later. I was huffing and puffing and grabbing my side, trying to staunch the stabbing pains. Wayne was as silent as I was loud.

He spread out his suit jacket and we sat down side by side, carefully sweating in tandem. There was no mowed grass up here on the top of the hill. Just weeds and wild wheat. But the view was great. We could see the whole memorial gathering below us. Or what was left of it. Elaine was gone. And so were most of the people who'd assembled earlier. Only Ed and a few of Sid's relatives were still there, cleaning up the picnic tables that had been loaded with food.

"So?" I gasped, finally turning to Wayne.

"I love you," he murmured, eyes cast down. "That's all."

"Oh, Wayne," I said and collapsed into his arms. It was an easy collapse. I was exhausted.

Unfortunately, it was a harder climb back down the hill, but at least it was faster than going up. We made it in twenty minutes and climbed into the car to drive to Elaine's. It was very quiet in the Toyota as I drove. I was just as glad. If Wayne didn't feel like talking, I didn't feel like confessing.

When we got to Elaine's, I parked on the street below the house as she'd requested the last time we'd visited, and we hiked up the long tree-lined driveway, my muscles still protesting our earlier trek.

Finally, we got to the top of the driveway. Elaine's BMW was parked diagonally, skewed across the blacktop. She must have been in a hurry, I thought. She was blocking her own garage. Well, I was in a hurry too. I was sick of this whole business.

"Don't go any closer," Wayne ordered suddenly, his hand on my arm.

But my legs kept on moving. Because my eyes had already seen.

Sunlight was glinting off of something sticking out from under the BMW. Gold threads. Gold threads woven into black stockings.

NINETEEN

And then I saw the lone shoe. One shoe, more than a yard away from the car. A black shoe with one long, slender stiletto heel and one big gold bow.

My limbs froze beneath my soggy clothing, finally receiving the signal to halt. Too late. Why hadn't I stopped when Wayne had told me to? Before Wayne had told me to? Because now I could see the other shoe too, still on Elaine's left foot stretched out from beneath the BMW. And her legs, encased in black stockings with gold threads glittering in the sun.

"Dead?" I heard and then realized it was my own voice asking.

"Must be," Wayne's voice came back, barely audible.

I wanted to turn his way, to see if he was all right, but I just couldn't move my head. Or my eyes. I couldn't stop seeing. The gold threads seemed to be glowing now. In fact, everything seemed to be glowing. And tilting. No, spinning.

I was sitting on the blacktop before I knew I'd planned to. But I was moving again. At least, parts of me were. All my limbs seemed to be shaking. And my stomach was doing a new dance step I didn't want to learn. I took a deep breath and looked up at Wayne. He'd stopped in his tracks too, eyes closed, body swaying.

I stood up fast. Too fast. But I ignored my own wave of dizziness and grabbed Wayne around the waist, steadying us both at the same time as I leaned into him.

"Sit," I told him.

His eyes popped open.

"Sit," I repeated.

So he sat, and I sat. And we had a little conversation.

"She'd be moving if she was still alive, wouldn't she?" I asked.

"Think so," Wayne agreed.

I didn't want to check. Because to check I'd have to get closer. To check I'd have to touch her. Could you get a pulse from an ankle?

"There's a whole BMW on top of her," I pointed out. But I still knew I'd have to check. What if she were dying right now as we spoke?

"Her torso must be crushed," Wayne added. I didn't think he wanted to check either.

"Ambulance," I suggested. "We need to call an ambulance."

"Or the police," Wayne agreed, nodding. Then he heaved a big sigh and stood up. But he didn't move toward the house. He moved toward the BMW. Quickly. Toward Elaine. Before I had a chance to join him.

I turned my head involuntarily as he knelt down to touch her.

"Dead," he announced a few breaths later. "Can't find . . . can't find . . ." His voice shriveled into a croak.

I spun my head back around and saw him bent over, one hand on the BMW bumper, the other on his stomach, his eyes closed again.

I was up in a heartbeat and holding him, keeping my eyes averted from what was left of Elaine. I helped Wayne stand up again and together we walked slowly toward the house, ringing the bell when we got there. We had to get inside to phone. But, of course, no one was home.

By the time we figured out how to get into the house through the garage, we were both feeling better. Dizzy, sick, and dry-mouthed, but better.

We went back out to sit on the blacktop again, our backs to the BMW. I would have liked to have sat further away, but Wayne was worried that someone else might turn up before the police.

"Who?" I asked, my mind still too muddled by shock to think clearly.

"Elaine's children," he answered quietly.

The image of Dawn, Elyse, and Eddie Junior walking with their aunt Ursula filled my mind with the full sensory detail of virtual reality. I just hoped they were with Ursula still. I hoped they'd be with Ursula for a long time. She seemed to like them. Maybe to love them. And their mother . . . their mother—

That was when I began to cry.

Fortunately, it was the police who came sirening up the driveway before any of the Timmons family did. A man and woman in uniform jumped out of the first car. The woman sprinted toward the BMW. The man strode toward us.

"You the ones that called it in?" he asked.

Wayne and I nodded simultaneously.

"You touch anything?" he asked.

"No," I answered just as Wayne answered, "Yes."

A tremor jerked my shoulders. Wayne had touched the car. And Elaine. Would they think . . . No, no, I told myself. Whoever killed Elaine didn't lift the car onto her body. They drove it over her. I took a quick breath, wishing I hadn't thought that one out in detail.

Detective Sergeant Gonzales had joined the party before Wayne even had a chance to explain why he'd touched the car. And then we both had lots of time to explain. Separately. Wayne on one side of the driveway first, then me on the other. Why were we there in the first place? Why had Elaine asked us there? Why had we entered the house to call? Why had Wayne touched the body? How well did we know Elaine? Who and what did we see as we came up the driveway? Who and what did we see and hear at the memorial service? Why did Elaine want to talk to us specifically? How did I really feel about Elaine Timmons?

I had a feeling Gonzales was going to begin with the Miranda rights routine again when Chief Irick arrived on the scene.

The chief oozed out of an unmarked car and hitched up his pants before strolling toward Sergeant Gonzales and me. There was a big smile on his red face.

"Well, if it isn't my favorite little murder lady," he called out. "Right on the scene again. Making a habit of it, aren't you? You didn't happen to kill this woman here, now, did you?"

I shook my head. "No, sir," I added, trying to funnel respect and sincerity into my tone. And trying to weed the revulsion out. Implied lechery and absolute authority are not an appetizing mixture.

Irick was still smiling. But Gonzales wasn't.

"We have the situation under control, sir," the detective sergeant told his chief. "If you'll just—"

"Just what, Gonzales?" Irick interrupted, the smile never leaving his face as his head swiveled around to face his sergeant. "Just retire so you can take over?"

"Sir!" Gonzales hissed.

I turned my head, embarrassed for both of them. Especially for Gonzales. Much as he scared me, he was a professional. I wasn't sure what Irick was.

Unfortunately, I turned my head too far. There was yellow

crime scene tape all around the BMW now, but Elaine's legs were still sticking out from under the car, glittering in the sun. My stomach starting practicing that new dance step again. I brought my head back fast. Back to face Chief Irick.

Irick's interrogation was decidedly more casual than Gonzales's had been. And a lot faster. Did I kill Elaine Timmons? Did I know who did? And did I have anything important to add?

"Then you and your boyfriend can get on out of here," he finished up.

I could almost hear the sound of Sergeant Gonzales's anxiety attack from where he had stomped off behind us. I peeked over my shoulder. Nothing was coming from his lips, but the air was crackling around him as he imploded. And I couldn't really blame him.

But I wasn't about to take any time out to console the man. I grabbed Wayne and we drove off before either Gonzales or Irick decided to ask us anything else. I wanted out of there.

"Do you suppose anyone's thought to intercept Ed Timmons?" I asked Wayne once we were safely in the car heading back down the road. "And Ursula and the kids?"

"Hope so," was his only reply.

In fact that was all he had to say for the rest of the trip home. But Wayne made up for what he lacked verbally with his big, gentle hands. He massaged my shoulders, and patted my arm, and stroked my head and neck over and over as I drove. If C.C. had been there she would have been jealous. And it began to work. His big hands were wiping out the pictures I'd seen. Maybe for him too. If only they could wipe out my thoughts.

Because I wanted answers as much as Sergeant Gonzales did. Why *had* Elaine wanted to talk to me? Had she known who Sid's killer was? If I had talked to her earlier, would she still be alive?

Of course I didn't have any answers by the time I pulled into my own driveway. But at least when Wayne and I got out of the Toyota we finally got to hold each other. And we held each other tight. So tight, we could have broken bones. Somehow, Elaine's death had gotten to both of us more than Sid's. Was it because of the children? Or the way she'd looked—

The sound of a car driving up behind us broke our clinch. Simultaneously, we dropped our arms and turned toward the incoming vehicle.

It was a turquoise vintage '57 Chevy. Driven by Felix Byrne, my friend Barbara's boyfriend, the pit bull of newspaper reporting.

Wayne and I exchanged a look of panic. Was there time to run away? Then Wayne's eyebrows dropped into protect mode and his shoulders swelled into their bodyguard persona. No one but me would have believed the look of panic had ever been in his eyes now. I tried to copy his expression and posture. As much as a person of my size and shape can.

Felix slipped out of his Chevy cautiously, eyeing Wayne as he approached us. Felix was small and slender with a luxurious mustache and soulful eyes. And a lust for information that the whole of the Internet wouldn't satisfy. He'd badgered me unmercifully to get gory details for his articles so many times that I could almost predict his approach. Anger, hurt, then bargaining. But Wayne scared him.

Not enough, unfortunately.

"Howdy-hi, Kate. Hey, big guy," he greeted us with a wide smile. "Heard through the grapevine you two discovered a stiff in Gravendale today."

I nodded. Wayne just glared. Smart man. I vowed to keep my head immobile from here on in.

"Care to share a little information with your old pal, your *compadre*—" Felix began.

"Go away," Wayne said quietly.

"Now wait a friggin' nanosecond here," Felix objected. Nope, not scared enough. "You both were there when the first stiff got fried too, and you guys never bothered to tell me! Me, your friendly crime reporter. Holy moly, what are friends for?"

He stared our way, his soulful eyes full of obvious hurt. Too obvious. Felix could have had a career on the stage.

When neither Wayne nor I said anything, Felix changed directions.

"Man, that Gravendale cop shop is a gonzo place, huh?" he tried this time. "Thinking two nice guys like you could off a couple of Kate's old buds." He shook his head sympathetically.

I was dying to ask him if the Gravendale police really thought we did it, but I kept my mouth shut despite my thumping heart. Gravendale was in Sonoma County. I had a feeling Felix couldn't suck information there like he could here in Marin. And anyway, I didn't believe that Irick and Gonzales could agree on anything, even if it was our guilt.

"How about a little info trade, huh?" Felix offered. "My poop for your poop—"

"Go," Wayne said again slowly. "Away." Only this time he took a step forward.

Just one step. But it was enough.

Felix took a step backwards.

"Hey, big guy," he said, smiling widely again. "Just asking the question, man. If you're uptight now, maybe I'll make it back here a little later."

Wayne took one more step.

Felix jumped into his vintage Chevy and backed out of the driveway, popping gravel.

"Later, man," he yelled out his window. And he was gone.

Wayne and I walked up the front stairs and were through

the doorway before we dared to look at each other. Because the moment we did we started laughing. We laughed all the way over to the couch and held each other until all the laughter was gone.

Completely gone. At exactly the same time. I rubbed my arms. Suddenly, my whole body felt numb. But not my mind.

I looked into Wayne's now serious eyes.

"Who—" I began.

"You spent yesterday interviewing people," he stated.

I could feel my shoulders slump as I nodded. And I reminded myself, no more snooping. Hadn't Elaine's body been proof enough that the murderer was serious?

"Who did you talk to?" Wayne asked.

"Pam, Lillian, Jack, Aurora, and Natalie," I told him. No more lies either. But should I tell him about the telephone threat?

"And . . ." he prompted.

"And Pam loves Charlie," I replied on cue. "Charlie's worth a million dollars, by the way." Wayne blinked in surprise. I went on. "Lillian is a great sculptor. Jack's a manic-depressive with suicidal tendencies, and Aurora . . ."

I stopped to think. Aurora was so many things. Worried mother. Hypnotist. Saint? Manipulator?

"Aurora's a witch," I finally finished. "But I'm not sure if she's a good witch or a bad witch."

"And Natalie?"

"Natalie's a concerned boss and about as stressed out as you can be and still walk," I concluded after a moment's thought. If Natalie's jerking gait even counted as walking.

Damn. I wanted to find out who did it. Snooping or no snooping. Because until I did, there was always going to be a threat to Wayne. And who knew what the murderer thought counted as snooping? Coming to Sid's memorial may have been enough by itself.

I'd find out who the murderer was. It was that simple. My chest opened up with the decision. I took a long breath in and tried to imagine that breath was courage.

"Kate, if you talk to anyone else, will you take me with you?" Wayne asked as if he'd heard my decision.

"Absolutely," I agreed. Because if we were always together, Wayne would be safe. Or at least more likely to be safe.

Wayne blinked again, unbelieving for a moment.

"From here on in, we're in this together," I insisted, straightening my shoulders. "Where you go, I go. Where I go, you go. Deal?"

I stuck out my hand.

Wayne took it and shook it, looking into my eyes, searching. I returned his look without flinching. I wasn't going to tell him about the threat. We would find the murderer and it would be over.

The majority of my brain cells were already gathering for a protest march, screaming in anticipation. But I ignored them and took Wayne into my arms again. And then we made love until I could feel again.

The next morning, true to our deal, Wayne and I were seated together on a vinyl couch between a woman with a yowling orange cat in her wire carrier and a man with a black Scotch terrier choking on its leash. It was time to talk to Mark Myers, veterinarian. I wondered if we should have brought C.C. as a cover. Mark had a partner in his practice. Her name was on the door. Maybe she wouldn't appreciate our just dropping in like this any more than Mark would.

So far, I hadn't seen anyone at the desk, so Wayne and I had just sat down. I peered sideways at Wayne. His brows were dropped in a scowl. Yesterday, the idea of investigating together had sounded good to both of us. Today, it was a little different as we both took more time out to neglect our respective businesses. But then again, that might not have been why Wayne was scowling. It might have had more to do with the terrier, choking on its leash, trying to get to the cat just two bodies away. The terrier that was frantically clawing Wayne's thigh in frustration.

The whole office was bursting with the sound of animals. I could hear chirping and yelping and squealing from the inner offices. I just hoped none of it was human. The smells were definitely animal, though, and pungent despite the antiseptic base.

When I turned my head back, magically there was a woman seated behind the receptionist's desk.

"Can I help you?" she asked us, a smile on her square freckled face.

"Well, yes," I answered quickly, smiling back as widely as I could. I remembered my recent fiasco at Nusser Networks all too well. "My name's Kate Jasper and this is Wayne Caruso, and we're friends of Mark. We were in the neighborhood, so we thought we'd just drop by." I paused and added earnestly, "And I promise we're not solicitors."

The receptionist leaned her head back and laughed. That was a relief.

"Just stay where you are," she told us. "It might take a little while. Mark's giving a Russian Blue her shots, but he's always glad to talk to friends."

So we sat on the couch for a few more minutes until another woman came in with another caged cat. Wayne graciously rose and gave her his seat, his scowl disappearing completely with the action.

When the woman sat down, the terrier went really crazy, snuffling and leaping in the air, and choking on its leash, as the cat inside the new carrier hissed and cursed the terrier's ancestors. At least, that's what it sounded like. The woman with the new cat shoved up against me, trying to pull the cage out of terrier range.

I never heard Mark walk up over the din. I jumped nearly as high as the terrier when he tapped me on the shoulder.

"Hey, Kate! Wayne!" he shouted cheerfully. "Enjoying the local fauna?"

"Oh, sure!" I shouted back.

Mark winked. But his intense eyes were alert in his round face. Maybe that's what gave him such a youthful appearance. Even with the receding hairline, he looked younger than any of the rest of the class of '68. A good twenty years younger than Becky, I thought sadly. And his wiry body was in shape too.

"Thought we'd ask a few questions if you've got a minute," Wayne put in seriously from his side.

Mark's eyes narrowed for a moment, looking even more intense. But then he motioned us past the receptionist's desk with good humor.

"Follow me to my private kennel," he offered, and we did, down a hallway past a couple of rooms with open doors. A tall woman was wrestling with a poodle in one of the compartments. An animal container whose contents were hidden to my eyes howled alone in the other one.

"Kennel" was a good word for Mark's office. The whole space must have measured all of six by ten feet, barely enough room for its battered wooden desk and the equally battered chairs on both sides. A bird cage hung from the ceiling with two little yellow birds, chirping away. We squeezed into the room and took our seats, the door still open to the sounds of the less cheerful animal mayhem surrounding us.

"Betcha a potbellied pig you're here to talk about Sid," Mark opened the conversation, plopping down in his own chair.

"You'd win," I replied, happy to cut to the chase.

"Ask away," he ordered and spread his arms wide in acquiescence. At least, as wide as he could without denting the walls.

"Did you see Sid at all during the years between high school and the reunion?" I asked.

Mark leaned back in his chair, his eyes rolling up in their sockets as he thought.

"A few times right after high school, I think," he answered, rolling his eyes back down finally. "In town once. And a couple times at restaurants. But nothing for the last twenty years or so." Then he smiled. "It'd been donkey's years, if you know what I mean."

Wayne took over then, ignoring the animal humor.

"Seemed like you really liked Sid in spite of his . . ." He faltered for a moment.

"His homophobic put-downs?" Mark finished for him, tilting his head.

Wayne nodded.

Mark shrugged. "I've heard worse," he told us. "Listen, I've been compared to more species of animals than I've practiced on. Sid wasn't actually that bad. Teasing me was just one more joke for Sid, like teasing someone fat or disabled. Or female for that matter. In his own way, he was an equal opportunity offender."

"So you liked him?" I prodded. I still wasn't sure.

"Well, I wouldn't want to marry him," Mark shot back wryly. "But Sid was fun. And fun to watch. He was a real puppy, you know. All full of life and knocking into things by mistake. And he wasn't afraid of my homosexuality. He actually shook my hand. A lot of men won't do that anymore."

I tried to remember if Wayne had shaken his hand. Or if I had.

"Who do you think killed him?" Wayne asked before I could remember whose hands had shook whose.

Mark leaned back again for a few moments, then said, "Elaine seemed angry enough. Though not at Sid, apparently."

I stiffened. Mark didn't know Elaine was dead. Of course. Or else he was an awfully good actor.

"Where'd you go after the memorial yesterday?" I demanded.

Mark's intense eyes peered into mine for a moment before he answered me.

"Back here, to the office." He paused, then asked, "Why?"

Wayne and I looked at each other. Then Wayne turned back to Mark.

"Elaine's dead too," he said quietly.

Mark's whole torso jerked forward in his chair.

"Elaine?"

"Murdered," Wayne added.

"God," whispered Mark, his skin color fading from rosy to creamy white. "What's happening to us?"

He certainly looked like a man in real shock to me.

He shook his head slowly. "So the question is whodunit," he murmured softly, as if to himself. He looked up in the direction of the bird cage, his eyes out of focus. "Natalie's uptight. Jack's depressed. Becky's an alcoholic. God, who knows?"

Finally, he brought his eyes back down and looked across at us, looking first at Wayne and then at me.

"Animals are easier than people, you know," he told us. "Nicer too, sometimes. And when they die—"

But whatever Mark was going to say was lost as an orange cat came racing into the room and jumped onto the wood desk. The black Scotch terrier wasn't far behind, skittering in through the door, its leash trailing behind. The dog spotted the cat and leapt triumphantly.

TWENTY

Mark caught the orange cat in his arms just as Wayne picked up his foot and stepped on the terrier's leash, choking the dog to a stop in midair. The dog dropped back to the ground and Wayne grabbed its leash by hand.

"Hey, buster," he muttered, not unkindly, and pulled the dog to him with one hand, the other hand outstretched palm up.

The terrier whined and tilted its head at Wayne, with a very human plea in its eyes. *Cat, please. Oh, please, let me at the cat.*

Wayne just shook his head.

Maybe all that karate practice had done Wayne some good. He was tough. And his reflexes were certainly fast enough. So were Mark's for that matter. But this probably wasn't the first flying cat Mark had ever caught in his practice.

"That's all right, sweetie pie," Mark soothed the cat, who was nuzzling and clawing his chest simultaneously as if trying to climb inside to safety.

Mark was smoothing the cat's ruffled fur gently when the receptionist and the man who owned the terrier came racing into the office, neck and neck. It was getting a little crowded in the small space. Wayne handed the man his dog and Mark passed the orange cat to the receptionist. Finally, the woman who owned the cat came running in a late third, huffing and puffing with each step.

"Is Camellia all right?" she demanded breathlessly.

"Perfectly all right, Mrs. Harvey," Mark assured her as the receptionist passed the cat in question to her rightful mother. "And Camellia's fast too. Not bad for a cat her age."

Mrs. Harvey smiled then, preening a little in Camellia's reflected orange glow.

It was more than a little crowded in Mark's six by ten office now. Animals and humans alike were jammed in as tightly and haphazardly as the contents of my kitchen junk drawer. Luckily the receptionist was between the terrier held by its owner and Camellia held by Mrs. Harvey. But it was still hard to breathe. Even the little yellow birds had stopped chirping. Wayne and I looked at each other and stood up. We wouldn't be able to ask any more questions today. Time to go.

Wayne stuck out his hand to Mark.

"Good talking to you," he said.

"Oh, you don't have to shake my hand," Mark teased him, squeezing around the table. "Just give me a big fat hug."

Wayne chuckled and did just that.

I gave Mark a hug too. Then we said goodbye to all the various species of human and animal that we'd met and threaded our way carefully out of Mark's office.

Once we were back in the Toyota, I took a moment to breathe in the lovely silence. No barking, no yowling, no chirping. Heaven.

"So?" Wayne demanded, interrupting my moment of bliss. "What did we learn?"

"Cats are faster than dogs when properly motivated?" I answered.

I have to give him credit. He tried to smile. But his heart wasn't in it. Nor were his brows.

"I don't know what we learned," I admitted finally. "It's hard to believe that Mark could be a murderer . . . but you never know."

Wayne nodded glumly. "Where next?" he asked without any obvious enthusiasm.

"Charlie's?"

Wayne looked at his watch. We were still in Mill Valley. Charlie's place was a good hour and change away.

"Better call first and make sure he's there," Wayne suggested.

"Home?"

"Home, James," he ordered, and I started the Toyota.

Unfortunately, home smelled a lot like Mark's office when we got there. Especially at the bottom of my filing cabinets. The spraying cat had sprayed again while we were gone.

"That's it," I hissed. "First I'm getting a squirt gun and then I'm finding that big black cat—"

"Are we sure it was that particular cat?" Wayne asked rationally. "Just because he was in here doesn't mean he's the one, or one of the ones, doing the spraying. From the size of him, he might have just stopped here for a snack."

His words pulled all the steel right out of my spine. Rationality can do that to righteousness. Rationality can be a big pain. I slumped. Wayne was right. For all I knew, my own cat was the guilty party. C.C. showed up on cue, meowing sweetly as she strode in the room. Too sweetly. I stared at her, wondering if female cats ever sprayed their own homes, while Wayne walked over to the phone.

"Charlie," I heard Wayne say. "Thinking of coming by today . . ."

Good. Charlie was home. I turned back to C.C.

"Confess," I whispered, glaring in an imitation of Sergeant Gonzales.

For all the good it did. C.C. turned gracefully and stalked

out of the room, her tail high. I could almost hear her say, "Some detective," as she left.

A half an hour later, after scrubbing the bottom of my file cabinets and the rug they sat on, Wayne and I were on the road again, passing familiar brown hills, green oaks, and cows of many colors as we headed up the curving blacktop to Charlie's place out in the hills beyond Gravendale. I drove while Wayne navigated as per the directions Charlie had given him over the phone.

"Maybe we should have talked to Felix," I said as we rounded a particularly panoramic curve. There were horses on this hill as well as cows.

Wayne turned to me, his eyebrows raised as high above his eyes as they'd go.

"Why?" he demanded. You would have thought by his tone that I'd asked him to join a satanic ritual group.

"Felix gives information as well as takes it," I explained. "I know it's easy to forget that when you actually have to listen to him, but—"

"Like what?"

"Like who has a criminal record, who's been in the paper, that kind of thing." I paused, negotiating another curve. "Maybe we should give him a call."

Wayne furrowed his brows and thought for a few more turns of the road.

"I'd rather be stuck in a locked kennel with the terrier and the orange cat," he finally concluded.

He had a point.

It really was a beautiful drive. In spite of our discussion of Felix. And it got more beautiful as we neared Charlie's. The rolling hills turned green for the last few miles of the ride. I wondered who or what had supplied the necessary water. And then, finally, we arrived.

There was no way to miss the place. Suddenly, there were

acres of paradise to the left of us, filled with fruit-laden trees, neat lawns, and flower beds. All behind vast wrought-iron gates.

I pulled off the main road and headed toward paradise. Once we were parked in front of the gates, Wayne got out and made a phone call from the adjoining sentry box. All under the moving eyes of the surveillance cameras. And then those magnificent wrought-iron gates opened magically and silently wide. We traveled up a long, winding drive until we saw the main house itself nestled between two hills. It looked like something out of a children's story, made of stone and wood with multilayered stories completed by turrets and chimneys and stained-glass windows.

Charlie's cottage was at least a half a mile further past the main house, made out of the same materials but not in such dramatic proportions.

What Charlie's cottage might have lacked in proportion however was made up for by the vast ocean of lupines that surrounded it. Stalks and stalks of gloriously blooming lupines in blues and whites. And pinks and purples. And creams and yellows. All gently swaying in the light summer breeze. The effect was astonishing. And dizzying. No wonder Charlie wrote children's stories. Charlie lived in fairy-tale land.

We walked up the rambling stone pathway through the lupines to the cottage and knocked on the wooden door set into its stone front. There was no doorbell. Except for the crazed barking from within. I guessed it was our day for animals.

Charlie opened the door and two Labrador retrievers came bounding out, tongues lolling, ready to lick.

A pink tongue had just reached my hand and was heading toward my face when Charlie shouted, "Down Donner, down Blitzen!"

I looked anxiously for the rest of the team, but there were only those two. They were enough.

Charlie alternately shouted commands at the dogs and apologized to us as he led us into his cottage. Donner and Blitzen trailed behind, making little begging noises.

The inside of Charlie's cottage was spacious, mostly stone except for the wooden roof, doors, and window frames. If it hadn't been for the thoroughly modern skylights, the cottage could have been from another century. It even had the right smell, of must and cooking and animals. Books filled the room, mostly in piles, some in bookcases obscuring the stonework. And in one corner, a built-in shelf held a bank of small TV screens. No, not TV, I corrected myself as I saw the estate from twelve different angles. Surveillance screens.

"Um, have a seat?" Charlie offered, motioning us to the only couch in the room as he gazed up at the ceiling over our heads. The couch was large and covered in a rainbow crocheted afghan. Which was itself covered in dog hair.

Wayne and I sat down and the dogs sidled close to either side of the couch as Charlie pulled up an easy chair covered in another rainbow/dog hair afghan and lowered his lanky body onto it, his eyes still focused on the ceiling.

I felt a cool moist nose nuzzle my hand from the right side of the couch and gave a surreptitious pat to either Donner or Blitzen's head.

"Been looking into this thing about Sid," Wayne began brusquely.

Charlie brought his gaze down from the ceiling and looked into Wayne's eyes, locked in by the man-to-man approach.

"Sid," Charlie repeated as if hypnotized. "Right."

"Need to make sure no one else is in danger," Wayne went on. Charlie's dreamy eyes widened as he leaned forward in his chair. "Especially the women."

"Pam?" Charlie whispered.

I wouldn't have believed Wayne had that much manipulation in him. But he certainly had Charlie's attention now. And he was milking it too, taking his time before answering Charlie.

"Pam's okay, isn't she?" Charlie demanded more loudly, halfway out of his chair now. The dog to my right sidled in a little closer. I gave it another pat for reassurance. Mine, not his.

"Pam's fine," Wayne told him. Charlie sank back into his chair with an audible gasp of relief. "As far as we know," Wayne added. Charlie looked at him again. "If there's a murderer at large, we can't be sure who's safe," he finished up.

"Wow," Charlie whispered. "What can I do?"

"Answer a few questions," Wayne suggested. "Offer a few observations."

"I'll be glad to," Charlie agreed. "If Pam is in danger, maybe I should stay with her. Or bring her up here where she'd be safe." His voice took on speed. "Pam's an incredible woman. I'm sure she can take care of herself, but still—"

"Back to Sid," Wayne broke in quietly but firmly. "Why wouldn't you talk to him about Vietnam?"

"Huh?" Charlie responded.

"Sid asked you about your experience in Vietnam and you didn't answer him," I translated.

Charlie looked up at the ceiling again. "I suppose I didn't want to talk about my experiences with Sid because he might have been one of those guys who liked killing people over there," he answered. "I hate that stuff." He brought his eyes back down again, squinting in confusion. "But what does that have to do with anything?"

"Gotta cover all the angles," Wayne growled, detective-style. Charlie still looked confused.

"Who do you think killed Sid?" I asked before Charlie could get unconfused enough to see where Wayne's question had been heading.

"Gee," he answered slowly, looking down at his hands

now. "I just don't know. Becky's kid was sure mad at him, but . . ." His voice trickled away. I opened my mouth to prompt him, but he started up again before I had to. "And Mark was mad for a little while, but Mark's too nice a guy. And anyway, everyone was mad at Sid, I think. I was and I didn't kill him."

"Who would Rodin Rodent believe killed him?" Wayne asked quietly.

Charlie's shoulders straightened with the question. His dreamy eyes came into clear focus. Damn. It was working. I'd compliment Wayne later. He was getting good at this stuff.

"Hmm," Charlie murmured. I could almost see his whiskers twitch. He popped up a finger. "One, someone who kept their real anger well hidden at the barbecue." Another finger came up. "Two, someone who was capable of careful planning. Three, someone who hated Sid a great deal or had a lot to lose with him alive. And four, someone incapable of empathy, at least for Sid."

"Who?" I demanded when he ran out of fingers.

Charlie squinted his eyes for a while, then flung his hands in the air.

"I don't know," he admitted, and he was Charlie again, slumped shoulders and all. He gazed at the floor. "I can't imagine any of us doing it."

I wanted to fling my hands out too. But one of my hands was too busy petting the Labrador, whose chin was now on my knee.

"Where did you and Pam go after the memorial?" I asked casually.

"Oh, I came home," he replied just as casually.

"But I thought you were going to take Pam back to San Francisco," I objected.

"I was, but it turned out that Anna May, the woman who sang for the memorial, was practically Pam's neighbor, so Pam decided to hitch a ride with her instead of putting me to the trouble." Charlie sighed. "At least, that's what she said."

Did this give Pam an alibi for Elaine's murder? I wondered happily.

"Anna May said they just had to pick up a couple of things at Elaine's first," Charlie rambled on.

My hand froze mid-pet on the Lab's furry head. Pam and the singer went to Elaine's? My mind buzzed. But if the singer was a stranger to Pam, the two couldn't have conspired to kill Elaine. So they must have arrived before the murderer. Because if they had arrived after the murderer, they couldn't have missed what we'd seen. I shook off that thought. But what if Pam had actually seen the murderer—

"Did Pam seem to know this Anna May previously?" Wayne asked, interrupting my thoughts.

Charlie shook his head. "No, they just got to talking and found out they lived close by—" He stopped mid-sentence. "What's all this got to do with Sid anyway?"

I looked at Wayne and nodded. I wanted to see Charlie's reaction to Elaine's death.

"Elaine Timmons was murdered," Wayne announced without any softeners.

"What?" said Charlie, his dreamy eyes looking even more confused as his head jerked back. "You mean Elaine from high school?"

We nodded.

"But why?" he asked, his voice dazed.

Was Charlie shocked by the news of Elaine's death? His voice sounded dazed, but I wasn't sure if it was any more dazed than usual.

"Did you or Pam leave the memorial first?" Wayne asked Charlie.

"Huh?" he responded. Back to square one. Maybe he really was in shock.

After what seemed like close to a half an hour of careful questioning, Wayne and I had elicited very little from Charlie about who left where, what, or when at the memorial. Charlie told us that Pam had left with Anna May and then he'd left right afterwards. Apparently, he'd been so smitten with Pam that he hadn't noticed anyone else's departure, not even Elaine's.

And then somehow, as the Lab eased his head onto my lap and his paw onto my knee, Charlie had stopped talking about the memorial and segued back into a listing of Pam's virtues.

". . . never fully appreciated her before," he told us. "She's strong, like one of these women detectives in books, but so kind and compassionate—"

"Like Mother Teresa," I interrupted.

"Well, kinda," Charlie agreed, startled by my interruption.

"Charlie, Pam is a real woman," I told him. "If you make too much of her, you'll blow it. She's wonderful, but she's not Superwoman. She gets mad. She gets scared. She's real."

"Yeah," he muttered, blushing now, looking off to the side, having run out of other places to look while avoiding our eyes. "I really know that. I've had girlfriends, you know. I know real women aren't really like Rolanda."

"Rolanda?" I asked. Who the hell was Rolanda?

"Rolanda is Captain Penelope Page's ship rat, remember?" Charlie answered, looking at me now with hurt in his eyes.

"Oh, right," I said quickly. And it really was coming back to me.

Rodin Rodent lived on the evil captain's boat. And Rolanda lived on Penelope's. Rolanda was a brave female rat with silky brown fur, a scrap of red velvet for a cap, and a two-inch hat pin for a sword. And the evil captain had taken Penelope and all her hands prisoner in the last installment.

"So how do Rolanda and Rodin save Penelope from the

evil captain?'' I asked to prove that I remembered. And because I really wanted to know.

The hurt look left Charlie's eyes. He even smiled as he
answered, ''Oh, Rolanda and Rodin chew through Penelope's
bonds. Then Penelope frees her whole crew and they get their
ship back and escape. Including brave Rolanda.''

''But what about Rodin and Rolanda's relationship?'' I objected, caught up in the story again.

''Rolanda is faithful and must leave with her mistress,''
Charlie answered, his eyes on the far beyond ocean of lupine.
''So she leaves Rodin alone once more. One little rat embrace
and then she waves her red velvet cap goodbye. And she's
gone.'' He sighed, then added more cheerfully, ''But they may
meet again. Maybe in the next book.''

''Would Rodin kill to protect Rolanda?'' Wayne interjected
before I could ask for more details.

''No,'' Charlie answered without pause. ''He'd find a way
to save her without killing.''

''How about in real life?'' Wayne pressed on. ''Would you
kill to protect Pam?''

''I wouldn't kill,'' Charlie insisted. ''Unless there was absolutely no other way to protect her. But that's not the case.
Pam was never in any danger from Sid.'' He looked Wayne
in the eye. ''Rodin Rodent doesn't believe in killing. And
neither do I.''

And that was that. We left paradise very soon after.

''We have to find a phone,'' I said once we were settled in
the Toyota once more, driving back the way we'd come, the
wrought-iron gates closed silently behind us.

''Why?'' asked Wayne.

''What if Pam saw the murderer arrive?'' I proposed.

''What if Pam is the murderer?'' he counterproposed.

''In conspiracy with a singer she met that day?'' I shot back,
shaking my head. ''No way.''

"Not likely," he conceded. He thought for a moment. "Gravendale's the nearest place for a phone."

"Why don't we visit Aurora's bookstore at the same time," I suggested, inspired. I was sure she'd let us use her phone. And I wanted to talk to her anyway. The woman had real moments of insight. It would be interesting to know what she'd make of what we'd uncovered. More than interesting.

Wayne found the card with the address for Aurora's store in my purse, but he didn't recognize the street name.

He reached in the glove compartment for a map.

And pulled out a fuzzy purple windup toy.

"What the hell is this?" he demanded.

"Oh, that?" I said, looking over. "Just a practical joke from Sid. It jumped out of the glove compartment the last time I opened it. With Sid's card attached."

"And you didn't tell me," he accused quietly.

"Well, no—" I began defensively.

"What else haven't you told me?" he asked just as quietly.

TWENTY-ONE

"What do you mean, what haven't I told you?" I sputtered as I pulled back onto the main road. "Nothing, nothing at all."

Except for that little old death threat, it was pretty much the truth.

I drove a few miles in silence, looking at Wayne out of the corner of my eye, hoping he wouldn't see me do it. His brows were pulled three quarters of the way over his eyes, his face set in gargoyle mode. All he needed was a fountain of water spouting out of his mouth and they could clamp him onto the wall of a castle alongside the drawbridge.

"Nothing important anyway," I amended. Wayne usually knew when I was lying anyway.

He didn't move a hair.

"You know," I followed up, finding myself suddenly more than defensive. Finding myself angry. "I don't have to tell you everything. You could give me credit for being able to assess what's important and what's not. For being able to decide what you need to know and what you don't." Self-righteousness was pumping into my bloodstream now, obliterating that pesky old rationality.

"What am I supposed to do?" I finished up in full snit.

"Give you a complete written report every time I come home?"

I tromped out my anger on the gas pedal, taking the curves like I was in Wayne's Jaguar instead of my own Toyota. Kate-io Andretti at the wheel.

"Is this why you want a traditional marriage, so I'll be a good little traditional wife—"

"Sorry," came a whisper from my side.

I wasn't actually sure I'd heard it at first. I risked another quick sideways glance as the car zoomed ahead. Wayne's face was no longer made of stone. It was made of soft vulnerable flesh again. Soft, white, vulnerable flesh.

"Kate?" he requested, his voice low and quiet. "Could you slow down a little? Not that there's anything wrong with the way you're driving," he assured me quickly. "But just because it would make me feel more comfortable?"

Those brown hills were whizzing by pretty fast. Actually, they were a complete blur, along with most of the road. I squinted at the speedometer and eased up on the gas pedal immediately. Jeez, no wonder Wayne was white. I eased up on my snit too as the Toyota slowed to a more reasonable speed.

"I know you don't really want a traditional wife," I told him. Then I let out a long sigh made up of righteousness leaking away. "If you did, you'd be asking someone else to marry you. But, Wayne, really, that's what I'm so afraid of. I like living with you. Most of the time I love living with you. I love you! I just don't want to screw it up."

"You're right," he murmured, and a wave of guilt carried away the last prickles of my self-righteousness with it.

By the time I saw Aurora's Illuminations Bookstore, we were both insisting that whatever the other one had been saying all along was probably absolutely correct. Ethically, practically, and emotionally.

I braked, cutting short Wayne's admission that his insecurity was at the root of any and all the problems we had and would ever have, and parked under the rainbow glow of the ILLUMINATIONS BOOKSTORE sign. Some people are just impossible to fight with.

Aurora's bookstore was packed, and not just with books. The smell of incense vied with the scent of aromatherapy oils. Celestial strings and Tibetan bells played in the background as a number of customers browsed and talked. And there were crystals everywhere, catching the light and refracting it in competing illuminations across books and jewelry and artifacts. Maybe these rainbow flashes were the illuminations that had inspired the bookstore's name, though I had a feeling something a little less physical and more metaphysical was probably the source.

"Do you have singing bowls?" a gray-haired woman was asking a larger red-haired woman behind the counter. A red-haired woman who was not Aurora. Damn. What if Aurora wasn't here? Everything and everyone else was.

I looked down one row of bookshelves, neatly labeled, "Astrology, Enneagram, Kabbalah, Tarot, Shamanism," and didn't catch a glimpse of Aurora. Though I did see one of Lillian's bronze busts, staring back regally. I looked down another row, "Recovery-Continued, Tantric Yoga, Sacred Languages, Ayurveda," and finally at the end, near "Buddhism," I saw Aurora listening earnestly to a young woman with a long blond braid that snaked down past her waist.

"But isn't that just attachment too?" the young woman was asking her. Demanding of her. "Thinking that one individual's oppression is important enough to worry about. I mean just look at Tibet . . ."

Aurora took that moment to look instead over the young woman's shoulder at Wayne and myself. A flutter of concern traveled over her serene face. I gave her a quick wave, hoping she'd abandon the young woman in favor of us and feeling guilty at the same time. The young woman was probably a paying customer. Then again, maybe she wasn't.

"Excuse me, dear," Aurora said, placing a gentle hand on the young woman's arm. "I must take care of something."

The young woman stopped talking mid-sentence and then began looking around for another victim as Aurora left her. An older bearded man came walking innocently down the row of books.

"Have you studied Buddhism?" the young woman asked him.

I would have advised a firm "no" as an answer, but of course he didn't receive the benefit of my psychic warning.

"Well, a little—"

The young woman interrupted, demanding to know whether the man had read *Zen in America* just as Aurora reached us. When he admitted that he had, she began to quiz him about the tenth chapter of the book.

"The Gravendale police called me a few minutes ago about Elaine Timmons's death," Aurora announced quietly without any other greeting. "Did you know?"

"Uh-huh," I answered her briefly, not telling her yet that we'd found the body. I was relieved to hear that the Gravendale police were finally moving on Elaine's death. I'd wondered why they hadn't contacted Charlie or Mark yet. And then I took a brief moment to ask myself if Sergeant Gonzales would be angry that Wayne and I were the first to speak to the two men about the murder. I clenched my teeth. Of course, he'd be—

"Kate needs to use your telephone," Wayne greeted Aurora just as brusquely as she'd greeted him.

"About Elaine's death?" she asked.

"Yes," he answered.

Aurora stood stock-still for a moment, peering through her

thick glasses into Wayne's eyes, seeking something. The truth about Elaine's death? The truth of the universe? A more polite request?

"I'll explain while Kate phones," Wayne promised.

Aurora just nodded then and took me by the arm to a tiny room in the back with a desk stacked with paperwork. It looked like my desk at home except for the crystal paper-weights and incense bowls. And another of Lillian's statues staring down at us from its niche in the wall.

"Feel free to make any calls you need to," Aurora told me, pointing at the edge of a lavender phone sticking out from under a tipped-over pile of ledgers. Yeah, a lot like my desk. Then she left and closed the door behind her.

I sat down at the desk, if sitting is the term for leaning forward on a chair that supports your knees more than your bottom, set my purse on top of the least precarious set of papers, and found Pam's business card. I dialed her number eagerly, ready to ask her what she'd seen at Elaine's, even ready to ask her if she'd known the memorial singer before, but instead of hearing her lively voice on the other end of the line I ended up in the seemingly endless maze of voice mail. In the midst of punching random digits and pound signs, I looked at my watch. It was almost one o'clock. Pam was prob-ably out to lunch. I hung up without leaving a message, un-willing to run the maze any longer. I'd try Pam again later and hope that I could catch her in real time.

I got up to leave, then looked back down at the desk, con-sidering rifling Aurora's papers for some clue of a link to Sid or Elaine's death, but the impulse died of its own will in less than a moment. There was nothing here but business. I walked out of her tiny office to enter metaphysical wonderland again.

Wayne and Aurora were huddled together, still standing, in a far corner of the store devoted to some of the larger items. Meditation cushions, Buddhas, altars, gongs, and shamanic drums, among other things. It was relatively quiet there, the celestial strings, bells, and customer conversation a muted backdrop for the sound of Aurora's firm, deep voice.

"Jack and I left the memorial service together in his truck," she was saying. "We talked on the ride back to Gravendale. Really talked. I truly believe Jack's beginning to heal now. The shock of Sid's death has made the preciousness of Jack's own life awaken in his consciousness. How this lightness can come from such darkness is truly amazing, but it has. Still, the darkness must be addressed. We must figure out who's doing these terrible things."

"Where did you go once you got back to Gravendale?" Wayne asked, skipping the more philosophical issues, however much they might have tempted him. And I was sure they did. Wayne was a sucker for a philosophical conundrum.

I joined them silently, waiting for her answer.

"Jack dropped me off here at the store," Aurora said, nodding brusquely to note my arrival at the same time. "I believe he went to Karma-Kanick then to meet Lillian."

"Was Lillian there?" Wayne pressed.

"I assume she was." Aurora peered at him again. "Was that when Elaine was murdered?" she asked. "After the memorial?"

Wayne opened his mouth to answer. I elbowed him gently in the ribs. I wasn't sure that we should be giving out information so freely anymore. I didn't want to hear from Sergeant Gonzales, or Chief Irick for that matter, about interfering in an official police investigation. It was a little late for discretion, but still.

"Sergeant Gonzales didn't give me any details except to say Elaine Timmons had been murdered," Aurora went on. "And to demand my presence at his office." She looked down at her watch. "In approximately an hour."

"Yes, it was after the memorial," Wayne told her. "We

found her body." So much for discretion. Maybe I should
have elbowed him harder.

Aurora paled slightly, looking older now.

"But why?" she muttered, looking around her absently.
"Why Elaine? Because she was Elaine? Or because she knew
something about Sid's death?"

Or both, I thought as she pulled out three meditation cushions and set them on the floor, taking her place cross-legged
on one and motioning us to the other two.

Wayne and I took our places on the remaining cushions,
not quite so gracefully as Aurora had. She looked at me for a
few heartbeats, then at Wayne.

"I have no answers," she declared finally. "Do you have
answers?"

We shook our heads as one. If we had answers, we would
be talking to the police, not here in Illuminations, overdosing
on incense and metaphysics.

Aurora bent forward. "I'll be honest," she said, her voice
hushed. "I don't believe anyone in my family is involved in
these two deaths. I didn't kill either Sid or Elaine. And I truly
believe neither Lillian nor Jack is capable of such an act."
She closed her eyes for a moment before going on. "Though
I do feel I must tell you something that you may find out
anyway. Jack's father killed himself. A year after you all graduated Gravendale High."

A tiny shock buzzed up my spine. Poor Aurora. No wonder
she hovered over Jack. I reached over and patted her hand
impulsively. No wonder she was searching so hard for answers
to the human condition.

She smiled at my touch and held my hand in her cool, dry
ones for a moment before going on. "Manic Kanick, they used
to call my husband." Her eyes softened. "He was an incredible man, full of energy. An architect. Alive and loving. But
when the despair would overwhelm him, it really over-

whelmed him. The pain was too much for him. He took an overdose of pills in 1969. That was when Jack began having real problems.'' She straightened her spine, her posture yoga-perfect. ''But my husband turned it inward, you see. Jack turns it inward too. Not outward.''

Wayne nodded sagely. He was the one who read all the pop psychology books. I wondered if he was nodding in real agreement or just being polite. I also wondered if despair turned inward necessarily precluded anger turned outward.

''And if I rule out my own family, then who?'' Aurora went on. ''You kids all had your own challenges to face. All of you. Becky, Pam, Natalie, Charlie, and Mark. And you, Kate. None of you came from completely functional families as far as I could see.'' She bent forward and whispered, ''Of course after all my reading, I've come to the conclusion that there is no such thing as a fully functional family in any case.''

I looked around furtively, remembering once again that we were in a bookstore and hoping that no one in the recovery section had heard her. But no one seemed to be listening to us anyway.

''Do you remember the order in which people left the memorial?'' Wayne asked, cutting back to the chase.

Aurora frowned in thought. ''I was talking to Pam and that singer, Anna May, a little before they left—''

''Did they mention visiting Elaine's?'' I cut in.

''Yes!'' Aurora's head jerked up. ''They did. Or at least the singer did. Something about something she'd left. Oh, I wish I could recall more clearly.'' She closed her eyes, her face tight with concentration. ''I believe she said, 'If we have time, do you mind dropping by Elaine's? I left some of my songbooks there.' '' She opened her eyes again. That sounded pretty damn clear to me.

''So, it wasn't Pam's idea,'' I said gratefully.

''No,'' Aurora agreed. ''It was the singer's. And it wasn't

definite the way she mentioned it either. Just a possibility.''
She tilted her head to the side, looking at Wayne.

"Go on," he said. "Pam and the singer left. And then
what?''

"Charlie left as soon as Pam did. The poor man is so obviously in love.'' A smile curved her lips, then disappeared.
''And then Jack and I left in the truck.''

"Was Elaine still there?'' I asked. Because a sudden insight
told me that if Elaine was still there, Pam and Anna May could
hardly have dropped in on her.

"I think so," Aurora answered, her firm voice wavering a
little. "It's hard to remember.'' She closed her eyes, concen-
trating again. Her voice had a trancelike quality when she finally spoke, a quality that raised the hair on the back of my
neck. "Ed Timmons was there. And his children and sister.
And some family members, all gathered around the food table.
Yes, I can see them now. And Mark and Becky, I believe,
talking. And Natalie. And Elaine, yes, now I can see her, down
near the pond. Yes, Elaine was there.''

Her eyes popped open suddenly, her irises still rolled up
under her eyelids. I shivered again as they rolled back down.
But whatever worked, worked. And I was happy. Because if
Elaine had still been there, I doubted that Pam and Anna May
had ever followed up on their tentative plans to visit her. Unless, of course, they had gone and waited for her. Damn. I
wished I hadn't thought of that.

"Some recall," I said to Aurora.

"All a matter of imaging," she replied briskly. "I have a
book somewhere," she began, turning to look at her shelves.

Then she turned back, waving her hand in front of her face.
"Forget the book. Sometimes it's hard to remember I'm not
always here to sell books.'' Her tone grew deeper. "We must
resolve this matter. Not just for our own sakes, but for the
murderer's as well. The darkness must be almost impossible

to bear.'' She closed her eyes for a moment and clasped her hands before going on. ''If the police haven't found the solution by this weekend, I propose we all meet again. We all have different resources. Between those of us who are left, I believe we can solve this mystery collectively.''

The weekend seemed a long way away, but Wayne and I agreed to the proposition, even splitting up a list of names to call on Friday for a Sunday meeting if the murderer hadn't been identified by then.

I was just rising from my cushion on cramped legs when Aurora's words brought me plopping back down.

''Please, stay for a moment,'' she requested quickly. ''If it's not too personal, may I ask you two something?''

I nodded. Wayne tilted his head back, waiting for the question. A much more sensible approach.

''I sense discord between the two of you,'' Aurora pressed on. ''I believe it's about your wedding plans. Am I right?''

Wayne and I exchanged quick glances. Another psychic like my friend Barbara? Just like my friend Barbara, I decided, intuitive on the little things, but useless when it came to identifying murderers.

''Well, Wayne has never been married before,'' I told her uncomfortably. ''So, of course, he'd like a real all-out wedding with all the trimmings—''

''But Kate has been married before,'' Wayne interrupted me. ''So, understandably, she'd like less formality. If any wedding ceremony at all. And I can't blame her—''

''And you both love each other,'' Aurora finished up for us, smiling largely. ''But you both detest the other's plans. Because weddings are about ritual, meaning, and metaphor. And your metaphors don't match.''

I glanced sideways at Wayne. He was frowning in Aurora's direction.

''For Wayne, a traditional wedding represents solidity, a

marriage that can never be broken,'' Aurora went on. ''But for Kate, it represents just the opposite, the marriage that can be and was broken. Your metaphors don't match.''

''So?'' asked Wayne, his tone of gentle confusion robbing the word of its potential rudeness.

''You must create your own individual ritual!'' Aurora pronounced triumphantly, throwing her arms out as if to embrace the concept.

She rose abruptly and gracefully from her cushion and was back within moments, two folded flyers in her hand. ''Creating Your Own Wedding Ritual,'' they declared proudly.

''Read this,'' she ordered, handing one to me and one to Wayne. ''A friend of mine offers these seminars. She's a woman of great imaginative awareness. She can guide you in creating a ritual that you two can agree on, one that blossoms out of both of your life experiences. Give it a chance. Make a metaphor that each of you can enjoy.''

''Well, it's certainly an idea,'' I said, rising from my cushion, ignoring the pains from my startled, cramped calves.

''Right,'' Wayne said, rising from his cushion. ''An idea.''

''You will find your ritual,'' Aurora assured us confidently and gave us each a hug before leaving us on a rescue mission. The young woman with the long blond braid was haranguing someone else about the true meaning of Buddhism, an elderly woman with a cane and a look of pure panic on her face. Aurora trotted off in their direction, determination in her gait.

Wayne bought a few books on the way out the door. I knew he wouldn't be able to resist. Two were on the mind-body connection, one of his favorite subjects, but I didn't see the title of the third until the red-haired woman behind the cash register ran it through the scanner. *Creative Conflict Resolution*. I should have known. I resisted buying a crystal in self-defense.

We closed the door of Illuminations behind us, and the sound of celestial strings and Tibetan bells faded away. Then we climbed back into the Toyota for the ride home.

The smell of incense lingered, though, as I drove past those all too familiar brown hills. And Wayne livened up the ride as well, reading me passages from the creative wedding pamphlet and telling me about some of the weddings its author had arranged.

"Listen to this," he said. "These guys had a firewalk wedding. They walked on hot coals all the way up to the altar to prove their commitment."

"I hope the bride didn't wear a full gown," I muttered, imagining flames creeping up white lace. I doused that horrible thought, and then began to wonder if they made the flower girls walk on the hot coals too.

"And these other guys got married in a hot air balloon."

"Must not have had a lot of friends," I told him. "How many people can you get in a balloon?"

"Maybe a whole bunch of balloons, all bumping together in space—"

"Excuse me, excuse me," I offered for sound effects.

Now Wayne was laughing.

"How about bungee jumping?" I suggested.

"Roller Derby," he countered.

"Mud wrestling—"

We were both laughing by the time we got home.

But after we'd finally climbed the front stairs, closed the door behind us, sniffed for further cat attack, and endured another round of Pam's voice mail, we sat down at the kitchen table and looked across it into each other's eyes.

"Aurora was right," I said softly.

"I know," Wayne replied just as softly.

And then we stood up to match our metaphors with a kiss. Our lips had just touched when the phone rang.

I pulled my mouth back reluctantly and picked up the phone.

It was Becky. I rolled my eyes at Wayne.

"Oh, Kate. Jeez, I'm glad I got you," she said. Wayne motioned toward a frying pan.

"Hungry?" he mouthed.

I nodded violently. It was way past lunchtime.

"I gotta talk to you," Becky went on. "I gotta tell someone . . ." Her words dribbled away.

"Tell someone what?" I demanded, my ears perking up.

"Oh, Kate!" Suddenly, I could hear her sobbing. "Can you come over now? I'm at home—"

"Can't you just tell me over the phone?" I countered. But my blood was perking up too. Why was she crying? Did she want to confess?

"Oh, please, Kate?" I heard through the sobs.

I sighed and looked up at Wayne, putting my hand over the receiver.

"It's Becky," I told him. "She wants to talk. At her house."

He looked wistfully at the frying pan, then put it back on its hook, nodding his agreement.

"We'll be right over," I told Becky.

But I hadn't even hung up my phone on Becky's tearful apologies when Wayne's business phone began to ring.

TWENTY-TWO

✜

"Gah, I know I'm awful," Becky was whimpering. "I'm so sorry . . ."

"Hello," I heard Wayne on his business line. Then, "No, no, have you tried . . ."

"Becky," I said as quietly as I could. "You're not confessing to murder, are you?"

"Murder?" she mumbled, and her sobs turned to giggles. Hysterical giggles.

"The whole system is down?" Wayne was saying.

"No way, Kate," Becky finally answered me, gasping as if she'd been running the Bay-to-Breakers marathon. "I mean, I know I'm a complete dope, but I'd never murder anyone. I don't think I'm even efficient enough anymore." She had a point. "I'm so messed up . . ."

Wayne looked over at me, throwing one hand into the air. So much for leaving his restaurant/gallery to the assistant manager for the day. A combination of frustration and desperation showed on his face.

". . . you are coming over, aren't you?" Becky was asking meanwhile, her last word dissolving into the first note of a renewed sob.

"Yeah, sure," I put in quickly, though I had a feeling I was going to be visiting her alone. "See you soon."

Then I hung up.

Wayne was not so lucky.

"Hold on," he told the guy on the other end of the line. Then he put his hand over the receiver.

"Computer's down," he growled.

I knew what that meant. Either he spent anywhere from twenty minutes to three hours working the assistant manager through the whole system over the phone or he went into the city in person.

"You stay here and help Gary on the phone," I suggested. Wayne would be safe here at home. I was the one visiting a suspect. "I'll go to Becky's by myself."

"But she could be dangerous, Kate," Wayne objected.

"Becky?" I countered, raising my eyebrows.

"Well . . ."

I could see he was wavering. Of all the suspects, Becky Vogel certainly seemed the least threatening. She'd said it herself. She just wasn't efficient enough to be dangerous. Especially in hysterics.

"Listen," I offered. "Here's what we'll do. I'll go to Becky's and talk to her. She's crying her eyes out now. I can't believe she's dangerous. Still, she might know something—"

"But—"

I held up my hand.

"I'll call you to let you know I'm all right in exactly a half an hour from now on my phone line," I went on. Then I could make sure he was safe too, but he didn't have to know that. "You've got Becky's number. If you solve the problem early, just call and come over. She's only ten minutes away."

He frowned, his eyebrows dipping below the horizon of his eyes, his hand still over the receiver.

"If you go," he murmured finally, "tell Becky that I know you're there."

"Will 'Wayne says hello' be enough?"

"Yeah," he agreed, a foolish smile hovering on his lips. "Guess I'm going a little overboard."

Actually, as I gobbled a couple of rice crackers with soy cheese and picked up my purse to go, I began to think he wasn't going overboard. Because I was beginning to worry myself about leaving Wayne alone in the house. I checked the back door. It was locked. I opened the front door and looked out at the street. I didn't see any suspicious cars lurking. Not that I would have known which cars to consider suspicious in any case.

"Listen, sweetie," I whispered in his ear as he told Gary what keys to punch on the computer. "Don't let anyone in while I'm gone, all right?"

"Right, right," he said, waving his hand.

I was pretty sure he was talking to me.

"Love you," I told him and kissed the side of his craggy face.

"Love you too," he murmured back, still preoccupied with Gary. Then suddenly he jerked his head around. "Kate, be careful," he warned, his tone deep and deadly serious.

I told him I would, and he blew me a kiss as I walked back out the front door and locked it ever so carefully behind me.

There were two surprises waiting for me on the doorstep of Becky's small stucco house. One, D.V. wasn't home. He was still at school, according to Becky. And two, Becky seemed to be sober.

"Oh, Kate," she said as she stepped back from the doorway. "Thanks for coming. I had to talk to you."

When I walked over the threshold, she gave me a hug. And she didn't smell of alcohol. At least, not of new alcohol. There was a whiff of that stale, pickled smell that heavy drinkers often have. But nothing on her breath. For a change.

And her step didn't waver as she led me indoors.

She motioned me to a seat in her living room, and I looked around the inside of her house for the first time. The small room was pleasant and light, with comfortable-looking furniture in soft yellows and beige and ivory. There was a cast paper piece of artwork hanging on the wall above her couch. The layers of paper depicted a woman flying, or maybe dancing, under a moonlit tree complete with an owl. There was a sense of childlike freedom in the piece, but also an undercurrent of sadness. Or menace. I couldn't decide which. It was like something out of a dream.

"Sarah Glater," Becky murmured from behind me.

"What?" I replied, startled out of the dreamlike trance the piece had inspired.

"Sarah Glater is the artist who did that one," Becky told me. "I've got a lot of her work."

And then I turned back to Becky and sat down. She might not have been drinking, but she didn't look good. Her open blue eyes were red and nearly swollen shut. Her fragile face looked almost battered, it was so blotchy and dry. She wasn't wearing her usual makeup, I realized. No makeup and she looked sixty years old. I tried to repress the shudder that raised the hairs on my arms but couldn't. The transformation was like something out of a horror movie. I just hoped Becky hadn't noticed my reaction.

Actually, I had a feeling Becky wasn't noticing much of anything as she sat down across from me. For once, she wasn't smiling. And though she wasn't wavering, her hands were shaking. She wrapped her arms around herself suddenly and closed her eyes.

"So?" I prompted. I was here. Wayne wasn't. And I was getting impatient.

She took a deep, rasping breath. Oh God, I hoped she wasn't going to cry again. Her swollen eyes didn't look like they could handle any more tears.

"So," she replied softly, opening those eyes. "I'm a drunk and a drug user. A substance abuser. An idiot. And since you're investigating—"

"Who told you I was investigating?" I interrupted, a spike of worry jerking my shoulders. The voice on the phone had told me to stop snooping, and even Becky knew I still was. Probably everyone knew. And Wayne was home alone. I'd try to make this talk with Becky short, I decided, glancing at my watch. It had only been fifteen minutes since I'd left Wayne.

"Mark Myers told me," Becky answered, her swollen blue eyes widening for a moment. As much as they could, anyway. "He said I needed to tell you what was going on with me. Because I've been drunk, I've been acting inappropriately, acting like a real dope actually, and doing all this weird stuff that might look suspicious if you didn't know. But I'm not a murderer, I'm just a drunk."

I looked at her and believed her. Still, I believed everyone. But Becky— A memory of Becky smoking dope and giggling at sixteen bounced into my head. She had always done more than anyone else, done to excess, even then.

"Did Mark suggest you stop drinking?" I asked curiously. Because someone or something had made a difference.

"Yeah," she answered, one side of her mouth going up in a lopsided smile for the first time. "I don't know why, but finally it seemed like good advice. And he's damn well not the first one to give it to me. Jeez, everyone's been after me forever. D.V. and my boss, especially. Even my ex-husband. My boss told me he'd pay for me to go to one of those dry-out clinics. But I just ignored him. But when Sid died, I . . . I . . ."

Tears began to form in her eyes. The smile was gone.

"One day without drinking and look what a mess I am," she whimpered. The tears rolled out of her swollen eyes. "I don't know if I can do it—"

"Then take your boss up on his offer," I suggested. I tried to keep my tone gentle, all the time wanting to take her by her collar and drag her to a clinic bodily if that's what it took.

"But what about D.V.? I can't just leave him here alone," she shot back. She put her face in her hands, muffling her voice. "Still that's just an excuse, I know it. I know it. Jeez, I just can't seem to get myself together."

And then amazingly, she did seem to get herself together, taking her wet face out of her hands and sitting back against the cushions of her chair.

"Marijuana in high school, speed in law school, cocaine after. And alcohol the whole time. Every once in a while I realized the drugs were a problem, but I didn't even count the alcohol—" She waved her hands suddenly, cutting herself off. "But the reason I'm telling you all this is because you asked me about going out with Sid and I didn't answer you. Kate, it wasn't because I was holding back on you. It was because every time I saw him I got staggering drunk. And I couldn't remember anything the next day."

"Did you sleep with him?" I asked.

Her blotchy face reddened. "I don't even know the answer to that," she told me. A lone tear rolled out of one eye. "God, I'm so awful."

Damn. I didn't want to go down that road again.

"How did D.V. feel about your relationship to Sid?" I asked, partly to distract her and partly because I really wanted to know.

"Oh, Jeez, D.V. hated him," she whispered, shaking her head. "He was so mad. I'd been on the wagon for a whole week before I went out with Sid the last time, but—"

Suddenly she stopped. Did she just realize the implication of what she was saying?

"D.V.?" I prompted, hoping to get her rolling again.

"No, not D.V.," she replied seriously, leaning forward. "He wouldn't kill Sid. He's just a kid. A messed-up kid, but a kid. Honestly, all that scowling and stuff is just an act."

She looked at me beseechingly through swollen lids.

I nodded my understanding. In fact, I believed her. I could see why D.V. might have killed Sid, but Elaine? I gave myself a mental shake. Here I was believing everyone again.

"Listen," Becky said urgently. "D.V. hangs out with me so I won't get bombed. That's all." Her voice got quieter. "But I found out he's been drinking himself, and smoking dope, and cutting classes. Oh shit, Kate, I'm such a failure—"

"No, you're not," I cut in hastily. "You're a practicing attorney, for God's sake! And you have a kid who loves you enough to protect you. You must have done something right."

"Jeez, Kate," she said, a hint of that lopsided smile on her brittle face. "You're still just the way you were in high school. You always made me feel good. You and Robert." She sighed and wrapped her arms around herself again.

"Gad, I loved Robert," she murmured. "I think Mark was right. Robert probably was gay. Jeez, here I was sleeping with everyone but him, and he was the one I loved." She closed her eyes for a few moments. I couldn't tell what she was thinking. "Life is just weird," she finally concluded. "Especially sober. At the memorial yesterday, I couldn't help but think of Robert. Even more than Sid. And the fireworks. Those awful fireworks—"

"What did you do after the memorial?" I asked her, cutting her off at the catharsis.

"I came home and got even drunker," she answered, swollen eyes opening again. "What else?"

No wonder she looked so bad. As I remembered, she'd been pretty well marinated before she'd left the memorial. It was a wonder she'd never hurt anyone driving. Or maybe she had. How would I know?

"Well, Sid would've approved," I told her, trying to lighten the tone. "He was no lightweight in the drinking arena himself."

"Actually, he was," Becky corrected me seriously. "He always seemed to be drinking, but it was always just one bottle of beer. Or one glass of wine, or whatever. I think he had to be in control. If only to pull off all those wacko pranks of his."

"I got a fuzzy purple windup toy in my glove compartment," I told her.

"So did I," she said, the smile returning to her face. "Only mine was orange."

And then we were off and running, at least our mouths were, reminiscing about Sid's pranks. We couldn't seem to stop. Suddenly they all seemed funny instead of obnoxious. The fake rubber vomit that he carried with him everywhere he went. And the rubber chicken. And the skeleton he managed to borrow or steal from somewhere and hang from a tree branch that spread out over Main Street. No one had actually run off the road when the skeleton came flying down, but there were a lot of near misses. Becky and I were still giggling about that when she remembered the time he'd sawed off the stop sign in the dead of night and then, just as furtively, tried to put it back up again when Pam convinced him the trick might actually get someone killed.

"Remember when he rigged the toilet so that it sounded like a nuclear explosion when you sat down on it?" I asked. Of all his toilet tricks, that was my favorite.

"Well, at least he thought it up even if he didn't actually rig it," Becky answered, gasping with laughter now.

But my own laughter dried up abruptly. I could hear my heart pounding in the sudden internal silence.

"What do you mean, he didn't rig it?" I asked.

Becky's eyes opened as far as they could between swollen lids.

"Jeez, Natalie was the one who really rigged it," she said.

"Natalie?" My mind began to race to keep up with my pounding heart.

"Yeah, I guess I thought everyone knew. Natalie was the one who really did the work on the complicated ones. You know how much into science she was. Sid couldn't rig those things himself—"

"How do you know it was Natalie?" I demanded, though suddenly it was all making sense to me. Sid hadn't been good in science. He hadn't even been mechanical. But Natalie had been.

Becky closed her eyes for a moment, thinking. She opened them abruptly.

"Now I remember," she muttered. "Natalie told me in the restroom one time. At school. She was crying. I think she was really pissed. She told me that Sid got her to do all the work on the really complicated gags—you know, the electronic ones—and then he took all the credit. Like the backwards light switch and the spooky voice when you rang the doorbell. But she told me not to tell anyone else. I thought she had a crush on him or something, so I . . . I never told." Becky's voice slowed as she leaned forward. "In fact, I'd forgotten all about it until now. God, Kate, do you think—"

"Natalie rigged the pinball machine?" I finished for her.

Becky and I stared at each other for a few moments. Neither of us knew the answer to that question. If Natalie had rigged the pinball machine, I hoped for Becky's sake that she'd forgotten she'd ever told Becky that she was the one who actually carried out the mechanics of Sid's gags.

I shook my head. I was making some awfully long leaps in logic. Long and sideways. Just because Natalie had helped Sid with his pranks twenty-five years ago didn't necessarily mean she'd do it now. I thought of Natalie's correct and icy reserve. Would she? Could she? And if she'd rigged the final prank, the one that killed him, what would her motive have been? I looked back across at Becky, wondering for a moment if *she* was telling me the truth. If Becky was lying—

I looked down at my watch suddenly. Wayne. I was fifteen minutes late in calling Wayne at home. I was surprised he hadn't called me.

"Becky, I need to use your phone," I rapped out, jumping up from my seat.

Becky led me to a phone in her kitchen, without asking for any explanation. And left me to use it in private.

But when I called my own number, all I got was my own answering machine.

I even left a message. A long message, hoping Wayne would come on the line any minute.

Twenty-three

␢ut he didn't. I babbled and babbled onto my own tape and Wayne's voice never came on to interrupt me.

I left Becky's in a hurry, hastily hugging her and wishing her luck in her new sobriety, while pleading a forgotten appointment as an excuse for my exit. Her fragile, battered-looking face registered surprise but no affront as I ran out the door. Maybe I hadn't given her enough time.

Once I was in my Toyota on the main road again, I floored it, hoping to make the ten-minute drive in five. And hoping Wayne was all right. Where the hell was he? Why hadn't he answered the phone as planned? I came up with plenty of answers. Maybe he was lost in the intricacies of computer land on his other phone. But would he have forgotten he was supposed to pick up my call in half an hour? He couldn't miss hearing it from his position at his own phone. I shook my head and pressed the accelerator even harder, back wheels shimmying as I took a curve. Had he gone into the city to solve his computer problem on the spot? No, he would have called me. I was certain of that. Unless he couldn't find Becky's phone number. But it was listed in the phone book—

I wouldn't think about Wayne until I got home, I told myself. I'd think about Natalie Nusser instead. Was Natalie the murderer? She'd acted stressed, even angry, most of the times I'd seen her. But that seemed to be her natural persona, even in high school. Sid had been working for Natalie though. That in itself suddenly seemed suspicious. But he probably really was a good salesman. Wayne had said that. Damn it, how could I have ignored the threat to Wayne's life? What if—

Not now, I told myself. Back to Natalie. She had the mechanical ability. But, hell, Jack was just as good a suspect. He wasn't just stressed, he was nuts. And mechanical. Then why hadn't he rigged Sid's pranks in high school?

Please, Wayne, I thought, if you're in trouble, just hold on for a few more minutes. Then I grabbed my thoughts and dragged them back to Natalie. Where had she been standing when Sid had died? I tried to get a fix in my mind's eye. And couldn't. Had she been at the barbecue?

Oh, God, I hoped Wayne—

No. I wouldn't think about Wayne. How about Becky? Was Becky necessarily telling the truth about Natalie engineering Sid's tricks? Probably. Why would she lie? Unless she was the murderer. But I still couldn't believe that.

Was anyone telling the truth for that matter? How could I tell?

Maybe Wayne had decided to come to Becky's to meet me there, I decided suddenly. But he hadn't called. I scanned the road frantically, but saw no Jaguars ahead of me or behind me.

Natalie, I reminded myself. I considered her tight face and jerking gait. And her unlikely reputation as a sexually active teenager. And her loyalty to her employees. Was there a motive in there anywhere?

Or should I look at the ones who really did have motive? Pam and Charlie. And D.V. And—

Wayne's Jaguar was still in the driveway when I came skidding in. I flew out of my car, not even taking the time to shut the door. I was up the front stairs and had the front door unlocked and flung open in less than a breath.

"Wayne!" I shouted as I ran through the doorway into the entry hall.

No one answered.

But then I heard the light wheeze of a snore.

I jerked my head toward the living room and saw Wayne, facedown on the coffee table.

Relief drained the adrenaline down through my body and out through my toes, leaving me limp and shaking. Wayne was just asleep. Why hadn't I thought of that?

But as quickly as that relief came, I caught movement out of the corner of my eye. From the other side of the room. Someone or something was behind one of the pinball machines, behind Texan. Or had I just imagined that flash of movement? I walked toward the wood-railed machine carefully, centering myself as in tai chi practice. And as I walked, a memory flickered in my mind's eye. Natalie Nusser, playing an old pinball machine in a pizza parlor years and years ago, her stiff body intent as she racked up another free game. Natalie Nusser who claimed she didn't play pinball machines. But that could be true, I told myself even as the memory still flickered. She might have played them then and not now. And C.C. was probably the one lurking behind the pinball machine. But—

I looked back over my shoulder at Wayne. Why hadn't he woken when I'd yelled? Adrenaline filled my body once more as fast as it'd drained from it. Faster.

"Wayne!" I shouted again, turning his way.

He didn't move an eyebrow. But he wasn't dead. I could hear the wheeze of his breath. Or could I? I took a step toward him and then stopped. I smelled something behind me, what was it? Something burning. Solder. That was it.

I turned slowly and cautiously toward the smell.

Natalie Nusser stood up from behind Texan and pointed a gun at me.

I stood stock-still. A gun. But this gun had a cord attached. And a smoldering red tip. It was a gun all right, a soldering gun.

"Wayne?" I said again, this time looking at Natalie.

Wayne's business phone rang then, exploding the quiet of the room as Natalie stood stiff and erect, holding the soldering gun out in front of her.

"What's wrong with Wayne?" I demanded, taking a step toward her as the answering machine kicked in. She was only a couple of yards away. I wondered how long the cord on her soldering gun was. Even if it wasn't a real gun, it could burn. I'd learned that the hard way many years ago.

"He's okay," Natalie told me, her voice uncharacteristically soft.

My heart leapt gratefully, believing her. But my mind wasn't so accepting.

"What did you do to him?" I asked, matching her soft tone as I stepped closer.

Natalie didn't answer me. She just stared at me, the whites showing all around her irises, her face set in an intensity of expression I'd only seen on the faces of certain mental patients and a few paintings of saints. Fanatical saints.

A voice boomed out of the speaker of Wayne's answering machine. "It's Gary." Wayne's assistant manager at the restaurant. Well, he could wait. "Why didn't you call me back? Where are you . . ."

I had to get that soldering gun out of Natalie's hand. Then I'd find out what she'd done to Wayne and fix it. I'd probably need help. But he was still alive. He had to be. I resisted looking behind me. One thing at a time.

"Natalie, put down the soldering gun," I said gently. I might have been talking to my cat for all the obedience I was getting. I kept walking in her direction, slowly. I stretched out my hand, palm up.

I was almost to her when she jerked the gun in my direction. I felt the sting as the red-hot tip glanced off the end of my middle finger. I yanked my hand away and back-stepped quickly. Even that brief burning touch had hurt, hurt badly.

I licked my stinging fingertip. It was time for a new strategy. I still didn't know what Natalie had done to Wayne, and I couldn't undo it until I got her under control. She was standing completely immobile now, soldering gun still outstretched.

I kept my eyes on her as I began stepping backwards toward the phone.

I was almost there when Natalie leapt in my direction, soldering gun first. I heard the cord pop out of the wall, but I knew the gun was still hot. In the second it took her to reach me, I sunk all of my weight into my left leg. Then I lifted my right knee and executed a lotus kick, sweeping my Reebok-clad foot in a circle that knocked the soldering gun from her hand. In that moment, I smelled burnt leather and couldn't believe I'd actually done it. When the Master had envisioned the uses of that kick, I'm sure knocking a soldering gun out of the hand of a computer programmer wasn't one of them.

I don't think Natalie could believe it either. She just stared at the fallen gun for a moment and then looked back into my face, her irises still rimmed with white.

"What did you do to Wayne?" I screamed. Maybe it was the volume. She finally began talking.

"Nothing that will kill him, just a sedative in his juice," she said quickly. Quickly and softly. But then her voice got louder. "Just to give me the time to rig the machine. It was hard enough to get him alone. I followed you and followed you, but you were always together."

The hair prickled on my arms. Natalie Nusser was crazy.

There was no way I was turning my back on this woman. But I had to help Wayne.

"What were you going to do after you rigged the machine?" I asked, giving myself time to think.

Natalie looked down at her feet sullenly.

"Tell me!" I shouted and advanced on her.

"I was going to do it to him too," she answered triumphantly. A glitter of something even crazier lit up her round eyes. "Just like Sid. You don't deserve Wayne. All your snooping. I told you to stop. I made you an offer. You refused it. Offer. Counteroffer."

"And Elaine?" I demanded. "Did you kill her too?"

"Yes," she answered, smiling lazily as if reliving the event.

My stomach was still processing that lazy smile when Natalie pulled the screwdriver out of her pocket. She raised it over her head and then jerked it back down, plunging it in the direction of my chest. In an instant, I turned to the side and the screwdriver sank into air. Then I lifted my arm and turned back, knocking the screwdriver out of her hand with the momentum of the turn.

This time I didn't stop to congratulate myself on the move. Not until I'd grabbed her and bent her arm behind her in a hammerlock. I hadn't learned the hammerlock move in tai chi. I learned it working in a mental hospital. But it worked. I used the leverage to push her facedown onto the ground and then straddled her, tying her arms behind her back with the cord of the soldering iron. Not easily. She was struggling with the strength of the mad. But I had the strength of a woman saving her sweetie's life. Either of us might have been burned by the still-smoldering soldering gun as I looped the cord around her hands despite her twisting and kicking. But I didn't care anymore.

"Wayne?" I called out as Natalie struggled underneath me.

I thought I heard a murmur from Wayne's direction. But it was lost in the sound of Natalie's muffled rage.

She began screaming as I dialed 911, turning her face from the floor.

"I killed the lying scum! I killed him. It was a fair deal. It wasn't nearly as bad as what he did to me. Do you believe I had a crush on him once? But then he wanted to sleep with me and I wouldn't . . ."

I shouted over her screams into the phone, hoping whoever was on the other end got the salient points. Ambulance and police. Possible drug overdose. And, oh yeah, the murderer of Sid Semling and Elaine Timmons.

Then I pulled Natalie up off the floor as gently as I could manage, all the while my mind shouting to hurt her—hurt her a lot—and tied her bound hands to the leg of Hayburners, the nearest pinball machine. It seemed right. She wouldn't get loose there. And she could scream all she wanted.

She did.

And finally I ran to Wayne.

". . . he blackmailed me," Natalie continued to rage behind me. I was sure the "he" was Sid, not Wayne. "I was lonely and shy. I wanted friends. But he kept pressuring me to sleep with him. Cajoling, then threatening, then . . ."

I knelt next to Wayne where he was, his bottom still on the couch but his upper body slumped over the coffee table.

"Wayne, wake up," I ordered, my eyes blurred by a sudden rush of tears.

". . . I even did his pranks for him. But he wanted more. He said he'd convince everyone I was a whore if I wouldn't sleep with him . . ."

"Kate?" Wayne said dreamily, his chin still on the coffee table. He was alive!

I shook the tears from my eyes as I pushed his shoulders

gently back until he was in a sitting position on the couch. He was alive. And breathing. Warmth spread into my body again.

"You'll be all right," I told him, willing it so, and keeping one hand on his shoulder in case he slipped back. Should I keep him upright? Would he breathe better that way? Then I knelt on the couch next to him, keeping my hand against his shoulder.

". . . I wouldn't sleep with him. I couldn't sleep with him. I was terrified of getting pregnant and losing my scholarship. Look at what a mess Pam made of her opportunities. So the lying scum did it, he told everyone I was a whore. And they believed it. You believed it, Kate! Everyone did. Black is white and white is black. Sid turned day into night—"

"What kind of sedative did you give Wayne?" I cut in, imagining my voice with the authority of a drill sergeant as I turned in her direction. "And how much?"

I watched as Natalie's eyes slowly shrunk to nearly normal size.

"How much—" I began again, but she was already telling me.

"Ten or so sleeping pills, over-the-counter," she replied brusquely, her voice the voice of the Natalie Nusser who owned and managed Nusser Networks once more. "Don't worry, I didn't give him enough to kill him." Then her voice got dreamier. Her eyes began to widen again. "I brought him a bottle of his favorite apple juice, with a little sleepy-dust mixed in. I could tell he thought it tasted funny. But he's so polite. He drank it down like a good little boy. You don't deserve him, you know. You didn't care enough about him to protect him—"

My mind cut her off. I didn't want to hear any truth in her words. Coffee, I thought. Caffeine might counteract the pills. Maybe. But did I have any coffee in the house? I had herbal tea in twenty flavors, but coffee?

"Don't know," Wayne mumbled sleepily. "Don't know."

I put my arms around Wayne and pulled him to me, cuddling him like a baby. It wasn't easy. He was heavy, deadweight. No, not dead, I corrected myself hastily. Alive and breathing weight. His head flopped against my chest, cheek first. It couldn't be that comfortable, but he was still breathing.

"I love you so much," I whispered in his ear. "Come out of this. Feel better."

His breath wheezed in a happy little sigh. At least it sounded happy. I panicked for a moment. Maybe I should be shaking him instead of cuddling him. I had no idea. How many minutes had passed? Where was the ambulance?

". . . and then Robert blew himself up with his fireworks," Natalie was saying behind me, her voice almost calm again. I craned my neck to look at her for a moment. The fireworks. I knew there'd been a connection. "And Sid told me he'd convince the police that *I'd* been the one to give Robert the fireworks. And he could have. He'd already done it once. He'd convinced everyone I was a whore. He could convince them I was a murderer too. And I'd been out of town with my grandmother that summer. Everyone would've believed him. So I accepted his offer. I slept with him. I was Sid's graduation present . . ."

So that was why. God, no wonder she'd killed him. But Natalie's motives didn't matter to me now. Only Wayne mattered. Coffee, I thought again. I had a jar of instant, didn't I? Somewhere in the kitchen for a friend who couldn't visit without coffee. But where? I tried to visualize it on the shelves. Behind the herbal tea?

". . . Twenty-five years later, Sid shows up out of work as a salesman and wants a job. I do my own sales. I didn't need him. But he'd heard about my prospective contract with the Defense Department. From Elaine. The deal was almost closed. Then he said he'd tell the feds I was an addictive gambler. That's the one thing that would have scuttled the deal. You can be a child molester and the Defense Department will work with you, but not a gambler. They're afraid you'll sell their secrets to cover your debts . . ."

"Rosemary," Wayne gurgled. My ears perked up. Another woman? "And parsley," he added.

". . . And there was Sid again, telling me he'd convince them. And not just the Defense Department, but the rest of my customers too. He could have done it. He could have put me out of business." Natalie's voice rose to a shriek. "What would have happened to my employees then?! So I hired him. And two weeks later, he started in with the sexual demands."

"I'm sorry, Natalie," I told her, meaning it, feeling for a moment what hell it must have been. In spite of the man in my arms.

But she didn't seem to hear me anyway. I craned my head around again. Her irises were rimmed with white once more.

"Doggie," Wayne mumbled near my ear. At least that's what it sounded like. "Good doggie."

"Sid had to die," Natalie told me. Or maybe she was telling herself.

I was pretty sure I knew where the coffee was then, but something kept me there, holding Wayne in my arms. Could I leave him alone in the room with Natalie, even if she was tied up? I felt as if her rage alone could choke him. It was choking me. My knees and arms and back ached with Wayne's weight, but I couldn't move. I wouldn't move.

"So I killed him," Natalie said, her voice cold and distant now. "It was a fair deal. He made an offer. I made a counteroffer. I saw my mother die of leukemia when I was ten, you know, saw my father drink himself to death. A quick death is better. I did Sid a favor. It was a fair deal."

"Do you know the antidote for the sedative you gave Wayne?" I asked quietly. It was worth a try.

"Sleep," she replied brusquely. "He's fine. I keep telling you that. You just don't know what's important."

I held on to Wayne's warm body. Wayne was important. I knew that. And he'd be all right soon. Ten or so sleeping pills couldn't hurt anyone too much, could they? I couldn't see my watch with my arms around Wayne. But it seemed like hours had passed. Damn it, where was the ambulance?

"I thought about it a lot over the years," Natalie went on, her voice suddenly intellectual, speculative. Calm. "Sid was jealous of me because I was an A student. More than jealous. He hated me for it, and he wanted to sleep with me because then he'd have power over me. And when I wouldn't do it, he hated me enough to destroy me." She paused. "And twenty-five years later, he was jealous that I had my own successful business, so he decided to destroy that too."

I found myself nodding. She was probably right. At least about Sid's motives.

"But it wasn't just me," she added, cold rage replacing the calm in her voice. "It was my employees. They depend on me. If my business had gone down, they would have gone with me. But Sid didn't care. What if my employees were out of work? Do you think anyone would hire a woman whose husband's dying of cancer? No, they can't because of their insurance rates. Sid might as well have pointed a knife at her throat. I couldn't allow that. Offer. Counteroffer."

Then Natalie laughed. I couldn't remember ever hearing her laugh before. The sound was high and musical, pretty as an opera star's. I held Wayne closer, my arms cramping with his weight.

"Pretty," he murmured. "Pretty, pretty."

Was he talking about Natalie's voice? Or had he snagged the word "pretty" from my own mind? What was he seeing in his over-the-counter, drug-induced dreams?

"And then Sid submitted his proposal for his own death.

He asked me to rig the pinball machine for his party. To rig it to make menopause jokes when he pushed the remote control. So I did, but I had my own remote control. A double throw switch with a secure firing mechanism. I took the ground wire off each side of the machine and hooked it to a 220 transformer. I wasn't even sure it would kill him, but it was a good possibility with his bad heart. A calculated risk. And even if it didn't kill him, it would have scared him, scared him out of messing with me anymore. He would have lost his leverage."

"And you were going to electrocute Wayne too?" I asked through clenched teeth. I should have just left her alone, but I couldn't.

"Yes," she said, her voice too high now, defensive. "But not to kill him necessarily. It might not have, you know. Just so it would look like it was your machines that were at fault, so they'd stop looking for a murderer."

"Or," I countered, "so they'd think I was the murderer."

"I couldn't help it!" Natalie screamed. "I have responsibilities!"

And then I heard the sound of sirens in the distance. Were those sirens heading here? Was one of them an ambulance? The other the police?

"How about Elaine?" I asked quickly. I wanted to know now. Before the police. And the lawyers. And the psychologists.

"Elaine told me to come and talk to her after the memorial. She didn't ask me, she told me. So I left a few moments behind her in my car. She told me to park on the street and follow her up on foot. When I got up to her house, her car was still in the driveway. She ushered me through the front door like I should be honored and put her purse down on an end table. No one else was home. She didn't even ask me to sit down."

Natalie went silent.

"And . . ." I prompted.

"Elaine told me she knew Sid had blackmailed me to get a job. She said I deserved blackmail, that I was always 'stuck-up.' Can you imagine? Me, stuck-up? And then she asked if I'd helped Sid rig the pinball machine. I knew she knew then. And her purse was just sitting there. I grabbed it and scooped out her car keys and ran out the door. And the fool came running after me. I knew she would. I jumped in her BMW and revved the engine. Elaine ran in front of the car waving her arms, just like she wanted me to run her over. Offer. Counteroffer. So I obliged her. I knew I'd killed her the first time the car rolled over her skinny body, but I went back and forth a couple of times to be sure." She paused, then added calmly, "And then I wiped off my fingerprints and left. No one saw me leave."

I gulped down a wave of nausea and listened. The sirens were getting closer. They had to be the ones coming for us.

"When were you going to stop killing people?" I asked.

"I never meant—" Natalie began.

"How about Becky?" I interrupted. "She knew you did Sid's tricks."

"That's right," Natalie said slowly. I could hear the cool calculation in her voice. Did she still think she could get out of this? Kill me? Kill Wayne? Kill Becky?

"You were the one who started the false rumors, weren't you?" I pressed on. "Doing just what Sid did to you, only to the rest of us—"

"No, no!" she shouted. "It was different. I wasn't—I did it for my company. He was going to ruin it. Ruin me. Ruin all my employees!"

I heard the sirens in the driveway and held Wayne even tighter.

"Just a couple more seconds, sweetie," I breathed into his ear.

"My company's all I have!" Natalie shrieked. "Don't you understand? That's all I have!"

And then I heard the sound of footsteps coming up the front stairs.

TWENTY-FOUR

There was a knock on the door.

The Kanicks' door, not my door. Four days had passed since Natalie Nusser had confessed to murder. Once the local police had arrived, she'd babbled out her unsolicited confessions (and her unsolicited justifications) before they could even get their Miranda warnings in order. They kept on trying to shut her up, but she kept on talking. And talking. One of the uniformed officers had even put his hands over his ears like the hear-no-evil monkey. The whole scene might even have been comical, if it hadn't been for Wayne still half-conscious in my arms.

But luckily the paramedics had been less than a minute behind the police. No matter how long it'd felt.

Now the old gang, minus three, was having their final Sunday get-together. Aurora Kanick had insisted, even though the murderer had been identified. And she was right. If sharing something meant giving away a piece of it, I was all in favor of sharing my experience of Natalie Nusser with the rest of the Gravendale High class of '68.

Lillian Kanick opened her front door, and Mark Myers came through, smiling widely, his hands behind his back. For a moment, I thought I heard him mew. Maybe he had. He was a veterinarian, I reminded myself. Mewing might be contagious for all I knew.

It couldn't have been anyone but Mark at the door. Becky was already here, fidgeting on her wooden chair, but looking much better than she had on Wednesday. Pam and Charlie sat together on one of the navy-and-white-striped couches, glancing at each other furtively every couple of seconds and then turning away . . . and then turning back again. Aurora was perched on a floral easy chair, beaming serenely at her son Jack. And Wayne was sitting next to me on the remaining blue-and-white-striped couch, safe and sound. And warm and muscular and—

"Anyone for kittens?" Mark asked, bringing his hands out from behind his back, his left hand in a flourish, his right hand holding a basket containing four tiny mewling balls of fur.

"Oh, kitties!" Becky trilled, brightening. But then the light went out of her face. "But I won't— They'll have to wait—"

"I'll keep a couple of them for you until you're ready," Mark promised. Then he walked up to her and unceremoniously grabbed two of the creatures by the scruffs of their little necks and plopped them into her lap. Becky's fragile face held a childlike look of wonder as she bent over the tiny tiger-striped forms and began to make all the oohing-cooing noises that only kittens (or possibly baby otters) can inspire.

"They're orphans," Mark added, looking around the room, his ever-alert eyes round now like a seal pup's about to be clubbed. I kept my own eyes averted. C.C. would make my life completely miserable if I got another cat. Not to mention the other cat's. "Little baby orphans—"

"Kate was just enlightening us about the legal status of Natalie Nusser's case," Aurora broke in.

I was impressed. Aurora appeared impervious to the kittens. Maybe I should meditate more. Was that her secret?

"Perhaps Jack would like a kitten," she added.

Forget that meditation, I decided.

On the other hand, maybe Aurora was just as astute as ever. She wasn't talking about taking a cat herself. She was talking about Jack taking a cat. Jack would get to feed it, drag it to the vet's for shots, and clean up after it. And due to Mark's alacrity, Jack already had the third kitten in his big hand and was smiling down at it with a light in his eyes that all the medications in the world wouldn't have provided him. Lillian was next to him, an arm around his shoulders, staring down more thoughtfully at the newest member of their family. Was she wondering how a kitten would translate to bronze?

I looked back at Aurora. Her face was serene as ever. Or was that smug? She was sure to get visiting rights. Without any of the work. All right, all right. Maybe meditation did clear the mind.

Five minutes later, Mark had placed all four cats, the fourth going to Pam Ortega. I wondered how it would get along with Charlie's Labrador retrievers. It would probably terrorize them, I decided, looking at the squirming bundle in her lap. I thought I heard Pam whisper, *"Loca, loca."* I wondered if she meant herself or the kitten. She pulled it up to her ample breast and gave it a little kiss with Charlie looking longingly on.

"Go on, Kate," Aurora ordered.

For a moment I thought she meant to go on and get a kitten for myself. But there weren't any left. Luckily. So I went on with my story about Natalie.

"My reporter friend, Felix, told me that Natalie confessed once they got her to Gravendale, after a perfectly unassailable rendering of her Miranda rights."

Yes, my "friend," Felix. At least Felix was acting pretty friendly now. Downright charming, in fact. Of course that might have had to do with the fact that I'd called him once I was absolutely sure Wayne was out of danger, and told him every detail of my encounter with Natalie. Maybe because I knew Felix was the one person who would listen with relish, instead of horror and sadness. Felix was so grateful for the information, he would have cooked me a vegetarian meal . . . if he could have. Or so he assured me.

"Now Natalie's attorneys are trying to get her confession suppressed," I went on. "They're claiming it was tainted by her earlier guilty ramblings at my house. But Gonzales did it clean. It looks like they've got her."

"But isn't she insane?" Lillian asked softly, turning momentarily away from Jack as she spoke. "What's the word, 'cracked'?"

"*Por Dios*, she must have been," Pam answered just as softly. "If Anna May and I had dropped by Elaine's house and caught them—" She stroked the kitten in her lap furiously as if to stop the thought. "But we never did, because Elaine was still at the memorial when we left . . . still talking to Natalie." She shivered. Charlie put a sympathetic hand on her arm, and then slipped it downward as if merely petting the kitten.

Insane? Maybe not legally. But in any other human use of the word? I remembered Natalie's white-rimmed irises and the sound of her voice as she described driving back and forth over Elaine's body. I closed my eyes and took a big breath. And felt Wayne's sympathetic hand on *my* arm.

"She didn't just have a computer science degree, she had an electrical engineering degree too!" Mark Myers put in, shaking his head violently. He smacked himself on the forehead. "For God's sake, it said so right in the *Where Are We Now?* pamphlet. She was the one critter who knew how to use the right tools. Of course she rigged it."

"And Sid used the same MO on her as he used on us,"

Charlie added grimly. He glanced at Pam's face. She looked back, her lustrous brown eyes full of pain. And affection.

"Blackmail," Pam explained briefly. "Only neither of us killed him." She took her free hand and held Charlie's. "That's a line neither of us would ever cross. Especially you, Charlie. You're far too gentle."

Charlie and Rodin Rat, I thought, as I watched gratification and embarrassment battle on his pinkened face. Gratification seemed to win as he squeezed Pam's hand back. The kitten nuzzled their joined hands as if to pry them apart. Jealous already?

"But how could she actually kill two people?" Becky asked, her voice low with wonder. "I mean, Jeez, I'm a complete mess. But still, I can't even imagine doing such a thing."

"Her employees," I answered. "They were her life. I'll bet they were the only friends she had. Her only family. And Sid and Elaine threatened them. At least in her mind."

"The woman was nuts," a low, clear voice commented. I looked up, surprised to hear Jack, not only talking but speaking clearly. "I ought to have known. I've seen people like that before."

He didn't have to say in mental hospitals. I knew where he meant. I just nodded.

"Her employees have all offered to help with her defense expenses," I went on. "And they're going to keep the business going in her name. They really do care about her."

"I'm glad of that tiny bit of grace," Aurora pronounced. "She executed these terrible acts on their behalf, at least in the context of her own illusions."

"Or else she just did it for her business," Lillian put in cynically.

"Or just for her own revenge," Mark put in even more cynically. I remembered him saying animals were easier than people. Maybe he was right.

"Twenty-five years of festering hate," Wayne growled from beside me. Maybe only I could hear the sympathy in that growl for Natalie. For all she had done to him, I knew he still felt sorry for her. "She never forgave Sid Semling for his treatment of her. She lost her self-respect and her reputation. Maybe even her ability to ever relate as a normal human being. All because of Sid Semling's whim."

"And Sid was using and abusing her again," Aurora added sadly. "It must have seemed an infinite torture to her."

Mewing was all that was heard in the Kanicks' house for a few moments. Maybe we were all busy pitying Natalie Nusser. I was.

But then I thought of Elaine Timmons. And of Wayne. I turned to him, my chest tightening with remembered panic. He raised his eyebrows in recognition and gently stroked the back of my head and neck. He'd been about to call me at Becky's that afternoon with his new plan to work out his restaurant computer problems from Becky's phone instead of his. Then Natalie had knocked on our door. And Wayne had been as polite as ever. He'd not only invited her in. He'd drunk her bitter apple juice "like a good little boy."

"What happens to Elaine's kids?" Wayne asked quietly.

"Aunt Ursula," Aurora replied crisply. I should have known she'd have the information, if anyone would. "I've spoken to Ed Timmons. His sister, Ursula, is going to move into his house to help care for the children. She's an extraordinary woman: vibrant, joyous, and intelligent. And she loves those children. She's also single, a philosophy professor by trade. And from what Ed tells me, she's been there emotionally for the children all these years in any case. If anyone can help them transcend the experience, it's Aunt Ursula."

"Good," Wayne breathed, and I felt something within him relax. And something within me.

"Becky has some news," Mark said with a nudge in her direction.

"They don't want to hear," Becky murmured, her eyes down.

"Yes, we do," Aurora told her. "The saying of something can make it true."

Becky looked across at her, tilted her head and laughed.

"Maybe it can," she conceded, her voice stronger. "Okay, here goes. I'm going to a drug rehabilitation facility for two weeks, beginning tomorrow. And . . ." As she faltered, one of the kittens in her lap began a slow crawl up her blouse. Becky looked down at it, placed a reassuring hand on its bottom, and then went on. "And I haven't had a drink or any drug but Advil for four days. I think I'm going to be sober from now on."

She lifted her head and corrected herself. "I *am* going to be sober from now on."

She waved away the round of applause she got from everyone who wasn't holding a kitten. But there was pride and belief on her face now.

"I decided to go to rehab once I finally understood that I'd been too damned drunk to realize that it must have been Natalie who rigged the pinball machine," she told us seriously. There was no giggle in her voice now. "I was the one who knew that she'd rigged Sid's tricks in high school, and I didn't even stop to think how relevant that information might be. I could have saved Elaine's—"

"You don't know that," Aurora interrupted. "You can't second-guess life. Everything is exactly as it is. Maybe even as it should be."

"Thank you," Becky replied quietly.

"We can all forgive ourselves," Jack piped up unexpectedly.

I took a quick look at Wayne. And was relieved to see him

smile back. Wayne had already forgiven me for not telling him about the threat against his life . . . and for the unnecessary stomach pump. But I was having a hard time forgiving myself. I was just thankful that Natalie had only given him a mild dose of over-the-counter sleeping pills after all.

Aurora smiled at me too. Somehow, her smile made me nervous.

"Have you and Wayne thought of your wedding ritual yet?" she demanded.

We both shook our heads hastily, caught unawares.

"Wayne and Kate are going to have a very special wedding with their own unique ritual," she explained for us. Talk about unsolicited confessions. I wanted to put *my* hands over *my* ears. "Something that matches both of their metaphors."

"Jeez, you mean like something to do with what they both have in common?" Becky asked.

Aurora nodded. I wondered if my face was as pink as Wayne's.

"How about something with kittens?" suggested Mark. "I have plenty more where they came from."

"I had some friends who had opera singers sing their wedding vows," Pam threw in.

And then everyone was making suggestions.

". . . a ceremony in a bookstore because that's where they met . . ."

". . . virtual reality . . ."

". . . in a hot tub . . ."

". . . or you could . . ."

"Well, what *are* your common interests?" Mark finally broke in.

"Huh?" we both responded.

"What brought you together?" Mark kept on.

"Finding dead bodies," Wayne answered morosely, but I

thought there was a twinkle somewhere beneath his lowered eyebrows.

I imagined a wedding procession through an obstacle course of corpses. Stabbed, garotted, shot. I shook my head and looked at Wayne, healthy and nearly smiling despite his tone.

"And living to tell about it?" I suggested gently.

Wayne's eyebrows shot up as he laughed, his head flung back against the couch in his good humor.

When he was all laughed out, he put his arms around me and repeated just as gently, "And living to tell about it."

Maybe we'd have that wedding after all.